CROSS OF VENGEANCE

The Burren Mysteries by Cora Harrison

CROSS OF VENGEANCE

A Burren Mystery

Cora Harrison

This first world edition published 2013
in Great Britain and 2014 in the USA by
SEVERN HOUSE PUBLISHERS LTD of
19 Cedar Road, Sutton, Surrey, England, SM2 5DA.
Trade paperback edition first published
in Great Britain and the USA 2014 by
SEVERN HOUSE PUBLISHERS LTD.

British Library Cataloguing in Publication Data

Harrison, Cora author.
  The cross of vengeance. – (Burren mystery ; 10)
  1. Mara, Brehon of the Burren (Fictitious character)–Fiction.
  2. Murder – Investigation–Fiction. 3. Relics–
  Fiction. 4. Women judges–Ireland–Burren–Fiction.
  5. Burren (Ireland)–History–16th century–Fiction.
  6. Detective and mystery stories.
  I. Title II. Series
  823.9'2–dc23

ISBN-13: 978-07278-8320-9 (cased)
ISBN-13: 978-1-84751-492-9

All Severn House titles are printed on acid-free paper.

Severn House Publishers support the Forest Stewardship Council™ [FSC™],
the leading international forest certification organisation. All our titles that
are printed on FSC certified paper carry the FSC logo.

Typeset by Palimpsest Book Production Ltd.,
Falkirk, Stirlingshire, Scotland.
Printed and bound in Great Britain by
TJ International, Padstow, Cornwall.

For Eleanor and John
With love and gratitude for your appreciation

Acknowledgements

Thanks are due to my agent, Peter Buckman of Ampersand Agency, for his excellent advice, his enthusiasm and his appreciation of Mara, the Brehon, even after ten books about her; to my editor, Anna Telfer for her positivity and excellent advice and to the team at Severn House for their continued interest in publishing these books about an obscure law, set in an obscure place in the west of Ireland.

Thanks are also due to Michael MacMahon whose article about the double-armed cross set in stone on the gable wall of the medieval church at Killinaboy first roused my interest in the pilgrims who may have come to see the relic of the true cross housed in the round tower beside the church.

One

Uraicecht Becc
(Small Primer)

There are three grades of Brehon (a maker of judgements):

The first grade may only decide on matters which relate to the lowest in society, such as craftsmen. He or she has an honour-price of seven séts, three-and-a-half ounces of silver or four milch cows.

The second grade is learned in law and in poetry and has an honour-price of ten séts, five ounces of silver or five milch cows.

The third grade is named as 'the judge of three languages' and he or she is competent in traditional law, poetry and canon law and has an honour-price of fifteen séts, seven-and-a-half ounces of silver or eight milch cows. This Brehon may administer the laws of a kingdom in the name of its king.

When Mara, Brehon of the Burren, set off on 14 September 1519 from the law school at Cahermacnaghten to attend Mass at Kilnaboy Church, it was just another boring duty in her busy life as the king's representative responsible for the maintenance of law and order in that kingdom in the mid-west of Ireland. Kilnaboy was not her parish church, but the Feast of the Holy Cross was of great importance there as that church held an important relic: a piece of the true cross itself, housed inside a gold shrine, heralded by the huge two-armed stone cross on the church gable. The attendance of the Brehon at the service would be expected by all the parishioners.

The fourteenth was a lovely, bright, very warm September day. Despite having to go to Mass on a Wednesday, her five scholars from her law school in the west of the kingdom were in a mood of wild excitement. It was unusual for them to be back in school before the end of September, but they had all agreed to start the Michaelmas term early on the promise of a fortnight's holiday in the King's palace in Thomond during the month of

December. And so they had arrived back the evening before, two weeks earlier than usual and were still busily swapping stories about their summer holidays. Mara had worried they might resent the cutting short of their summer break, but now suspected that they were, in fact, pleased to be back in the companionship of their fellow scholars. She remembered her own days as an only child at her father's law school, and how delighted she was when the holidays were over on the feast of St Michaelmas and the old stone walls rang once more with shouts and laughter.

Slevin, a thirteen-year-old boy from Donegal, was telling some outrageous story about a cattle raid in the mountains near to his home, casting quick looks over his shoulder from time to time and lowering his voice so that the Brehon could not overhear. She smiled to herself and reined back her mare, allowing them to gallop on ahead. Slevin, thought Mara tolerantly, came from a long line of bards and storytellers and she would drop out of earshot and allow him to embroider his story to suit his artistic talents while she enjoyed the scenery at a leisurely pace. Domhnall, her fourteen-year-old grandson, was listening with a grin puckering his lips, but the two nine-year-olds, her own son Cormac and his foster brother Art, were wide-eyed with astonishment. As was twelve-year-old Finbar from Cloyne.

September was a favourite time of the year for Mara. The hedgerows and ditches of the Burren were still full of summer flowers: deep-pink fragrant orchids and yellow hawkweed framed the tall, pure-white, five-petalled marsh maidens on the verge, and the fluffy pincushion flowers cast a purple haze over the fields. Here and there late frog orchids, tiny but vividly yellow, still crouched in ditches, and pale blue harebells arranged themselves, as always, to flower in harmonious contrast beside the clumps of crimson cranesbills.

And yet, despite the summer flowers and the warmth of the morning, there was a slight crispness in the air and already the haws reddened on the hedges and the immature, pale green globes of sloes peeped out from the yellowing leaves of the blackthorn bushes. Swallows, chattering ceaselessly, were beginning to cluster on tree tops and on the roofs of barns, and brightly coloured fieldfares fed greedily from the berries. The sun's heat was like that of summer, but the year was moving inexorably into autumn and towards winter.

The air is very still; we might get thunder tonight, she thought, guiding her mare around a deep hole in the limestone road and walking for a while in the soft grass beside the ditch. There was a sharp sweet smell of water mint crushed by the hoofs and for a few minutes she rejoiced in it. The rounded swirling limestone hills, silver in the sunlight, and the majestic sweep of the stone-paved uplands were her favourite parts of the Burren, but there were times, like now, when she felt that the fertile valleys rivalled them as the most beautiful place on the earth.

'Shall we take a short cut and ride across the fields down through Roughan, Brehon?' called back her grandson, Domhnall, and she nodded her agreement. Domhnall was the eldest boy in the school and a great leader, a boy of brains and decisiveness. All the scholars looked to him for leadership. When the school was in session, the ancient enclosure which held the law school buildings and the fields around rang continuously with the cry of '*Doh-nall*' and Domhnall always gave an instant decision. Mara was usually happy to back his judgements. He was very like her own father, Brehon of the Burren until he died, and she guessed that when her time came to retire or to die that Domhnall would make a worthy successor.

In any case, thought Mara, today he had chosen the route well. The fields were dry and Roughan itself was one of her favourite places. The whole hillside was covered with ancient tombs, the slabs of limestone gleaming in the sunshine as though they were made from marble. The place had a special feel of old times, of continuity with the past, of sacred ritual.

'The church bell,' shouted Slevin, interrupting his saga, and Mara was roused from her ponderings about the race of giants who must have built these monuments and lifted the flat slabs to make the sides and tops of those wedge-shaped tombs. She shook her reins and joined her scholars.

'No hurry,' she said. 'Ride sensibly. We have a good quarter of an hour before the service starts. They ring the bell early here so as to alert the pilgrims who are staying in the inn over by the river.'

The church was packed by the time they arrived. She spotted many familiar faces, including that of Ardal O'Lochlainn, her closest neighbour, and friend for . . . for forty-six years, she thought with a slight feeling of shock. Ardal was a *taoiseach* (chieftain) of his clan since he was a very young man, a wealthy landowner and breeder of fine horses. He lived alone in the tower house of Lissylisheen, a quarter of a mile from the law school. For years Mara had tried to find a suitable wife for him, but now that he had turned the age of fifty she had given up in despair. He had become desperately religious, attending Mass on a daily basis, and had recently returned from a pilgrimage to the shrine of St James of Santiago, followed by a visit to Rome to see the Pope and the wonderful churches there. She tried to catch his eye, but he was gazing reverentially up at the small figurine of the crucified Christ, made from gold and alabaster, which hung beside the altar.

Mara gave up and exchanged nods and smiles with other neighbours. The church was full. As well as the local people of the Burren, there was, as usual, a group of badge-wearing pilgrims, come to pay homage to the relic; just six of them today – three women and three men. Most, thought Mara, looking at them with interest, would probably round off their pilgrimage within a few days with a visit to the Aran Island – Aran of the Saints, it was known. If so, they would leave Kilnaboy the following day, take a boat from Doolin to cross the narrow strait between the island and mainland, and then would stay there for another few days, visiting the various shrines and praying at the seven churches. And after that they might go to Galway and take a ship to Spain.

'The three ladies are from Wales,' murmured Nechtan O'Quinn in her ear as he slid to his knees beside her. He crossed himself ostentatiously and muttered a prayer. Mara waited. Nechtan O'Quinn, lord of the tower house just behind Kilnaboy Church, was a distant relative of her husband, King Turlough Donn O'Brien. He was a great gossip. She ought, perhaps, not to encourage him, but she was curious about the three women. Many pilgrims came to Kilnaboy month after month in order to worship the relic of the true cross, but these were the first women pilgrims that she had seen.

'The small, prim-looking one is a prioress,' whispered Nechtan. 'She comes from a convent near to the shrine of St Winifred in Wales. The other two ladies are her sisters. The older one, the big fat one, is a widow and the younger one – looks like a daughter, but she's a sister, too, apparently – very shy girl, terribly scarred, as you can see, after some accident when she was a child, I understand.'

He seemed to know a lot about these pilgrims, thought Mara, but she said no more. Her pupils were lined up in front of her and, although the three older boys, Domhnall, Slevin and Finbar, were devoutly fingering their beads and looking straight ahead at the altar, nine-year-old Cormac was using the squared tiles on the floor beneath their knees as a board on which to play a game of merels with his foster brother Art.

Since Cormac was Mara's son this was doubly reprehensible, but on the other hand, the tiny figures, which the boys were pushing into groups of three, were made from clay so dark that they hardly showed up against the grey tiles on the floor. And they were both kneeling quietly with bent heads. Mara decided to ignore them for the moment, at least until the service began, and allowed her eyes to study the pilgrims with interest.

'Who's the tall blond pilgrim?' she murmured to Nechtan, keeping her eyes fixed on the altar. The priest had not appeared yet. Father MacMahon would still be putting on his special red robes, worn only on this day every year; Sorley, his sexton, would be taking them out from the cedar chest, removing the small sour crab apples which kept the moths away from the silk, hanging them up to air and smoothing out the creases.

'That's Hans Kaufmann. He's from Germany, a rich merchant,' whispered back Nechtan. 'The small, dark-skinned one, the elderly-looking man, is a monk from Italy – Brother Cosimo – and the one with grey hair is a Dominican priest from the shrine of St James of Santiago in Spain. He's called Father Miguel.'

How does he know so much about them? wondered Mara, and then Nechtan's wife came drifting in from the side door that led to the path towards the tower house. Narait O'Quinn was Nechtan's second wife – a very good-looking young woman at least twenty years younger than her husband. It was the voluptuous figure, the dark eyes and the lusciously pouting mouth that had attracted him, and disguised the total absence of intelligence, Mara supposed, but now after a couple of years of marriage, she had the impression that both parties were bored and discontented.

Still, she thought, unlike in England where a wife would have to murder her husband to get rid of him – and risk being burned to death if her crime was discovered – here, Brehon law allowed for a peaceful divorce and an equable division of property. She smiled sweetly at Narait and noted with interest how the girl ignored her husband, but blushed and smiled across at the row of pilgrims, and how her eyes lingered on the pilgrim from Germany.

'We offered them supper last night,' said Nechtan to Mara, following the direction of her eyes. 'Narait met them soon after their arrival,' he continued. 'She thought that the inn would not give them a good meal.' Unlike the jolly, gossipy note of his previous pieces of information, his voice was toneless now and he did not trouble to reduce it to a whisper, but stared belligerently at his wife as she came to sit beside him.

An unlikely excuse, thought Mara. Blad, the owner of the inn, which was built on the banks of the River Fergus, only fifty yards from the church, was a wonderful cook. Even her husband, King Turlough, who loved his food, spoke of him with reverence. She looked around the church for Blad and could not spot him, though his daughter, Mór, was present. She, also, was looking across at the tall, blond young German pilgrim.

Did the German know how many women in the church were stealing glances at him, Mara wondered? He was an unusual pilgrim, very much younger than the customary people who made these voyages from shrine to shrine, across Europe and even to the Holy Land itself. The Italian and the Spaniard were well above middle age – the Italian perhaps approaching old age – and so was the prioress and her plump sister, the widow. Only the German and the unfortunately scarred woman could be called young.

And then all rose for the entrance of the priest, dramatically dressed in the special robes of red damask embroidered with gold thread. He mounted the carpeted steps to the altar, followed by a well-trained troop of altar boys and watched from the doorway by Sorley, the sexton and gravedigger. Mara smiled to herself to see the anxious look of the man. It was said on the Burren that Sorley was so immensely proud of having the responsibility of the round tower with its relic of the true cross in his keeping that he acted as though he were the king of Kilnaboy. Once the priest had genuflected to the altar, saying, '*Introibo ad altare dei*,' and the altar boys intoned the response, Sorley retired – no doubt, thought Mara, to make sure that all was in order for the ceremonial visit to the relic in the round tower once the service was over. The presence of a group of pilgrims, though there were disappointingly few today, would add to his consequence. This was usually his big day of the year – and even though the number of pilgrims was small, the people of the Burren, as usual, had turned out to worship the relic.

Mara automatically listened to the Mass and made the appropriate responses, but when the congregation sat to listen to the epistle – one of the many hundreds written by St Paul, a man who was no favourite of hers – her mind wandered back to the pilgrims.

What a strange thing to leave your home and to wander from shrine to shrine. Not something that would appeal to her, she thought, though it would be interesting to see some more of the world. She imagined she might like to go to France one day and to witness how they grow the grapes and make the wine, wander around vineyards, sample different vintages and . . . She suppressed a smile. She was a wife and a mother, and with her position as Brehon of the Burren, her responsibility for law and order on the Burren, investigating crimes, drawing up legal documents, counselling couples who wished to divorce, explaining to farmers about boundary obligations, drafting wills, giving advice on problems with common land, sitting in judgement three or four times every year – more often if necessary – and added to all that her teaching commitments to her young scholars, she was lucky if she got a couple of hours to herself, she thought, as she rose respectfully to her feet to listen to the gospel. That young man, that German merchant, she mused, as she solemnly signed her forehead, mouth and breast with her thumb, what was happening to his business while he wandered over lands and seas in the company of three women and a couple of elderly men?

He could not be more than about twenty-eight, she reckoned, as she looked across at him. An intelligent face, but with a slight look of a fanatic about him. Certainly, at the moment, he was not looking at the women who were eyeing him: Narait, Nechtan's wife; Blad's daughter, Mór; the three women pilgrims; and even herself. He was looking straight ahead, staring at the altar and its marble statues, its crimson carpet, the gold figure of the crucifix, the jewel-encrusted monstrance which the priest raised on high with the sacred host in its centre, and there was a stillness, a concentration and, she almost thought, a look of burning passion in his eyes. That was the explanation, she supposed. This man was not going on a pilgrimage for the company or the amusements or to while away the time; some burning belief, some religious fanaticism drove him to sacrifice his time and his money.

Well, thought Mara, it takes all kinds to make up a world. Religion to her was something very much in the background. And yet she was, she thought with a sudden insight, as fanatical about the law, the Brehon laws of her ancestors, as this man or Ardal O'Lochlainn was fanatical about the Church of Rome. A law which never shed blood, which ruled that the hungry and the insane had to be cared for, a law that gave rights to women and children, a law that relied for obedience to its judgements on the consensus of the community and not on savage punishments with whip and the hangman's noose – that law, she thought, as she stood up for the last Gospel, with a half-smile at her sudden fervour, was worth a certain fanaticism.

'May we go up to see the relic of the true cross, Brehon?'

'If you like, Art.' Mara suppressed a sigh. She had hoped to plead urgent business once the service was over and get away quickly, but Art was a genuinely religious boy and his mother, who lived on a farm near to the law school, would be eager to hear all about it when he visited her later on in the evening. Odd, she thought, that Cormac, her son, had been fostered with Art from the time that he was a tiny baby, had lived in the same house, slept in the same bed, fed from the same milk – and yet Art was religious like his mother and Cormac, like *his* mother, Mara, seemed to be sceptical about certain aspects of the Church's teachings.

Still, if Art wanted to see the relic and if he truly believed that it was part of the cross on which Jesus met his death, then he must be allowed to do so. She wondered for a moment about allowing Domhnall to be in charge of the party climbing up to see the relic, housed in its own little tower a few yards from the church, but although he was very responsible, for fourteen he was rather small and Father MacMahon might think it strange of her. In any case, she thought, Cormac was quite likely to wonder aloud how many pieces of the true cross existed in the world, and, being a mathematical boy with a love of figures, might start working out how many pieces of wood could be taken from a man-sized cross. And then he would probably take his findings to Father MacMahon and scandalize the good priest.

'It's my first time seeing it,' said Art as they crossed the churchyard, shepherded by Father MacMahon and ushered ahead of the pilgrims who were being placed in an orderly line by Sorley.

The stone-roofed round tower was quite small – probably only about ten foot across on the inside and made from stone. Mara and her scholars followed the priest up the ladder that led to the door, placed for security reasons a good six foot above ground level, and waited on the first wooden floor until Father MacMahon laboriously made his way up to the second floor where the relic was housed. It was a tight squeeze in the little circular room and Mara moved on to the ladder, allowing the boys to huddle together in an area not more than a couple of paces wide. It turned out that it was the first time for all of the scholars and they speculated freely, in discreet whispers, on what might happen by the sacred power of the precious relic. It was very airless and Mara was thankful when Father MacMahon finished his prayer and came back down again. She climbed the wooden spiral staircase and breathed thankfully the cool air that came from the four narrow window slits – facing north, south, east and west. She stood by the eastern one and allowed the boys to press forward to where the relic lay on a cushion of purple velvet, housed in a knee-high, beautifully carved gold shrine.

'To think that people cross the world to see something the size of that,' said Cormac. He sounded quite disappointed and, being Cormac, had a note of annoyance in his voice as though he felt that someone had tried to fool him.

'Across Europe,' contradicted Domhnall. As the son of a successful merchant who exported goods from and into the Anglicized city of Galway, he had a clear idea of the location of various countries. His father, as a boy, had met Christopher Columbus when the explorer had stopped off in Galway, and since then had taken a huge interest in the exploration of the Americas, and Domhnall was deeply interested in the idea that the world might be shaped more like a ball than a disc, as most people believed. He looked down at the relic now, bowed his head, but made no comment. He was a boy with a razor-sharp brain and a discretion beyond his years.

'It's very small.' Art also sounded disappointed, but he crossed himself reverentially and after a couple of minutes of silent prayer Mara led the way back down the staircase. The local people waited politely until the Brehon and her scholars descended, but now formed a queue, eager to see their parish relic before returning to work on the farms and households of the Burren. The place would then be cleared and the pilgrims allowed a longer time to pray uninterrupted. Five of the six pilgrims were wandering around the churchyard, looking at the slabs and examining the tombs, but the sixth, the German, she saw through the open door of the church, still lingered, on his knees, with head bowed. Mara nodded to herself with satisfaction. I'm right, she thought. He's probably a religious fanatic and wishes to say some very long prayers.

'Ah, Brehon, I was hoping to see you.' A rich voice from behind distracted Mara as she was about to hush Cormac from hoping that sight of the precious relic would help him to score a goal in the forthcoming hurling match against the MacClancy Law School. She turned to greet the innkeeper.

Blad was in full flow, inviting her to a meal at the inn in company with the six pilgrims and, of course, Father MacMahon and Sorley his sexton. Nechtan O'Quinn and his wife Narait were already walking down the path that joined the inn to the church. 'And all of your scholars as well,' he said. 'And I hope you are hungry, boys, because I have a table covered with food.'

It was the look on Finbar's face that made Mara change her mind about making an excuse. Finbar was always hungry. He was the son of a Brehon and had come from a law school in Cloyne in the south of Ireland. To her surprise the Brehon had sent his son to her when the boy was already twelve years old. She had seen after a day that Finbar was very much behind her other boys and had realized that his father had given up the teaching of his son in despair. She wished that he would just leave the boy to her now, but Domhnall, her grandson, had told her that Finbar's father made him work at the law texts during the holidays and that he went supperless to bed if he didn't answer questions correctly. Brigid, Mara's motherly housekeeper, had exclaimed at how very thin the boy was when he returned from his summer holidays.

So she changed her refusal into a hearty acceptance and was rewarded by a blaze of pleasure on all of her boys' faces. Brigid gave them plenty of good food, but the reputation of Blad's cooking had spread far and they could hope for something exciting from a meal at the inn. Brigid herself would be relieved not to have to provide a meal for the boys when they returned from the Feast Day Mass. This was a busy time at the farm attached to the law school and Brigid's husband, Cumhal, with the help of hired labour and friendly neighbours, was snatching a second cut of hay before the autumn rains began. Brigid would be on her mettle to feed them all well and would be pleased not to have to think about the boys and herself as well.

'And your neighbour, the O'Lochlainn, has promised to come also,' said Blad, with a look across at Ardal who stood courteously bending his head as Father MacMahon interrogated him, no doubt about his pilgrimage to Rome. It gave Mara a slight pang to see Ardal's once bright red-gold hair now so grey. He was only five years older than she and yet there was hardly a grey hair among the dark coils fastened behind her neck.

Two

Three things are required of an innkeeper or a hospitaller:
1. A never-dry cauldron.
2. A dwelling near a public road.
3. A welcome to every face.

The inn at Kilnaboy had been recently built. There had been an old monastery on the site, probably hundreds of years ago; certainly it had been a ruin even in the time of Mara's grandfather – her father had told her that. Ruined walls, piles of cut stone and huge stone roofing slabs had lain by the river until Blad had seen an opportunity.

Blad had been a farmer in Thomond until the last few years. When his wife died he divided his farm between his two sons and bought the site of the old monastery and a few acres of riverbank meadow from the church. The money he had paid had gone to buy a splendid crosier for the use of the bishop when he came to Kilnaboy Church, while Blad could now achieve a secret dream and build a splendid inn on the bank of the river, using the old stones from the ruin. He was a great fisherman and a man with a huge interest in good food and fine wines, and he had trained up his daughter to be as good a cook as himself. Mara had been responsible for drawing up Blad's Will and knew that he had endowed Mór with the inn and with the fields surrounding it where they grew vegetables and reared ducks, hens and geese for the table.

It had been, she thought, a fair arrangement. His sons had the farm and his daughter the inn. Normally a daughter could not inherit land – except enough to graze seven cows. It was one aspect of Brehon law that needed amending, she had often thought, though she knew the arguments about keeping clan land within the clan. But this was not clan land or property; it had been bought by Blad out of the profits from successful farming and so was now his own to do what he wished with. She was pleased for Mór's sake – a jolly, plump girl who was no longer a girl but was sliding rapidly towards an age when a future husband might need the inducement of her property before proposing.

The inn, indeed, was a property worth possessing. It was a well-planned building, with an undercroft filled with straw mattresses for the servants of the guests and for poverty-stricken pilgrims. Above that there was a spacious hall with three tall, narrow windows overlooking the river and three very small ones on the wall opposite giving sight of the courtyard. The bedchambers for the more affluent pilgrims were built above the hall and each had its own wooden staircase leading to it from the courtyard and another on the side of the river. The bedrooms, Mara was intrigued to see when Blad showed her around, each had washing facilities with pumped water – there was even a small latrine built into the thickness of the wall – and a chute led down to a small culvert to carry away the waste, an arrangement that had been retained from the time when there had been an abbey on the site. Clean river water entered the kitchen from upstream of the River Fergus and foul water and waste were returned eventually by a meandering stream, fringed with willows and filled with bulrushes and water lilies – a stream which entered the river well away from the inn. By this time the water would have been purified by the plants and the river weed. Blad insisted on showing her all the arrangements and she admired them to his heart's content.

Having viewed the bedrooms, Mara looked around the hall with interest. It was her first visit here. Kilnaboy was on the very south-eastern tip of her territory and she did not often ride in this direction. The room was a very simple one: walls of white limestone blocks, carefully and evenly cut, their surfaces still bearing the mason's marks, were left unadorned by tapestry hangings or wall carpets – just a couple of pale oak dressers laden with gaily painted flagons, mugs and dishes and numerous wooden and leather drinking vessels. The sun streamed through the windows facing south on to the river – the room well protected from the cold air by diamond-shaped panes of glass – and the white stone of the walls gleamed in its light. Two small windows faced north and allowed a view of the entrance court, and an oil lamp, suspended from the ceiling in the centre of the room, would supplement the candlelight on dark days and evenings.

'It's spectacular,' said Mara with a warm smile of approval. 'I like it so much.' She looked at Blad with interest. He was a very wealthy farmer; she had known this and had expected to see evidence of his wealth everywhere, but this room was a miracle of restraint. There was nothing in the room that was not needed, but everything that was needed was of the best quality: the finely-grained pale oak of the central table and the dressers, the tasteful decoration of small stylized flowers on the pottery – French, she guessed, and then wondered when she saw that they were painted with images of the tiny dark blue May-flowering gentians that grew everywhere on the Burren. Perhaps they grew in France or Switzerland also. Her father had spoken of seeing these gentians in the mountains on his pilgrimage to Rome when she was a girl – the Alps, she thought.

'Ah, here come the ladies!' Blad's ear had caught a sound from outside. 'You will be very interested to meet with Madame Eglantine, the prioress, a very travelled lady,' he assured Mara before hastening out to throw open doors and usher in the three women pilgrims. They were followed by Ardal O'Lochlainn, still recounting details of his visit to Rome to Father MacMahon, Nechtan O'Quinn and his wife, the priest from Spain and the monk from Italy. There was no sign of the German with the interesting face, but Mara took a few polite steps forward to greet the prioress.

'It's a great pleasure to meet you,' she murmured in English. Welsh was not a language that she knew, though it might not be too unlike her native Gaelic. She wondered whether the woman should be addressed in Latin.

'Oh, good, you speak in English. How wonderful! Like being back in civilization again,' said the prioress sweetly. She cast a disparaging glance around at the magnificent simplicity of stone and oak and whispered, 'Very bare, isn't it?'

'Not to me, Madame,' said Mara serenely, and was amused when the woman pressed a tiny delicate hand to her rosebud lips.

'Oh, *excusez-moi*,' she said, with what Mara assumed must be a Welsh accent. It certainly sounded like no French person that she had ever met. Her son-in-law, Domhnall's father, often had French wine merchants staying at his house in Galway and Mara, who had a gift for languages, loved to talk to them. Still, she smiled affably at the woman and remarked, 'When natural things are beautiful, there is no need for too much decoration.'

'Of course,' said Madame Eglantine politely, and then in lower tones, with a glance at Blad, 'I don't suppose that the innkeeper speaks English, so you don't need to worry about his feelings. Now tell me about yourself. Are you really a lawyer? I've never heard of such a thing. How do you manage? It must be terribly exhausting to go out into the world of men. I'm so lucky; I've led such a sheltered life inside my convent with my dear sisters.' She saw Mara's glance go to the other two women, and laughed shrilly. 'Not these sisters. I mean my sisters in Christ – the nuns in my convent.'

'But you journey with your sisters of the blood?' Mara lifted her eyebrows in a query and wondered how quickly she could get away from this woman. She had no notion of explaining how deeply satisfying her life was, and how she enjoyed the society of both men and women on equal terms, and that her voice was listened to just as eagerly, or even more so, as the voices of her male colleagues, MacEgan of Thomond and MacClancy of Corcomroe.

'Will you introduce me to your sisters?' she went on, moving a little closer to the other two women. They intrigued her. There was such a gap in age between the prioress and her sister the widow – both of whom looked to be in their late forties or early fifties – and the youngest sister, who judging by the skin on her hands and neck and the sheen on the blonde hair that escaped from under her hood, was at least twenty years younger. The widow, she found, was Mistress Narboath and the young girl Mistress Grace Bowen.

'What a very pretty hood you are wearing, Grace.' Mara

boldly addressed the youngest sister by her first name. It was, after all, the Irish custom, and Wales, she had heard, was like Ireland in lots of respects. They even had Brehon law there, though not, Madame Eglantine had assured her, in the north-eastern part of Wales where her convent was situated.

'But we are more English than Welsh. My convent is at Holywell, beside the well of St Winifred, almost in England,' she interrupted as Grace was telling Mara that the pattern was a traditional Welsh pattern and that she had woven the hood herself from wool that she had dyed with the juice from blackberries.

'Such a pretty rose colour and the pattern is most unusual,' commented Mara, ignoring the prioress. Did the two sisters live in the convent also, she wondered. If so, it was not a good life for Grace who was still a very young woman.

Father MacMahon was passing on to Father Miguel from Spain all he had learned from Ardal O'Lochlainn on the burning question of the ex-monk Martin Luther, who was expostulating about the abuses of the Catholic Church and about the relics. These sermons and talks of his, Mara gathered, were ruining business for the shrines all over Europe, and she wondered whether he had deterred the usual crowds that arrived at Kilnaboy for the feast of the Holy Cross. If that were the case, then Blad's investment in an inn opposite the church might not have been very wise.

He looked happy enough as he summoned them all to table and seated them according to his notions of status. Mara was on his right hand, with her scholars on a separate small table just behind her seat. The prioress was seated on Blad's left. The other two ladies were seated together opposite Father Miguel and Brother Cosimo. Father MacMahon was placed on Mara's other side beside Ardal O'Lochlainn, and they continued to converse gravely on the Pope's view of Martin Luther as the serving boys began to bring in the first course.

'Ninety-five theses, words criticizing the Church and its teachings about the salvation of the Christian soul – and he nailed them to the church door at Wittenberg!' Father MacMahon lifted his hands with horror. His voice rose to almost a squeak and everyone at the table looked towards him.

Cormac muttered something to Art and Art went a dark red and dived under the table. Mara glared at her son – Art was a terrible giggler and always found it hard to stop once he started. Cormac stared back at her with an angelic expression and she made a mental note to have a stern word with him as soon as they returned to the law school.

'What does this Martin Luther object to?' she asked to distract attention from the boys, and Ardal answered gravely.

'He speaks out against sacred relics and indulgences,' he told her. 'The Holy Father is very concerned.'

'I see,' said Mara. Indulgences were a fact of life in the Church – bargains with God, as she often thought of them. You did something difficult and unpleasant, like remaining on your knees for hours on end, or climbing a stony mountain called Croagh Patrick in your bare feet, and in return you got a printed document telling you that you would be let off a year or more's suffering in the fire of purgatory after your death. Did no particular harm, she thought. In fact, she understood that the climb up the mountain in Mayo was quite a sociable affair and the view over Clew Bay, with its myriad of tiny islands, was spectacular once you arrived at the summit. You could also buy an indulgence if you had plenty of money, and that Mara found less easy to accept. She wondered how many people truly believed in these.

'I'm sure your young scholars will know all about indulgences,' said the prioress. 'You, young man, do you know what is meant by a plenary indulgence?'

To Mara's relief she pointed at Domhnall and he replied, in very good English, after his usual careful pause for thought, 'A plenary indulgence is a full remission of all sins, Madame.'

'And you can buy that?' Cormac opened his mouth and widened his eyes. 'For ever? And then you could do what you liked for the rest of your life? How much is it?' His voice rose up full of excitement and most people at the table looked across at him – some indulgently, others with annoyance.

The door behind him opened and the tall figure of Hans Kaufmann, stooping slightly under the doorway and then straightening to his full height, came in. All eyes went to him but he walked up to the scholars' table, looking directly into

Cormac's large light green eyes. His handsome face was very serious as he said, speaking Latin with a strong German accent, 'Yes, my boy, you can buy this. There are Pardonners everywhere all over Europe who sell these indulgences. They have a basketful with them and when the basket is emptied they fill it up again.'

'They buy them cheap and sell them dear, is that the way of it?' Cormac had a sharp brain and, despite herself, Mara's lips twitched, though she resolved again to have a word later about guarding his tongue.

'And the money, Cormac,' said Father MacMahon repressively, 'is used for the greater honour and glory of God. Our own church has been repaired and the chancel rebuilt by the generosity of the pilgrims and the gifts of money that they have left. The beautiful carpet on the altar steps was presented by a wealthy pilgrim who had returned from the Holy Land.'

'Ah, indeed,' said Father Miguel, with an air of triumph, speaking a heavily accented Latin, 'and remember also, Cormac, that you can save a soul from purgatory by buying an indulgence for him.' By now Blad must have spread the word that this young boy was the son, not only of the Brehon, but also of the King of Burren, Corcomroe and Thomond. To Mara's annoyance, the pilgrims seemed interested in impressing him. Still, she thought, it was good for his Latin. Cormac hated not to understand everything and she could see from his eyes how he was concentrating intently on the words said to him.

'That's correct, boy,' said Hans, changing over to English as he strolled to the table and seated himself on the bench beside Grace, who blushed uncomfortably and shifted nearer to Mistress Narboath to make room for him. 'This is what they say, you know, "*Wenn die Münze im Kästlein klingt, die Seele in den Himmel springt.*" And in English that is, "*As soon as the coin in the coffer rings, the soul from purgatory into heaven springs.*" That's a thought, isn't it?' His English was good, though he spoke with a strong German accent.

Father MacMahon looked at him suspiciously, but made no comment. Didn't know English, thought Mara – and neither did Ardal O'Lochlainn, nor probably the other two clerics. The prioress lifted her hands to heaven and shook her head, muttering something about the wickedness of the world which misinterpreted God's works.

'But . . .' began Cormac.

At that moment, to Mara's relief, Mór pushed open the door and staggered in. Though a large, fat woman, she was weighed down by the tray that she carried and was followed by two of her kitchen maids carrying other trays. Blad got up from his seat and bustled around with a flagon of wine, the kitchen lad with a pitcher of ale. Cormac immediately lost interest in the sale of indulgences and licked his lips. Art forgot his giggles and picked up his wooden spoon. Even the adults stopped talking and got out their knives from pockets and pouches and looked with interest at the food.

Most meats and fish had been spit roasted, and were attractively laid out on iron skewers arranged on wooden trays with bunches of herbs and vegetables in between. There were partridges and quails, baked quinces, roast curlew, woodcock, all served with sauces of damsons in wine or hypocras, exquisitely spiced with nutmeg and cinnamon. Another tray held trout, salmon and small perch, with crabs and lobster, fresh from the nearby Atlantic Ocean, their scarlet and dull pink colours set off by the dark green of watercress and the small garlic-tasting cloves of *cainnenn* – a plant that Mara grew as much for its wonderful purple flowering heads in early summer as for its plentiful clove harvest in September. Slices of red-skinned apples formed a border on the tray and large leaves of cabbage, decorated with small heaps of glistening blackberries, were placed around and underneath the fish.

Mara helped herself to a partridge and accepted a generous helping of the spiced hypocras. There was no doubt that either Blad or Mór was an expert in food preparation. The spicy wine sauce went so well with the bird. She was pleased to see that her boys were tucking in as if they had been deprived of all food for many hours. She sent her compliments to the cook and chewed happily on the slices of fresh white bread and a helping of damsons in wine. She would have liked to talk to Ardal about Rome – her father had brought back many stories of the wonderful buildings there. Ardal, however, was fully occupied with the two priests and their discussion about this

Martin Luther so she turned her attention towards Hans Kaufmann. To her surprise he was flirting with the prioress, gallantly moving choice pieces from his to her plate and even, Mara overheard, admiring the sheen of her nails and dropping a quick kiss on the tips of the woman's fingers.

Mara concealed a smile. He was the sort of man who could have had any woman adoring him, but the shy, badly scarred younger sister was resolutely keeping her eyes fixed on her plate. The heavily built widow on Grace's other side was also enjoying the German's gallantries to her buxom person, though she did from time to time try to include Grace in the conversation. And after a few minutes of personal gratification the prioress also remembered her younger sister. Grace, however, would not respond and blushed fierily whenever the German tried to say something in his highly accented English. Mara began to feel a little sorry for the girl. Her elder sisters seemed to be making a determined effort to throw her into conversation with this rich German. Did they hope that he would offer marriage to her, wondered Mara? Otherwise, she would have thought that the prioress would be too pious to encourage an unmarried young girl to be on easy terms with a man who was no relation. Hans Kaufmann was the sort of man who would flirt with any woman, she decided, catching a rapid wink that he sent in the direction of Mór when the prioress was not looking.

'The king will be sorry that he has missed this feast,' she said to Blad, knowing that the slightest word from Turlough would have been more welcome to the man than a bagful of gold. 'What a shame that there are not more pilgrims here today,' she went on.

He nodded resignedly. 'Yes,' he said, 'and these few will be leaving as soon as the meal is over. Their luggage is all corded and ready for the packhorses and they will be on the boats to Aran within a couple of hours from now.'

Even as he said the words, Hans Kaufmann rapidly swallowed what was left on his platter and got to his feet decisively.

'I must see to my luggage,' he said and strode from the room. The noise of his boots sounded on the courtyard outside. Blad's eyes followed him with a disappointed expression. The magnificent meal which he had provided had not been appreciated by the German pilgrim. Mara could see him worrying whether a poor account of the inn would be carried to other Germans. In fact, she thought, I can never remember a pilgrim from Germany coming before now.

'Well, perhaps things will pick up,' she said consolingly. 'This Martin Luther business of speaking out against the worship of relics might be just a flash in the pan. Fashions come and go in pilgrimages.'

'Canterbury is not as popular as it was, but of course, Rome will always be the most important destination,' said Brother Cosimo smugly.

'The numbers of pilgrims at the shrine of the Blessed St James at Santiago has continued to rise,' said Father Miguel assertively. 'By the way, Master Innkeeper, perhaps you might hand some of these out to future pilgrims.' He dug deep into a leather bag by his side, producing first the small candle lantern that most travellers carried and then a rolled up bunch of small sheets of parchment. He unrolled one and showed it to Mara. It was written in Latin so as to be comprehensible to all travellers and it invited the pilgrim to see for himself, or herself, the huge spiritual benefits to be gained by visits to the shrine of St James at Santiago. There were even neat little pictures of the relics on show which were painted around the margins of the sheet. Blad accepted one glumly.

'We could do some splendid ones like that for you, Blad,' said Mara enthusiastically. 'It could show the church here with the two-armed cross in the gable and then the round tower with the relic. Finbar would do the drawings – he is very good at that. Cormac,' she looked severely at her son, 'needs to practise his script so he could write a few every evening for you.' She beckoned to the two boys to come up to the table and they obeyed, Finbar rather nervously, and Cormac stuffing a tasty chunk of venison into his mouth before he left his plate. They leaned over the scroll and admired the small pictures – at least Finbar did, and Cormac wisely confined himself to some vigorous nods as he chewed rapidly.

'And here's one for Walsingham Priory – I carry some of theirs and they carry some of mine.' Father Miguel delved into his pouch again and placed another leaf of vellum in front of her.

'The house of Mary, Mother of Jesus?' queried Mara. 'I thought that Walsingham was in England . . .' She stopped. After all, in the world of miracles, all was possible. Houses could be moved from Jerusalem to Norfolk in the east of England.

'And they have a small vial full of her breast milk there as well,' said Father Miguel. There was a note of sheer envy in his voice. This shrine business was competitive, not just for the innkeepers but for the priests and monks themselves. Soon the prioress would be weighing in with the account of St Winifred's miraculous bones at Holywell in Wales.

'Milk?' queried Cormac in a puzzled tone, and then saw Finbar blush to the roots of his fair hair and his jaw dropped and his lips formed the letter 'B'. Mara glared at Cormac, daring him to say anything more.

'Yes,' she said hurriedly. 'Go back to your meal, boys. We'll discuss this later. We'll show you a sample, Blad, and then you can see if you like what we do.'

The boys returned quickly as the two kitchen maids were now bringing in the sweetmeats: honey cakes and apple and pear pies and succulent mouthfuls of blackberries sitting inside pastry baskets. Mara took one for politeness and then a long hour ensued during which everyone ate and drank and talked – mostly about relics and pilgrimage shrines. Father MacMahon embarked on a long, complicated description of the history of Kilnaboy and the monastic site, and proudly explained to Herr Kaufmann how the right to sanctuary was still retained by the church.

'Sanctuary from what?' Cormac was leaning back, patting his stomach, and the word had caught his attention. 'Isn't "sanctuary" a sort of refuge – a holy place that shelters people? Didn't we have something in our Latin, something about Ajax . . .?' he finished vaguely.

'They have "sanctuary" in St Nicholas's Church in Galway,' said Domhnall. 'If you are in danger of being hanged or some-thing then you can go to the church and stand beside the altar and demand sanctuary – I think that it only lasts for forty days and that you have to stay beside the altar for all of that time. Is that right, Brehon?'

'What about if you have to go . . . well, you know . . .' queried Cormac with interest, and Mara sighed and thought about moving her son to another law school.

'No one hangs people on the Burren so sanctuary is no good here,' observed Art.

'Except that the English ruled here for a while a couple of hundred years ago, before they were defeated at Dysart O'Dea,' put in Domhnall. 'They might have needed sanctuary then. The English hang people even for stealing a loaf of bread.' Thankfully he spoke in Gaelic to Art and the rest of the company just looked at him with polite interest. Mara hastened to intervene.

'It will be an interesting subject to discuss when we go back to the law school,' she said emphatically, and was glad to see them look distracted by a fresh tray of tiny stuffed figs which had just been brought in by a kitchen maid. Domhnall was the only one of the boys who had ever tasted one before, and he gave such an enthusiastic account that Mara could guess that the other boys' mouths were watering before the tray came to them.

She was glad to see, after the trays of sweetmeats began to empty, that the remaining pilgrims were beginning to look out through the windows to where the sun had begun to move into the south-west. Like everyone on a journey they would want to move on to the next stage. And Mara wanted to get back to the reality of her life in the law school and leave relics to those who liked them. She pictured her husband's face when he heard, as he undoubtedly would from Cormac, about the vial of the Blessed Virgin's milk, and she bit her lips to disguise the sudden smile.

'You'll have a good crossing to Aran,' she said politely to the prioress. 'The sea can be rough sometimes, although the island is only about six miles from the port at Doolin. There may be a storm tonight, but tomorrow will be a lovely day – or so my farm manager tells me, and he is a great judge of the weather. He plans haymaking tomorrow, so it will definitely be dry and calm,' she continued, seeing the alarmed look on the faces of three women. The Irish sea between Wales and

Ireland was notorious for storms, high winds and rough waves; the pilgrims probably already had an unpleasant crossing. They would have been worrying about the trip to Aran. The other pilgrims finished their meal hastily but waited for Father MacMahon to say a solemn Latin grace after meals before standing up also.

'I'll take leave of you now, and wish you God speed,' said Mara graciously, exchanging bows with the three ladies and then with the two clerics. Not a very interesting or, except for the timid Grace, a very likeable group of people, she thought, and decided that she would not demean her office as Brehon by standing around in the courtyard while the usual bustle of loading goods and mounting horses took place. She summoned the boys to make their farewells also and they did not disappoint her with their polite bows and the ease with which all, except for Finbar, were able to switch between Latin and English. She dismissed them then back to their own table with a quick nod. There was no reason why they should not quickly finish up the left-over sweetmeats while the visitors were getting going. She herself went to one of the small open windows and looked out on to the courtyard. Hans Kaufmann was already mounted on his horse, though the others had not yet arrived out.

Mara stood at a discreet distance and observed him. Blad was not there, but his daughter Mór emerged from the stable. She took a quick glance around and then stood on her toes, leaning coquettishly on the shoulder of his horse. He stooped down, kissed her on the lips and then impulsively dismounted and took the woman in his arms. This time the kiss was very prolonged and seemed to Mara's interested sight to be extremely passionate. She doubted that it was the first embrace and wondered about the sleeping arrangements of the night before. Still, it was none of her business and she turned away quickly before any of the boys joined her at the window. As she crossed the room towards them, she heard, through the open door in the passageway, the noise of horses' hoofs. Hans Kaufmann could not wait to depart. He had gone ahead of his fellow pilgrims and would probably reach the coast well before the other five.

Mara watched the boys eat for another minute. No expense had been spared on this meal. Cyprus sugar was cheap enough in Galway – she had tasted it, beautifully blended with vinegar, in one of the sauces that had accompanied the fish – but the cakes of refined sugar from which some of these sweetmeats had been made were very expensive indeed, and of course the figs, imported from somewhere in the south, would have cost Blad a good few pieces of silver. And then there would have been the cost of the transport of the sugar, and the wine, across the mountain that lay between the city and the Burren. Mara bought wine and some other luxuries from Galway, but Domhnall's father, her daughter Sorcha's husband, Oisín, delivered hers free whenever he had an order for goods in the neighbourhood.

'Let's go into the kitchen and thank Mór for the lovely food,' she proposed when she saw the hand to mouth action beginning to slacken. She was meticulous about insisting on courtesy from the boys, who, if they passed all of their examinations, would have the responsibility of acting as Brehon – with all the peace-keeping and diplomatic implications of that position – and so she never passed up an opportunity to show them how to behave to others.

In any case, she had her share of curiosity and wondered whether Mór would reveal anything about this intriguing Hans Kaufmann. How wonderful if he was to propose marriage, but Mara feared that it may not have been marriage which was on his mind.

Mór, to her pleasure, was in great good humour, admiring how grown-up Domhnall had become since she had seen him last, flirting a little with the handsome Slevin, and trying to kiss Cormac who had often been at the inn when accompanying the king to Thomond during the summer holidays.

'I'll only put up with it if I can have a sweet pastry,' he said with a grin, and Mara did not scold him for his outrageousness because she saw how Mór was looking for an opportunity to work off her high spirits. What had Hans Kaufmann said to her during those few minutes out in the courtyard? Had he told her that he would call in again on his way back from the Aran Islands? Or perhaps they had been together in that hour when he was missing from the table. Mór's colour was high and her dark blue eyes were sparkling. Despite an excess of weight, she was a very pretty girl. And, of course, it had been surprising that the German should have left the hall without partaking of the sweetmeats and the malmsey wine. Perhaps that wink exchanged between himself and Mór had been an agreement for an assignation – it had been a little odd that she had allowed her kitchen maids to serve the sweet course and had not appeared herself with it. Mara remembered thinking that Blad had not looked too pleased either. His good manners as host had not allowed him to leave the ladies on either side of him, but she had seen him look towards the door to the kitchen in a puzzled fashion. Mór had been somewhere else. Hans Kaufmann had not gone to his room; there had been no sound of footsteps going up the steps – he had crossed the cobbled surface of the courtyard and then had gone . . . where?

And then, above the exuberant shouts, laughing comments and the exaggerated smacking of Mór's full lips as she chased Cormac around the room, there was a thunder of heavy boots in the passageway outside and Sorley, the sexton, burst into the room. His face was red and his grey hair, cut very short, seemed to stick straight from his head. He glared at Mór.

'Where's my key?' he shouted. 'It's gone from my jerkin. And I left my jerkin here in the kitchen. Who touched the key to the tower?'

Mara took a quick step forward. There was a note of hysteria in the man's voice. He was an odd fellow. Perhaps digging graves and shovelling old bones aside every week of his life for as long as she could remember had had a strange effect upon him, but she had never seen Sorley smile. His face was white now and small patches of red appeared in places, one right in the middle of his forehead. The boys stopped laughing and stared at him uneasily.

Mór had flushed a bright poppy-red, but now her face grew pale at the look in his eyes. Mara stepped forward quickly. 'It'll be somewhere, Sorley,' she said soothingly. 'It's such a big key that it won't be mislaid. And Father MacMahon has his key, doesn't he?'

His face turned even redder. 'I'm talking about *my* key,

Brehon,' he said. She had a feeling that only respect for her office stopped him short of shouting at her. He nodded stiffly, but managed to keep his mouth shut after that. His angry eyes swept from Mór to the two aghast faces of the kitchen maids. Mara saw them exchange looks and guessed that they knew something about the key. Quickly she intervened again.

'You probably lost it in the courtyard,' she stated. 'Come along, boys. Let's all go and search. Come with us, Sorley. You can show my scholars exactly where you walked.'

His hand went to the empty cord dangling from the belt of his jerkin and he looked once more around the kitchen. Sorley had been offered the same meal as they had, and probably plenty to drink also, but he had dined in the kitchen. Even now, with the door ajar, with the windows widely opened to the river, and the fire reduced to embers, the place was hot. When they were cooking there would have been charcoal braziers burning as well. He would have removed his jerkin and hung it up before sitting down to his food and ale. Just as she thought of this, she saw his eyes go to the floor beneath the row of hooks on the wall at the far end of the kitchen. But Mór ran an efficient kitchen and there was not even a crumb to be seen. Mara touched his arm reassuringly.

'It will be found,' she said with conviction, and signed to him to go ahead of her in the wake of her young scholars.

'What is the best way to find it, Domhnall?' she asked once they were all in the courtyard and Sorley was safely surrounded by her young helpers.

'Search the whole area,' he replied decisively. 'It's difficult to remember exactly where you've walked. We'll do the whole thing, Sorley. Don't worry. It won't take long. Cormac, you measure two paces from the wall. Art, the next two paces . . .'

'Did you go into the stables at all, Sorley?' asked Mara with feigned anxiety. 'That would be more difficult with all the straw . . . No? Well, that's good. Let's walk along the path towards the church together. The sun should pick up a gleam from the metal. Where were you when you noticed that it was missing?'

At that moment there was a shout from Domhnall. 'It's been found, Brehon.'

With a feeling of thankfulness, Mara turned back. She had better things to do than searching fields and roadways for a key. She was not, moreover, surprised to be summoned back so quickly. Mór was bold and decisive.

'Found it under that chest near the hooks,' she was shouting, waving the large key triumphantly. 'You must have dropped it and it got kicked under there when we were serving.'

It was a possible story. The kitchen would have been hectic with the three women and the serving boys dodging in and out of each other's way, carrying heavy trays, their eyes stinging from the heat of the fires and the smoke from the braziers. Sorley, however, looked sceptical, and as he tied the key back on Mara observed the complication of the knot which secured it to his jerkin and guessed that he was not convinced that it could just have fallen off and then been kicked under the chest. He drew in a long breath and Mór looked at him defiantly.

However, at that moment Blad came out with Father MacMahon and Ardal O'Lochlainn on either side of him. Ardal was, as usual, grave and slightly withdrawn, but Father MacMahon was positively merry with a broad smile on his lips and a slight stagger to his walk. Blad had, Mara guessed, drowned the memory of an unsatisfactory amount of pilgrims with a bowl of brandy and the priest had taken his full share.

'Wonderful day, Sorley,' he said exultantly. 'All the pilgrims praised how beautifully you keep the tower. They thought our arrangements so much better than at other places of pilgrimage.'

None of them had said anything of the sort, to Mara's knowledge, but, she thought charitably, perhaps a priest had a God-given ability to read minds. She hastened to add her morsel towards obliterating the painful memory of the missing key.

'Everyone must admire the tower,' she said solemnly. She had heard again and again how Sorley and his father had built that little tower when the church of Kilnaboy had purchased the relic of the true cross from a church in Rome. 'It is so wonderfully built and so cleverly designed. It's like Jacob's ladder ascending to heaven,' she concluded. That was, she modestly considered, a stroke of genius. For the first time during the day, Sorley smiled the smile of a satisfied man.

Father MacMahon positively beamed. He cleared his throat pompously and turned to the boys. 'What is it that the Bible says?' he demanded, and then without waiting for an answer he continued: '"*And he dreamed, and behold a ladder was set up on the earth, and the top of it reached to heaven: and behold the angels of God ascending and descending on it.*" That's right, isn't it?'

He hiccupped slightly, and while Domhnall assured him solemnly that he was correct in his memory of the quotation, Cormac and Art, once more overcome by giggles, bolted across the courtyard and set off running towards the church, followed by Slevin and Finbar. Mara smiled at Domhnall.

'Better get them back,' she said with a glance at the stables where her Arab mare, a gift from King Turlough ten years ago, was standing patiently in the cool shade, tolerating the companionship of the boys' ponies. 'Such a marvellous meal and a wonderful occasion, as always, but now we must return,' she said, addressing Father MacMahon and Blad. 'Will you ride back with us, Ardal?'

His reply was drowned by Cormac's shriek and then a deeper roar. In a moment the boys were back in the courtyard.

But their cries had gone before them and Sorley was hurtling through the gate before they reached it.

'Fire! Fire!' they yelled. 'The round tower is on fire!'

Three

Brecha Forloischche
(Judgements of Arson)

When judging a case of arson a Brehon must first decide whether the fire was caused by malice or by accident. The former merits a heavier fine.

Next the judge must consider whether death or injury to either people or animals was caused – if so, the appropriate fine is imposed.

Burning buildings such as mills, barns and animal pens will result in a heavier fine than other buildings.

Fire is violent and terrifying and the effect on the owner should be calculated as well as the amount of the loss. Recompense must be paid for both.

Mór was the first to react.

'Buckets!' she shrieked. Immediately her kitchen staff, who had followed her to the door when she restored the key into Sorley's anxious hand, dashed back into the kitchen. The stable boys, who were dining on a large basket full of left-overs from the lavish meal, up in the loft space above the horses, came vaulting down and grabbed more leather buckets from the store in the stable. Fire was an ever-present risk in stables and they automatically began to run towards the river.

'No, the round tower, in the churchyard!' Slevin's voice was hoarse with the effort of bawling across the field.

'The round tower!' Sorley's voice was a roar filled with despair. He began to run and Ardal O'Lochlainn followed and overtook him.

'The well, you numbskulls; there's a well in the churchyard,' shouted Mór, hitching her *léine* up through her belt. 'Get the water there.' And she set an example by seizing two empty buckets and sprinting through the gate.

'God and His blessed saints aid us in our hour of need!' prayed Father MacMahon.

Mara left him to his prayers, resolving not to display as much leg as Mór, but at the same time determined to reach the burning building before any of her scholars got themselves into a dangerous position. Surely, she thought, as she sped through the gate and across the field, a solid stone building like that would not be too vulnerable to fire. Until a couple of hours ago that churchyard was full of people, and even after all had viewed the sacred relic and Sorley had, as she was sure, carefully locked the tower, many people drawn by the annual Feast of the Holy Cross would have stayed in order to pray at the gravesides of dead relations and friends. The fire, she reasoned, could not have been going for more than an hour.

When she reached the church, she began to relax. Someone, probably Ardal O'Lochlainn, who was always good in a crisis, had formed the helpers into a line leading from the well to the tower. The thatched roof was not on fire, but there seemed to be a fire burning fiercely in the top room of the little tower, flames darting out through the small window slit on the south side of the tower. Sorley was on the top of the ladder, Ardal halfway up, and another man at the bottom was passing up the leather buckets filled with the water from the sacred spring of the daughter of Baoith, patroness of the church. Even as Mara arrived, the bright orange tongues of fire in the east window slit were replaced by a cloud of smoke.

Mara's heart ceased to beat so rapidly. Her scholars were in the back of the line, nearest to the well. Ardal, on the ladder, looked supremely in command and confident; a couple of his men were on the bucket-bearing chain nearest to the ladder, she noticed, and realized that the fire would soon be under control.

Sorley worked on doggedly, pouring bucket after bucket through the narrow opening and flinging the flat empty leather containers down on to the ground. Cormac, who liked to be on the move, now left his post and was darting to and fro, picking up the buckets and sprinting back with them to the more docile Art, still standing at the well. However, he was fast and efficient and in no danger so Mara did not interfere.

Already clouds of smoke were drifting out through the other three windows and the bright flames and sparks had died down.

Perhaps the fire had been caused by a stray spark from a bonfire, but there were no bonfires – it was too early in the year for leaf burning.

'Take over,' said Ardal abruptly to his young steward Danann who accompanied him everywhere. Mara thought for a moment that Ardal was tired – he had not looked well since he came back from the pilgrimage – but when he came straight towards her, she realized from the expression in his eyes that he wanted to speak and moved across the churchyard to a secluded spot where they could talk without being overheard.

'What is it?' she asked quietly. His lips were compressed and his eyes were full of anger. She began to feel alarmed. 'There wasn't anyone in there?' she queried swiftly, suddenly appalled at the tragedy that might have occurred if the door had been locked accidentally. But who could it have been? The pilgrims would have been the last to leave and Sorley would have waited respectfully in the churchyard until they reappeared, and then would have locked the door before crossing over to the inn to enjoy one of Blad's sumptuous dinners.

'No, not that.' But his expression did not lighten. 'The fire was on the top floor. I couldn't see much because of all of the smoke, and we daren't open the door until it is completely out – the draught would start it up again – but I have a terrible fear.' He stopped and passed his hand over his eyes, stroking down over the thin cheeks.

'What?' Mara stared at him, appalled. 'What are you trying to tell me, Ardal?'

'The relic,' he said dully. 'The sacred relic of the most holy cross of Jesus. I hardly dare say it, Brehon, but I fear that it may have been injured, probably destroyed.'

Oh, is that all? Mara bit the words back from the tip of her tongue. 'As you say,' she said evenly, 'we can't come to any conclusions before the fire is out.' She eyed his white face with concern and was about to call one of her boys to get him a drink of water when he left her abruptly and went to talk to Father MacMahon, who had just staggered across, his face red with exertion, anxiety, or perhaps, she thought mischievously, just plain over-eating and over-drinking.

She did not join them. Her mind was busy. A fire starting

on a thatched roof would have been one thing – these did happen from time to time – but this fire had not started on the roof, but in the small chamber that contained the relic of the holy cross. The chances of a spark being blown in through one of those very small openings, no bigger than arrow loops in castle walls, was small – and, in any case, there was no fire nearer than the kitchen fires in the inn.

So how did a fire start in the round tower? And on the top floor, too, not the bottom. Sorley would have seen that all was well before he admitted the six pilgrims – he would not have taken a chance that anyone could have dropped something that would sully the purity and the spotlessness of the shrine which he had watched over from a boy. All the Burren people would have been suspiciously supervised by him; he even checked that they cleaned their boots before climbing the ladder.

But what, she thought, if he had not bothered to check after the pilgrims left? He would expect them to treat the shrine with the same reverence that he himself felt for the sacred relic. It was quite possible that he had decided that he would do that after the meal was over and the pilgrims had departed.

And, of course, one pilgrim had stayed longer than the others. By the time Hans Kaufmann had descended, Sorley's stomach was probably beginning to rumble.

And then there was the case of the missing key.

Mara's eyes went to the top of the tower. By now only wisps of smoke were appearing from one of the windows and the others were clear. There had been no hurried shouts or running figures from the farmers on Roughan Hill, so the fire at Kilnaboy had gone unnoticed by the parishioners. Not much of a fire – there were no marks on the stone outside.

But it wouldn't have taken much of a fire to destroy the precious contents of the round tower. And the sooner the truth was known, the better. Mara looked across towards the two figures of Father MacMahon and Ardal O'Lochlainn just as Sorley came down heavily from the ladder following young Danann, and they both yielded their place to Ardal. Then she walked across and stood beside the priest. His old face was rigid with horror, his eyes almost starting from his head. Sorley came across and joined them, grey and exhausted as though he had been fighting a tornado for hours. Mara said nothing. Ardal would have to be allowed to check for himself. She would wait until the door was opened and their worst fears confirmed. By now her boys had joined her and she was glad to see that they all stood very quietly with solemn faces.

Ardal moved the ladder and repositioned it so that the top now touched the wooden door – uninjured, noticed Mara. As if by a signal, Sorley put his hand on the key and climbed up without a word. The cords that suspended the key from his jerkin were long enough to permit him to undo the lock without untying. He went straight inside and all held their breath while Ardal climbed up also. They would both now be in the tiny round first-floor room which had seemed so hot a few hours ago at noon. She expected them to pull in the ladder in order to reach the top floor, but they did not do so; the inside ladder must not have been damaged, proof that the fire had been relatively trivial.

Mara, followed by her boys, moved forward and gazed upwards. Yes, they had succeeded in climbing up. Perhaps, she thought, hoping for the best, the relic had escaped. All might still be well and she and the boys could go back to their peaceful law school and get on with their studies without having to spend time working on unravelling a mystery which did not interest her greatly. She strained her ears, hoping against hope, but heard no word from either of them.

Then the sound of returning footsteps came to them. In a moment, Ardal was back down again and one look at his face, drained of all colour, told her what he had found. Father MacMahon groaned aloud and the boys shuffled their feet with embarrassment.

'I think you had better look at this, Brehon.' Ardal's voice was very quiet and he held out a small object to her. The boys crowded around. 'Don't touch it – it's hot.' His left hand, she saw, had the mark of a burn on the fingers, but he did not appear to notice it, other than by using an unaccustomed right hand.

'You know what it is, don't you?' he asked, and she nodded.

'A traveller's lamp,' she said. Most travellers and pilgrims carried them in the satchels beside their horses. Small rounded lamps, the size of a baby's fist, with a perforated lid that could be lifted and a spike inside where the stump of a candle could be held upright and safely. It had a small ring of quartz at the base. A quick slash with a knife against the quartz would produce a spark and the candle could be lit and safely enclosed with the perforated lid. Once it had been made from bronze, probably, but now the metal had dissolved and then set into an ugly lump.

And yet, oddly, there inside the lid was something that was not metal.

'Vellum,' said Cormac, looking over her shoulder.

Ardal took the tip of his knife and levered up the lid, wincing slightly as the heat from the metal inflamed his burn. The small piece of calf skin had half-dissolved in the heat. Cormac picked it out with his nails and held it up, waving it gently to and fro to cool it.

'Why put a piece of vellum in the lamp?' asked Slevin with interest. 'Though vellum or parchment would burn well, wouldn't it, Domhnall? I remember we had a small fire in our barn once and a lambskin that was pegged up to dry was the first thing to burn – it's the fat in the skin, Brehon,' he added, and Mara smiled an acknowledgement. She liked the way boys of Slevin's age assumed that she had little knowledge of practical matters. They probably fancied that she did not know the origin of the parchment and vellum which they used in the law school.

'I think I know why that piece of vellum was used here,' said Domhnall. He and Slevin always worked well together; the more volatile Slevin often started an idea and Domhnall would then pursue it to its logical conclusion. His dark eyes now showed that concentration that made him such a good scholar. 'Perhaps it was originally a longer piece of vellum than the bit we've got,' he said slowly. 'In that case it might have had one end touching that velvet cushion and the rest of it tucked in beside the candle.'

'And the heat from the candle would warm the fat; it would blaze up quickly – and then the fire would travel along the line of the vellum.' Slevin looked excited.

'A clue! That vellum comes from the hand of the villain!'

exclaimed Cormac loudly and dramatically. He lowered his voice as Mara frowned, but whispered loudly in Art's ear, 'A pity it's not a murder. I'd love a murder to solve.'

'This is worse. A crime against God is a greater crime than a crime against man,' said Art piously.

'That's not true, according to the law. According to the law, the worst crime is the rape of a girl in plaits,' said Cormac airily.

'There's a word here, Brehon,' said Domhnall. He held up the twisted piece of vellum to the light.

'A number – the number 90.' Slevin peered closely.

'Funny letters,' commented Finbar.

'Let us see,' commanded Cormac, pushing Finbar to one side. 'T, A, G, E,' he spelled out the letters with difficulty.

Mara held out her hand for the scrap of vellum. She peered at the ornately curling letters intently. 'It's German,' she said slowly. She glanced over her shoulder but Father MacMahon had already come over and was standing just behind her and peering at the twist of vellum. Still, there was no help for it. The truth had to be uncovered and the matter dealt with by the law. A crime had been committed and restitution had to be made.

'I think, Father,' she said, 'this is an indulgence – an indulgence written in the German language. "90 *Tage*" would probably refer to a remission of 90 days' suffering in the fires of purgatory.'

'German!' Ardal's voice was harsh with suspicion. 'Hans Kaufmann?'

'Or possibly one of the other pilgrims,' said Mara. 'These people have been visiting lots of shrines. Indulgences are to be . . . to be acquired at all of those places – and the language would not necessarily alter their efficacy in the eyes of the pilgrims. Is that not right, Father?' She spoke from an automatic dislike to give a ruling before an investigation of the facts was completed, but she had little doubt in her own mind now that Hans Kaufmann was a follower of Luther and had destroyed the relic at his master's behest – perhaps others, also. And had shown his contempt of indulgences by lighting his fire with one of them.

'Get them back, all of them!' Father MacMahon's face was now so red that she feared he might have a fit.

Without a moment's hesitation Ardal shouted 'Danann!', and followed by his steward he set off at a run towards the stables in front of the inn. Nechtan O'Quinn followed him, shouting at his own steward to get other men.

The die is cast, thought Mara. She wondered what would be the end of this. She feared fanaticism of any kind – it upset balances and checks. Who would take charge of this case – a matter of petty arson, really? After all, what was destroyed: a carved shrine blackened with smoke, slightly melted, a few of its ornate decorations slightly damaged – it could easily be repaired; a small velvet cushion burned and saturated with water; and a one-inch piece of wood . . .

Valueless, or beyond all value? That depended on the belief of the assessor. Or did it depend on the beliefs of the injured party – and did the beliefs of the guilty party play a part also?

Despite herself, Mara smiled slightly. She so loved to wrestle with a complicated problem like this. The Brehons of Ireland had an annual meeting in August of each year, and she thought that the events of this year of 1519, when the world of religion in the European countries was beginning to change, might be a very interesting time for the lawyers of Ireland to debate. In secrecy, of course; the Pope might have a rule against laity discussing such matters. Yes, she thought, there could be an interesting discussion next year.

But in the meantime there was another problem for her to deal with. Her eyes went to Father MacMahon, now striding up and down as though he could not wait for the transgressors to be hauled back in front of him.

The law of the Church or the law of the king – which was in charge of this affair? Mara set her lips firmly. King Turlough Donn was away in the north of Ireland on an important mission. It was up to her, as the King's representative, to take this matter firmly into her hands and to render justice with mercy according to the tenets of Brehon law. This was a Gaelic kingdom, not England, not Rome. Still, there was no point in anticipating trouble. She turned to her scholars.

'Let's go and search the round tower and see if we find anything,' she proposed.

'Clues,' said Cormac enthusiastically, but it was the methodical Art who found the first clue.

At the bottom of the round tower, on its east side, just below where the door stood above head height, Sorley had planted a bush of fragrant lavender. Sheltered from cold winds, exposed to the sun and warmed by the retained heat from the stone wall behind it, the bush had flourished. It had reached a height of about four feet and then stopped growing, but year after year it had thickened and widened. On this fine day in early September the exquisite pale purple of the tightly-budded flowers seemed to glow in the heat and they were full of bees desperately seeking stores of honey before the winter.

But purple wasn't the only colour to be seen. Lying on the far side of the clump was a small patch of deep rose. Art, careful as always, had not touched it, but called Mara instantly. For a moment she stood there, standing as he had directed her, halfway up the ladder that led to the raised doorway of the round tower, and gazed down. The shape of the object was hidden by the stems and flowers, but the colour was distinctive and she had seen it very recently.

The object, she thought, may have been held in the hand of someone who stood there on the ladder – perhaps taken off in order to hear better and then dropped. Or perhaps the bonnet was removed to show the one beauty – the silky blonde hair of a woman whose other beauties had been disfigured by scars,

But why not picked up? There could, she thought, be two possible reasons for that.

Mara went back down the ladder, skirted the wide bush and picked out the small, neat, finely woven bonnet dyed in that distinctive colour by the combination of blackberries and bilberries. She held it for a moment in her hand, reconstructing the scene.

Could Grace have followed the handsome young German over to the churchyard, climbed the ladder leading to the round tower, stood outside its massive door, perhaps put her ear to the large keyhole, removing her bonnet to hear all the better . . .?

And then something disturbed her. Perhaps Hans Kaufmann and Mór had shown signs of coming out, or perhaps she could not bear the murmurs any longer. But, of course, there was another possibility.

Could she have wanted to burn the relic in order to please a man who had secretly expressed contempt for it?

Whatever had happened she had fled, leaving the small bonnet behind, hidden by the purple flowers and the clusters of bees until Art's sharp eyes spotted it.

When next Mara had seen Grace, her head had been demurely covered with the hood of her travelling cloak, her face almost invisible.

'It's Fachtnan,' shouted Slevin, just at the moment when Mara was regretting that her boys, even Domhnall, were too young to appreciate the nuances of adult love and the problems of a woman, badly scarred and yet deeply attracted by a man in whose company she had already spent weeks. Fachtnan, she knew, would be able to bring a mature understanding and compassionate heart to this problem.

Fachtnan was Mara's assistant teacher. He had first been a scholar in her school, had managed with enormous difficulty to pass the lowest grade for qualification as an *aigne*, and had stayed on as her assistant, trying desperately to pass the further examinations but finding a poor memory an insuperable handicap. Mara valued him immensely, not just for his gentle, kind nature but for his intelligence and his deep understanding. Eventually, when it became plain that he could progress no further, she had offered him this position as a permanent teaching assistant. It had been an impulse that she had never regretted, and now she often wondered how she could have managed without his companionship, his intuition and his caring relationship to the scholars that she taught. Six years ago he had become betrothed to Nuala the physician who owned property at Rathborney – only a couple of miles from the law school. As Nuala was Mara's cousin and as dear to her as a daughter, it had been one of the happiest days in Mara's life when Fachtnan and Nuala had married, and now they had three small girls – worshipped by their father.

Mara came forward now, her hands outstretched. 'Fachtnan,' she said impulsively. 'You are just whom I was wishing for. What made you come? How on earth did you know about this?'

'The O'Lochlainn sent one of his men to go to Caher-macnaghten, and Cumhal immediately sent someone down to Rathborney with a message,' explained Fachtnan. Mara nodded in understanding. Ardal would have known that she would value help and had thought of her even in the course of the headlong chase to arrest the passage of the pilgrims to Aran.

'That was like Ardal,' she exclaimed thankfully. 'Domhnall, you tell Fachtnan what happened. Art and Cormac, you go and have another look around the churchyard and see whether you can discover any more clues. Slevin and Finbar, go and ask Blad whether you could check the pilgrims' bedrooms to see whether anything may have been left behind.'

She waited till they were all occupied and then mounted the ladder and went into the small, windowless first-floor room of the tower. Yes, she thought, a very cosy and private place for an assignation. With the key in her possession, Mór would have not failed to take advantage of it. Mara remembered the wink and the whisper in the ear of the German. Had others noticed it also? Of that she could not be sure.

Four

Seanchus Mór
(Great Traditions)

And this is the Seanchus Mór. *Nine persons were appointed to arrange this book. Three bishops: Patrick, Benen and Cairnech; three kings: Laeghaire, Corc and Daire; two Brehons, learned in law: Rosa mac Trechim and Dubhthach; and one poet: Fengus. Nofis, therefore, is the name of this book that they arranged, that is the knowledge of nine persons.*

It was said of St Patrick that there were three offences which he particularly forbade among the Irish:

1. *Killing trained oxen.*
2. *Offences against milch cows.*
3. *Arson – in particular the burning of church buildings.*

The small group of pilgrims was dwarfed by the size of its escort. Ardal, or his steward Danann, had picked up additional men from the tower house of Lissylisheen and were riding in the van of the group. Nechtan O'Quinn's men, flamboyant in their red jerkins bearing the O'Quinn badge, and armed with prominent knives and throwing spears, were lined to the front and back of the three men and three women, enclosing them in a cordon of militant iron. And behind them, came another solid block of O'Lochlainn men, red heads flaming, blue eyes steady and cold. Ardal O'Lochlainn was a man who commanded the complete loyalty of his clan, and if he had not been totally loyal and devoted to his king, to Turlough Donn O'Brien, Mara would have been worried at the number of men-at-arms he kept, and trained, at his tower house so near to her law school.

Nechtan O'Quinn wore a triumphant air and his eyes avoided those of his wife, Narait, who had drawn near to the entrance gate as soon as the noise of horses' hoofs had sounded on the limestone road. The beauty of eye and colouring had failed her in this moment and she looked pale, older and rather frightened. Like everyone else in the churchyard she was looking at one man.

In the front of the pilgrims, riding boldly erect, was the magnificent tall, broad figure of Hans Kaufmann. He looked at the group of people awaiting the arrival – Narait, Father MacMahon, Blad the innkeeper and his daughter Mór, Sorley the sexton, the man whose life's blood had gone into enshrining, cherishing and guarding what he had considered to be one of the most sacred objects that the world held, a relic of the true cross – and then, unbelievably, Hans Kaufmann smiled. He smiled mockingly and lifted his hand to Sorley in a slight salute, as if to say, that was my lucky toss of the dice. Then he put his head back and roared with a great burst of laughter as though he were a spectator at some play.

Sorley started and glared at him. He took one step forward, fist raised, but Ardal O'Lochlainn, who was in the front of the cavalcade, shook his head firmly at the sexton and Mara felt a moment of thankfulness for his loyalty and his good judgements. She must, she made a mental note, remember to tell Turlough how very helpful Ardal had been to her. Turlough would be pleased. His opinion of the *taoiseach* of the O'Lochlainn clan on the Burren had always been high.

'Madame, Madame, Madame,' called out the prioress in agitated fashion, riding out from the group and towards Mara. 'Why have you brought us back here – I understand that it is by your orders that our sacred journey has been interrupted? You cannot possibly think that I or my sisters or these gentlemen could have had anything to do with such a terrible thing.'

'Probably not a crime, but an accident,' said Hans Kaufmann in a light, careless tone. Mara saw him look appraisingly around the churchyard and then cast a shrewd glance at Ardal O'Lochlainn. Ardal looked straight back at him and there was a cold look in his eyes. Ardal's suspicions, like her own, were directed at the German pilgrim, thought Mara. He had, after all, been recently to Rome and had heard all about the former German monk, Luther, and his impassioned outburst against such practices as the sale of indulgences and relics. Quite a few German pilgrims might be finding themselves under suspicion these days. Father Miguel, also, was looking at Hans Kaufmann and there was an ugly expression on his face. Mara felt a slight coldness go down her spine as she remembered the tales of the terrible Spanish Inquisition where thousands and thousands of innocent Jews and Muslims had been burned to death – and now the same thing was happening to Christians, who, like Martin Luther, rejected some of the teachings of Rome.

'This affair has to be investigated,' Father Miguel said, his sibilant Spanish accent lending a hissing quality to the Latin words. 'Do I understand that the relic of the true cross has been completely destroyed? What an appalling thing. I wonder it was not better guarded.'

He looked belligerently at Father MacMahon and the priest bowed his head in shame. Sorley looked from one to the other, but no one offered to translate the Spaniard's bitter words. However, the blazing anger in his eyes and the bitter note in his voice told its own story and Sorley, also, began to look shamefaced.

And yet there was a smugness about Father Miguel, thought Mara, which made her wonder whether the commercial success of the Spanish shrine was not also in his mind at that moment. Then she dismissed the thought. If the relic had been stolen, then the other pilgrims might have fallen under suspicion, but the destroying could only have been done by a person who rejected relics and all that they stood for.

Mara's eyes rested gravely on each of the pilgrims in turn, ending with Hans Kaufmann, and only then did she speak.

'I must ask each of you to dismount and to take your satchels into the church here,' she said. 'My assistant, Fachtnan, will accompany you. Could you,' she turned and aimed her words at a space between Ardal O'Lochlainn and Nechtan O'Quinn so that she would not appear to be favouring one over the other, 'escort the pilgrims and get them to wait until I come.' She watched the six go off between the two men, following Fachtnan into the church, and sighed. The balance of power was going to be a difficult one in this case, small though the crime was. Feelings, she guessed, would run high and the different players would be keen to maintain their power. Ardal was a *taoiseach*, the chieftain of the second largest clan on the Burren, and Nechtan was not. However, his tower house was situated beside the church of Kilnaboy and his family had been, since ancient times, the *coarbs*, the ancient heirs of the monastic lands, and still received rents from them.

Kilnaboy was an interesting place. She remembered her father telling her about the significance of that ancient site on the south-eastern corner of the Burren. It had belonged to a group of monks and they had held sway in the lands there, had owned the rich fertile river meadows, the hillside with its ancient tombs, and their sway had even superseded that of the ancient kings. The monks had held out against Turlough's ancestors on numerous occasions.

'Come, boys,' she said to her scholars once the door of the church had been closed by Ardal, 'the pilgrims' luggage will have to be examined and this is where you will all be so useful to me. Each of you must observe one of the pilgrims and never move your eyes from that person. Afterwards we will talk together and discuss our impressions, but in the meantime you must be silent and observant.'

Quickly she allocated the pilgrims to the boys: Domhnall had Hans Kaufmann; Slevin, Father Miguel; Finbar, the Italian monk, Brother Cosimo; and she, with the two younger boys, were to observe the three women – the nine-year-olds, she reckoned, were young enough to cause no offence to the prioress. And then she led them swiftly over into the cool shadiness of the church from which the noontime sun had departed. One by one the pilgrims had placed their leather satchels on a bench at the back of the building and one by one she demanded to see their travelling lamps and they fumbled in their bags and produced them.

Interesting, she thought, to catch glimpses of the contents of those satchels: something silk and trimmed with lace peeping out from Madame Eglantine's satchel – surprising from such a religious lady as the prioress; Cosimo, the Italian friar vowed to poverty, had an extremely valuable cross studded with precious stones that gleamed from the depth of his bag – Mara saw Finbar's eyes widen at the sight of it; and Father Miguel had a huge bundle of correspondence from something called *Tribunal del Santo Oficio de la Inquisición*.

However, all of this was none of her business.

What was her business was that Hans Kaufmann could not produce a travelling lamp. He shrugged with a pretence of coolness, but his eyes watched hers.

'I don't bother,' he said in fluent Latin. 'I have eyes like a cat. I see through the darkness. I never carry a lantern.'

Mara took from her own satchel the distorted lamp and held aloft the shrivelled piece of vellum.

'So these are not yours,' she said, and as he hesitated she added, 'The language is German – it is an indulgence. Am I right in thinking that you are against indulgences, that, like your leader, Martin Luther, you believe that the church is at fault in granting pardon for sins – that only God can forgive sins and that a piece of vellum or parchment will not, cannot, take the place of God in this matter? The person who burned the relic used this piece of vellum, this indulgence, to transfer the flame from the lamp to the velvet cushion which was placed underneath the relic.'

'What!' roared Father MacMahon. 'Is this man a disciple of that anti-Christ, Martin Luther? Has he desecrated the citadel of our sacred relic?'

'You devil, you fiend,' muttered Sorley. He took a step forward and Hans Kaufmann retreated, but it was no good. His fellow pilgrim, the Italian friar, was just behind him and Cosimo instantly rounded on him.

'So that is what you were at,' he snarled. His age-marked hands crisped into fists. 'And to think . . .' Suddenly he stopped. His hand went to his belt and came back armed with a long, thin, wickedly pointed knife. Without hesitation his arm went up and aimed the knife at the German's heart.

'Here, steady,' shouted Ardal. He spoke in Gaelic but the words seemed to penetrate through to the Italian. His arm and the deadly dagger were lowered, but by that time Hans Kaufmann was no longer there in front of him. Mara saw the German look towards the altar and the next instant he had left the bottom of the church, had bounded up the centre of it, gone through the screen, mounted the steps of the sacristy, and then he was beside the altar, one hand clutching the altar cloth.

'I claim sanctuary,' he shouted. 'Let no one touch me here. The Lord will protect me and woe to him who will break the Lord's sanctuary.'

The effect of his words was varied.

Father Miguel gave a gasp. He stood very rigid, staring at his fellow pilgrim.

The prioress said: 'Sanctuary – does this little church in the middle of the country have such rights?' And when no one answered her she turned haughtily to her sisters, lowering her voice, but not ceasing to talk.

In a moment the church was full of voices.

Father MacMahon said angrily, 'Sanctuary was never meant for an unbeliever, for one who denies the means that God gives to man to save his soul from the fires of purgatory.'

'I'll get him out of there, Father.' Sorley advanced three threatening steps.

'Liar, blasphemer, villain, maligner of honest men!' Brother Cosimo's teeth gleamed, set edge to edge behind his grizzled beard and moustache.

'Horsewhipping would be too good for him!' Blad had come through the small door on the south and had joined the group at the bottom of the church. 'He's destroyed my livelihood, Brehon,' he added in a low voice to Mara and she nodded. This was something that she felt Brehon law should take into account. This man had set up his inn in the sure and certain knowledge, as he saw it, that the relic of the holy cross would bring a steady stream of pilgrims to the remote church of Kilnaboy. She had, she thought, standing very still and waiting, as was her custom, for the storm of words to blow itself out, less sympathy for the priest – the church with its gold and diamond ornaments and its crimson carpet was of less importance to her than the livelihood of an honest, hard-working man and his daughter. Her scholars, she noticed, had moved a step nearer to the innkeeper, and Cormac, with his kingly father's sympathy for his subjects that might be in trouble, patted him on the arm.

'Death must be his punishment.' Father Miguel's voice was

sharp and decisive and now he spoke Latin without that slightly hesitant lisp. He did not look at Mara, but addressed himself to Father MacMahon. 'I take charge of this man in the name of the Holy Father and I will bring him to Spain where he will be tried by the *Tribunal del Santo Oficio de la Inquisición*. If he is found guilty, then he will burn. You,' he addressed himself to Nechtan Quinn, 'will give me men to ensure that this criminal is kept in safe custody until I reach the Dominican Friar in the city of Galway. From there I will take him in chains by ship back to Spain.'

Nechtan O'Quinn cleared his throat hesitantly. 'Well, the fact is that . . .'

Hans Kaufmann, Mara noticed, still stood quite erect by the altar, his feet firmly on the crimson carpet and his face turned from one to the other. When Father Miguel, the Dominican, spoke of the Spanish Inquisition he turned back towards the altar, took the altar cloth in a firm grip between his two hands and then turned back to face them. There was a murmur from the other pilgrims and Nechtan O'Quinn took a hesitant step forward and then moved back again. The door opened and the lovely face of his wife Narait appeared. Her large eyes travelled around the church and then saw the German standing at bay on the altar. She gave a sudden gasp and then stood clutching the door as if to support herself.

Ardal O'Lochlainn ignored them all. With a couple of strides of his long legs he followed the German up the church. The throwing knife in his left hand was stretched out and the other hand placed on the man's shoulder.

'The law of this country is the law of King Turlough Donn O'Brien and his representative here is the Brehon of the Burren.' His voice was clear and emphatic. As always, Ardal, *taoiseach* of the powerful O'Lochlainn clan from a young age, effortlessly exuded power and authority, and the German, big though he was, stood very still under that hand. Ardal waited for a minute, confident and wholly in command. Then he looked down at Mara and asked respectfully, 'What would you want done with this man, Brehon?'

At that moment Nechtan O'Quinn came forward. Gone was the hesitation that he'd showed earlier. Perhaps he was conscious that the eyes of his young wife were upon him, but whatever it was, his voice had cleared and the words came out fluently.

'Niall O'Quinn, my great ancestor who fell at the battle of Clontarf, fighting side by side with Brian Boru, was the man who caused this church to be built,' he said, spacing his words and giving even stress to each one of them. 'He it was who laid out the termon, who fixed its boundaries with the River Fergus to the south and west and the tau cross by the ancient tomb to the north and the spring well to the east. And he laid down that his descendants would be *coarbs* of the monastic grounds and would receive one-fifth of the rents from the eight hundred acres. And he gave to the monks' church the right of sanctuary for all that would seek it.' When Nechtan said the last words he looked not at Mara but towards where his wife Narait had been standing. She flushed and looked away, and then after a moment's hesitation walked out of the door with fast steps that seemed about to break into a run. And then she had gone from the church, allowing the door to crash closed behind her. Mara waited until the echoes subsided before translating Nechtan's words into Latin.

It was interesting, she thought, that those very religious people – the Dominican friar from Spain, the Benedictine monk from Italy, the three women pilgrims from Wales, and even Father MacMahon of the very church of Kilnaboy – should stare at the man who invoked the sacred right of sanctuary with such undisguised anger and disgust. After all, that ancient privilege of some churches had existed for over 500 years. Even the wife of King Edward IV – King of England when Mara was a child – had, she understood, sought sanctuary in the abbey of Westminster in London during a time of trouble.

'I have no objection to this man awaiting the verdict of the court in any place that seems fit to him,' she said, making sure that her voice was divested of emotion. 'All that I will stipulate is that he must not leave the kingdom until the hearing is complete and the fine is paid. In order not to inconvenience the pilgrims and delay them any longer than necessary on their journey to Aran, I propose to gather evidence this afternoon, if possible, and to hold the trial first thing tomorrow morning at the place of justice, Poulnabrone,' she continued briskly, nodding to Fachtnan to translate her words into Gaelic. Father MacMahon, Blad, Nechtan and Ardal would all know about the procedure for trying law cases and crimes at the outdoor location at Poulnabrone beside the ancient dolmen in the centre of the Burren, but there would, she guessed, have to be explanations to the others afterwards.

'But surely this man should be cast into prison,' said the prioress, interrupting Fachtnan.

'He is innocent until proved guilty,' said Mara sweetly, with a glance at Hans Kaufmann. 'And we have no prisons here in the kingdom of the Burren. The inhabitants are willing to be ruled by Brehon law and to pay the penalties given by the courts.'

Although the prioress spoke in English, Mara replied to her in Latin; she wished that her German was better, but though she had learned a little from her father when he came back from his pilgrimage she had found few opportunities for practice in recent years. Still, the man understood Latin and that was good enough. Latin was the common language for all European countries – as soon as any scholar entered her law school she began to teach them Latin, even at the age of five years. Fluency in that language was essential for their future as lawyers.

Deliberately she moved away from the pilgrims and up towards the altar. By now the German was sitting on the luxurious crimson carpet, lounging in a comfortable way, his back resting against the top step. He did not look alarmed at her progress towards him, but sat up as she approached and gave her a warm smile. Domhnall, despatched by Fachtnan, carried up a chair for his Brehon and placed it politely at the foot of the altar steps.

Mara sat down and with a gesture invited Hans Kaufmann nearer. Fachtnan beckoned to Domhnall and with his usual tact managed to get the other pilgrims to withdraw a little towards the back of the church. Brehon and the accused faced each other in the dim light.

'It would make things much easier for me,' Mara said frankly, 'if you would just admit, now, that you were the one who set

fire to the relic. After all,' she could see by the half-smile that
puckered his lips, that she was on the point of winning, 'you
only did it in order to gain publicity for the views of your master,
Martin Luther. You want people to understand his message
– is that not true? Why not admit it now? Your reasons can
be given in public tomorrow to the inhabitants of the Burren,
as well as to your fellow travellers. You will have an audience
and, who knows, news of your gesture will be all over Europe in
a year or so.' Deliberately she kept her voice very low. These
were not words that she wanted to be overheard by the other
pilgrims.

He looked at her and a smile puckered his lips. 'You're a
very original woman,' he said, his voice also muted. He spoke
Latin with great fluency, she noticed.

'Save me trouble,' she said, ignoring the compliment, but
still finding pleasure in it. 'Save me the trouble of gathering
evidence and agree to plead guilty tomorrow. The sentence
will be a fine – a fine to make restitution to the priest.' Poor
Blad, she thought with a moment's compunction, but she could
not really see how she could interpret the law so that he would
be considered a candidate for restitution. Perhaps Father
MacMahon would be able to buy a new piece of the true cross
and then all would be well, she thought cynically. 'Just tell me
now that you plead guilty,' she said aloud, and when he made
no response she added, 'and then your fellow pilgrims can all
go to one of Blad's suppers and to their beds and ride off for
the ferry to Aran tomorrow. You, I think, will have to return
to England – I don't really want you to commit any more
outrages on my king's territory.' She gave him a friendly smile
and he responded with an attractive grin.

'Back to Wexford?' he queried.

'Back to Wexford,' she said firmly. And then could not
resist adding, 'You could always go to Walsingham and view
the vial of the Virgin Mary's milk. It should be an interesting
experience.'

'What will the fine be?' There was a cautious note in his
voice, but his very blue eyes sparkled.

'I'm not sure,' said Mara frankly. 'I will have to look up my
law books. Not more than you can pay, I should imagine.'

He took a deep breath. 'I'll do it,' he assured her with a nod. 'I'll plead guilty.'

'Good,' she said. 'Now, do you wish to ride back with me?' She turned and beckoned. 'Perhaps, Ardal,' she said as he approached, 'you would be kind enough to give Herr Kaufmann a bed for the night and make sure that he attends the hearing at Poulnabrone tomorrow.' No need, she thought, to spell it out to Ardal that the man should be kept under close watch so that he did, indeed, attend the hearing on the following day. Justice, in Brehon law, always had to be seen to be done.

'No,' said Hans Kaufmann. His reply was swift and his eyes went towards the Spanish priest, a look of apprehension in their very blue depths. The threat of the mighty Inquisition was a potent one. Even here in the remote west of Ireland tales were told about the burning of those who disagreed with the Roman doctrine. 'No,' he repeated. 'I have claimed sanctuary and let him burn in hell whosoever breaks it.'

'Very well,' said Mara. Brehon law did not countenance violence and after all the man was, in theory, innocent until sentence was passed at Poulnabrone. 'I'll leave you now and make sure that you have everything that you need for the night. No need to go supperless to bed. Our Brehon law is concerned with compensation, not with revenge. Make full admittance and confession tomorrow and be prepared to pay the fine that is demanded of you, and then you can leave – but go east, not west, or the long arm of my law will pluck you from the remotest hiding place.'

'I will go east,' he said with a nod. 'My work is only beginning.'

Mara got to her feet feeling happy and satisfied with herself. An interesting fellow, this pilgrim! In some ways she would have liked to stay and to debate matters with him, but her consciousness of her position as Brehon of the Burren, and of being the representative of the king forbade her to indulge in a moment's fancy. Her duty now was to clear up this affair and to make sure that there were no repercussions. She gave him a nod and returned to the group.

'Hans Kaufmann, the pilgrim from Germany, has made a full and frank confession,' she said. 'He has agreed to be taken from here tomorrow morning to the judgement place at Poulnabrone and there to be sentenced according to the law of this country. In the meantime,' her eyes wandered over the little group of pilgrims and the men from her own kingdom, 'he prefers to remain here under sanctuary of the holy church. I have promised that he will be well treated and that supper and other necessities will be supplied to him.'

'What happens if that man escapes in the night?' Father Miguel, the Dominican priest, seemed to be the only one who seemed to be concerned about this. Grace, the scarred sister, had retired to the darkness at the western end of the church. Mara thought she overheard a sob and the sound of Bess talking in a flow of soft Welsh. The prioress herself, despite her angry words earlier, was looking between her sisters and Hans Kaufmann and there was an air of irresolution about her. Brother Cosimo, also, seemed deeply uneasy. Perhaps Hans Kaufmann knew something about him. A picture of the ornate, bejewelled cross in the Benedictine monk's satchel flashed into Mara's mind. What was it that Brother Cosimo had accused the German of? '*A maligner of honest men*', those had been his words. All except the Dominican priest would probably prefer if the German was set free tonight. It was not something that she could square with her conscience to do, though, she thought. A crime had been committed and retribution had to be exacted.

'Father MacMahon, will you give the key of the church to Blad?' She turned to the innkeeper. 'The kingdom will pay the bill for his meals, but food, drink and all other necessities he must have. When he has all that he needs you may lock the church and keep him there until the morning when he will be taken under escort from Nechtan O'Quinn to the judgement place of Poulnabrone where I shall pass sentence on him.'

'The church cannot be locked,' said Nechtan. There was an unusual ring of authority in his voice. 'The rights of sanctuary allow the man to leave the church in order "*to take the air, to visit the lavabo and for the relieving of his necessities*" – that's what the monks laid down. But he must not go beyond the boundaries of the churchyard.'

'I'll stay here tonight, if Father MacMahon will give me room,' said Ardal O'Lochlainn. 'I'll assist you to patrol the boundaries, Nechtan. My steward will be with me. And the stables. They must be guarded to make sure that he does not take his horse, until he has paid his fine and can depart from the kingdom, of course. We can work it out between us, Brehon. You have no need to concern yourself. All will be well. We'll patrol the boundaries. He has no right to go further. What do you say, Nechtan? Danann and I will do whatever you order.'

A tactful man, Ardal O'Lochlainn, thought Mara as she gathered up her scholars and once more reassured Blad that the kingdom would pay for the extra night lodging for the remaining pilgrims and for the supper for the guilty one. Why should the innkeeper lose more revenue, she thought, looking at his face, mottled red and white with anger and anxiety? Life would be a worry for him from now on. Without the huge incentive of the relic of the true cross, the flood of pilgrims arriving at Kilnaboy would soon dry up.

Nechtan and Ardal were chatting amiably about guards and boundaries and throwing knives and other weapons. Grace's tears were being efficiently scrubbed away from her cheeks by her widowed sister. She appeared to make some tentative moves towards the guilty pilgrim, but was instantly intercepted by her sister and borne off in the wake of the prioress, in whom the word 'supper' – and at someone else's expense – seemed to operate a powerful force drawing her towards the inn. Mara quickly stepped in her way. Father Miguel and Brother Cosimo stopped abruptly behind her and looked enquiringly at Mara.

'There is now no reason why you should not go on your journey tomorrow,' she said, 'but there will be no boat to Aran until tomorrow afternoon so I think it best if you stay in the inn until then. I shall come over first thing tomorrow morning and we will all ride together over to Poulnabrone, the judgement place for this kingdom. There you will see how justice is done and retribution paid under our laws.'

It was possible, she thought at the time, that some words from the pilgrims about conversations with the accused man,

Hans Kaufmann, might prove of use to her in deciding the punishment for this very unusual crime. And also, she acknowledged to herself, it would afford her great satisfaction to show these people from other countries how law and order could be maintained without the use of savage punishments or shedding of human blood.

Five

Uraicecht Becc
(Small Primer)

The heir to abbey lands, even if not in holy orders, has the same honour price as would have an abbot to that monastery.

The honour price of the abbot of the largest abbey in the country is 42 séts, 22 ounces of silver or 22 milch cows.

The honour price of the abbot of a small abbey is 10 séts, 5 ounces of silver or 5 milch cows.

Where a monastery no longer exists, the coarb *is in receipt of the revenues from the old monastic lands.*

The coarb, *also, bears responsibility to safeguard the ancient privileges of the former abbey or monastery.*

Mara felt tired but contented when she, Fachtnan and her five scholars set out from Cahermacnaghten Law School on the following morning. She had sat up late going through all of the books which her father had left to her, as well as the many manuscripts which she had collected during her twenty-five years as Brehon of the Burren, but had found little to help her until she had come across some notes that her father had made on the history of the monks of St Columba. In his precise minuscule script he had noted the presence of those *Ceile Dé* (companions of God) on the shores of Lake Inchiquin and of the church that they had built at Kilnaboy on the southern edge of the kingdom of Burren. Their lands had extended to the foot of Mullaghmore Mountain and their rights had included that of sanctuary to anyone who claimed it by touching the altar within the church. At the very bottom of the page, squeezed into the tiny space left, her father had written damage to the church must be repaid to the abbot or to his heir, the *comharbae ecalso*.

Nechtan was the man to whom recompense should be paid,

and this was an easy matter. Nechtan, as the *coarb*, would
have an honour price of ten *séts* or five ounces of silver. For
a long time she puzzled over how to estimate the value of the
property destroyed, but then she had a sudden brilliant
inspiration. Of course, she thought triumphantly, slamming her
law book closed and getting to her feet ready for sleep; *Críth
Gablach*, as usual, had the answer. Hans Kaufmann must restore
the value of what has been lost.

And how would he do that? Well, thought Mara as she
climbed the stairs to her bedroom, that was a matter between
him and the officials of Kilnaboy Church; between him and
Father MacMahon and Nechtan, the *coarb*, the descendant of
the ancient line of O'Quinn.

I'm sure, thought Mara, that if I see Nechtan beforehand,
the fine that we collect from the German can be transmitted
immediately as a donation to Father MacMahon. This, she
planned, she would announce as soon as she finished sentencing.
Notice had been sent out, by Fachtnan, to various churches,
mills and other places, of this unscheduled hearing at
Poulnabrone, but probably since this unexpected spell of fine
weather was ideal for taking a second cut of hay from the fields
before autumn and winter set in, or going to the bog, or taking
a load of seaweed from the coast for fertilizing the fields, not
many would bother turning up for a case against someone
who was just passing through the kingdom.

And it was a glorious day. The night had been stiflingly hot
and with a heavy downpour a couple of hours after sunset.
Mara had feared the thunderstorm would bring to an end the
fine weather. But weather was hard to predict here on the fringe
of the Atlantic and this morning a light, fresh breeze had sprung
up, blowing straight in from the west and making their ride a
time of great pleasure. The early morning sun sparkled on the
silver-grey lichen that clung to the stones on the wall, and the
shiny coral red berries of the guelder rose shone like jewels.
To their left, as they rode down the steep slope of Roughan,
the mountain of Mullaghmore gleamed in swirls of silver. Mara
looked up at the pathway that wound around the slopes and
promised herself that she would climb it again when Turlough
returned from Donegal – just the two of us, she thought. They

had too few moments together; Turlough had his duties as king of three kingdoms, and she hers as Brehon of the Burren and *ollamh* (professor) of the law school. The last occasion when she had climbed Mullaghmore – the holy mountain as it was known – had been on the eve of *Bealtaine* on the night before the first of May, the day of the big ceremonial occasion when every move, every word spoken by either their king or their Brehon would be watched and listened to with reverential interest by the people of the Burren.

'Let's approach by this way,' she said to Fachtnan. 'I would like to have a quick word with Nechtan O'Quinn before I see Father MacMahon – and the German pilgrim . . . or follower of Luther,' she amended. She doubted whether he had ever been a pilgrim; his mission was other. No doubt shrines all over Europe were now bewailing the destruction of some cherished relic. What was going to happen in the future, she wondered? Would the doctrines of Luther have any effect on the Church of Rome? Whatever happened, she hoped that here in the west of Ireland it would not affect them too much. She and her fellow countrymen and women had come to a comfortable compromise with the more rigid doctrines of Rome. Many monks were married men who had the discretion to send their wives and children on visits to relatives when inspections were threatened from England – and quite a few priests were fathers of sons as well as fathers to their religious congregations. And frequently a son inherited his father's position in the religious hierarchy. The church of the early *Céile Dé* still lived on in this remote spot.

'If we turn this way, we will ride through the clump of trees and no one will see us arrive,' said Fachtnan, breaking into her theological musings.

'Good idea,' said Mara, and told him of her conclusions.

He nodded. 'And we should make sure that the other pilgrims are on their way to Aran straight after the trial so that there is no trouble between them and Hans Kaufmann,' he said. 'I'll have a word with the O'Lochlainn and tell him that I heard the boat was leaving early because of the thunderstorm last night.'

'Good idea,' said Mara. Ardal would not question any message from her and would speed the pilgrims on their way while the German was still under the court's protection. It was clever of Fachtnan to have thought of this. She reflected, with a moment's regret, that he would have made a wonderful Brehon. He was thoughtful, intelligent and always very aware of the feelings of others and the need for careful handling in matters where pride and precedent were of the utmost importance. Still, his loss was her gain. She could ask for no better sounding board for her thoughts and worries.

'Ride on ahead, boys, but wait for us when you come to the wall,' she called, and then turned to Fachtnan and began to tell him her conclusions about the recompense due from Hans Kaufmann after the burning of the relic. Fachtnan was more religious than she and could probably spot any flaw in her solution.

The boys had taken her permission to ride ahead with the exuberance of their age and their delight in the fresh and lovely September morning, and she had hardly finished her sentence to them before the noise of hoofs pounding on the limestone almost drowned the sound of her voice. She smiled to herself. There was something very endearing about them all, she thought, enjoying their energy and their sense of fun.

'So that's the way my mind is working,' she finished, 'and I was wondering . . .' and then she stopped. Somehow in the last few moments the pounding noise of horses' hoofs had stopped. She frowned, puzzled. Had something happened? They couldn't have reached the churchyard wall so quickly. And those horses' hoofs had not slowed gradually as they would have done had they seen their destination.

No, they had stopped abruptly.

And there were no sounds of young voices.

'Quick,' she said to Fachtnan, and clapped her heels to the sides of her old mare.

A moment later she and Fachtnan burst through the trees into a small, rounded space open to the sky – a space where the grass grew oddly short, as though cropped nightly. It was almost completely surrounded by prickly gorse bushes and was often used as a circle to gather sheep. In the centre of the vividly green grass was a sloping mound and on top of that mound was a low tomb, shaped like a wedge, made from two thick slabs, propped up on their sides, sloping towards each other and crowned by an enormous capstone of lichen-encrusted limestone. The boys, each holding a pony, were grouped around the stones. The first thing Mara saw was the white face of her son, and then, automatically, she counted heads. All were there . . .

And then she saw what they were looking at.

There was a naked body on the tomb.

In silence Mara dismounted from her mare, handing over the reins to Slevin and walking forward steadily as Domhnall and Finbar stood back to let her take their places.

The man was dead. The eyes, like blue pebbles, stared up at the sky above. She touched the wrist: stone cold.

But that was not all.

The naked body was arranged in the shape of a cross. The arms were stretched out, fingers touching the outer edge of the capstone. The feet were placed side by side.

And there was a spot of blood in the centre of each palm and in the centre of each foot. And, she observed, a knife wound in the side.

'He's been crucified.' Art's voice broke on a sob and Cormac awkwardly put an arm around his foster brother's shoulders.

'No.' Mara's voice was sharp. 'No, Art, he's been murdered, and it's for us, for the Brehon and her helpers, to find out who did this terrible deed and punish them.' The unknown murderer, she noticed, had even gone to the trouble of cutting off a few twigs of holly from a nearby bush and twisting them together with some woodbine to form a rough crown.

'It's not a crucifixion, Art,' said Domhnall consolingly. 'Look, you can see that these are not real holes in the hands – just someone twisted a knife . . .'

He stopped abruptly as Art heaved noisily. Fachtnan seized him by the arm and dragged him over to the bushes, and the boys stood in silence listening to the sounds of him vomiting. Cormac was very white, but glared when Mara stretched out a hand to him, so she left him. His pride was very important to him. Both he and Art were too young for this, she thought, gazing down with horror at the sight. Death they knew – there had been killings on the Burren – but never anything like this twisted, vile horror. The symbolism was obvious – or was it? Perhaps it was meant to imply that Hans Kaufmann was a Christ-like figure, but she doubted it. More likely some perverted religious instinct had deemed this was the ultimate punishment and humiliation for a man who had desecrated the relic of the true cross.

'Don't touch,' said Mara as she saw Cormac's hand go forward towards the crown of thorns.

'There's something there, Brehon,' he said. 'Look, Domhnall, there's something under the pieces of holly – down there by his ear.'

Mara leaned over. 'You're right,' she said. 'I didn't notice it before as the holly was over it. I can see it now.'

'Looks like a piece of vellum – just like the one that we found inside the lamp, the one that was used to set fire to the cushion,' said Slevin.

Mara put out her hand carefully and without touching the corpse plucked out the small scroll. It was not the same; she knew that. The scorched piece of vellum which had played its part in destroying the relic of the true cross was safely in her own satchel. She had hoped to confront the person responsible for that misdeed today, but now he was dead and she was faced with a far greater crime – the greatest of all – the taking of a human life.

'Looks the same,' said Slevin, as she unrolled the small leaf of vellum. 'It's decorated in the same way around the four margins.'

'So it is,' said Mara. 'But not written in German – look.' She flattened it and held it out towards her scholars so that they could read the Latin words.

'"*God is not mocked*",' said Domhnall thoughtfully, and then continued, '"*Be not deceived; God is not mocked: for whatsoever a man soweth, that shall he also reap.*" Do you think that the murderer wrote that, Brehon?'

'I don't think so,' said Mara, 'look how faded the ink is. This is something from one of the epistles of St Paul to the Galatians, if I remember aright. Pilgrims carry these prayers with them. It's apt, though, isn't it?'

'The murderer tried to make a fool of God by burning the

piece of the true cross and God has had his revenge,' said Finbar dramatically.

'Birdbrain,' said Slevin with a curl of his lip. 'Do you really think that God has nothing better to do than to set up this – pretending that the man was crucified?' He waved his hand at the figure spreadeagled across the tomb.

'He'd just send down a thunderbolt and have it over and done with.' Cormac was recovering and eager to show how tough he was.

Mara nodded absent-mindedly. She retained the leaf of vellum in her hand, but crossed over to where Fachtnan stood with his arm around the shivering Art.

'Poor Art,' she said compassionately, touching his clammy skin. 'You don't look well; perhaps you've eaten something that did not agree with you. Fachtnan, would you take Art back to Brigid – and Cormac, you go too to help Fachtnan.'

'I'll take him up in front of me; my horse will easily take the weight and Cormac can lead Art's pony,' said Fachtnan, and Mara nodded. This would be a face-saver for Cormac, and Art looked most unwell.

'And Fachtnan,' she said after he had hoisted up the boy, 'I need Nuala. We must have a physician look at this body as soon as possible. He must not be moved from here until then. Do you think that Nuala can leave her hospital?'

'There won't be a problem.' Fachtnan as Nuala's husband was reassuring. 'Peadar can cope with anything. In fact Nuala gets a bit annoyed that people keep asking for her as she thinks very highly of Peadar.'

'That's the Burren for you,' said Mara, glad to find something that relaxed her lips into a smile. 'Memories are long. Peadar will always be the boy from Scotland and Nuala will always be an O'Davoren of the Burren, descended from a long line of physicians.' Then she noticed her son's face, struggling between his strong affection for his foster brother and his desire to be manly and stand beside the naked dead body with the other scholars. She said hurriedly: 'Will that pony be too much for you, Cormac, as well as your own? Should I send Domhnall with you?' And then bowed her head meekly as he told her scornfully how very competent he was to lead one pony while seated on another. She waited until they had gone before turning to the three remaining scholars.

'Well?' she said, and there was a query in her voice.

'The man is dead and he didn't die of anything natural,' said Slevin promptly.

'Was it God that struck him down?' faltered Finbar, looking with shrinking fascination at the body.

'I told you, birdbrain; God has enough to do without going around and stripping clothes off people and laying them out, stone dead, on a slab,' said Slevin scornfully. There was a slight note of hysteria in his voice so Mara did not reprove him, though she tried to ban such expressions as 'birdbrain' when they were discussing legal matters.

'Not suicide,' said Domhnall. He seemed the only one of the boys to be unmoved by the sight of the naked and dead body. 'There's no sign of a knife anywhere – I've looked on the ground all around the tomb and I haven't seen anything.'

'Where are his clothes?' asked Finbar in a voice that he strove to make sound steady.

'God took them up to heaven,' snapped Slevin.

'Let's do a thorough search, and for the knife,' put in Domhnall. 'I suppose it's just barely possible still that it might have been suicide and that he might have had the strength to have thrown it away before he died. I was just thinking that he would have dropped it. Do you think that he pricked his hands and his feet, stuck himself in the ribs, then pulled the knife out and threw it away so as to make himself look like a crucified Christ? Not likely,' he finished, answering his own question.

'Not likely,' agreed Mara, 'but you are quite correct in considering the question, Domhnall. The law only gives a verdict after all possible aspects of the puzzle have been carefully examined. Let's look for the clothes, too.'

She joined in the search with the boys, though she was fairly certain in her own mind that this was not a case of suicide. Herr Kaufmann was not overwhelmed by any guilt that he had burned the relic of the true cross. Everything in his bearing had demonstrated a satisfaction with himself. He had, perhaps, been alarmed for his own safety, especially with the threat of the Spanish Inquisition hanging over him. His demand for sanctuary had stemmed from that, but he had not, she was sure, felt that he had done anything wrong. A fanatic she had thought him to be, before she had known anything of his crime, and she guessed that she was right in that deduction. Fanatics, in her experience, never felt guilt but were invariably sure that they were right in what they did.

'Well, the clothes are definitely not in the circle,' said Domhnall eventually. His eyes went across the body on the tomb. He was a very steady-nerved, mature boy, thought Mara. Would have made a good physician as well as a lawyer – his face bore no emotion other than a slight exasperation that there was a puzzle which he could not solve.

'Is the heart on the left or the right side, Brehon?' asked Slevin, joining him and taking one more look at the body.

'Feel your own heart,' said Domhnall, lifting a hand to his ribs. 'Remember the twelve doors to the soul. Remember what Nuala told us – nearer to the left – so that knife would have gone straight through the ribs and into the heart, I'd say.'

'He must have been killed first and then stripped. His clothes will be soaked in blood. When you stick a pig,' said Slevin, a farmer's son, 'there's buckets and buckets of blood. It would be all down the stone and in the grass here, if he had been killed here, but there's not a sign.'

'True,' said Mara, marvelling at how quickly all of the boys had got used to the sight of the dead body. 'So you think that he was killed elsewhere and then carried here?'

'And that puts suicide out – you're right, Slevin,' said Domhnall. 'Still, let's have a good search on the path between here and the church to make sure that the knife is not anywhere there – dropped by the murderer on his way back, or the clothes, either.' He turned away and then turned back again. 'He would be very heavy to carry,' he said, wondering. 'Look at the size of him! What do you think, Slevin?'

'Could be as much as a couple of hundredweight,' said Slevin, no doubt calling on his knowledge of dead pigs, thought Mara. 'Take two men to carry him and they'd have to be strong.'

'And then they stripped him and laid him out on top of that old tomb,' said Finbar. He was always anxious to join in with the two older boys, but they just shrugged and moved off, going down the narrow pathway, bending over the grass and searching it thoroughly.

'Or carried him here and then stripped him.'

'We'll probably find the knife first; it would glint in the sun,' said Slevin. 'Let's start with the bushes.'

They were thorough in their search, Domhnall allocating to each an area of the path, and then they swapped areas and searched again, but nothing was to be found – neither the knife, nor the clothing.

'Don't search too hard for the knife,' said Mara. 'It doesn't look like suicide, so the knife is probably still in the possession of its owner. Most people carry a knife in their pouch. One good wipe and it could be put back in. Concentrate on looking for clothing.'

The path to the ancient tomb was a short one, but the boys then extended the search, going right back to the churchyard, and then coming back to start rooting under the gorse bushes that blocked the circle around the ancient tomb; they searched around in front, behind and on both sides of the sheep-shearing enclosure; they even looked up into trees and bushes, but nowhere was there a sign of the man's clothing.

Hans Kaufmann must have been naked when he was killed.

And then carried out here and laid on the capstone of the ancient wedge tomb, his arms and legs arranged in semblance of the crucified Christ.

Six

Óire
(Payments)

A man's foster brother is nearer and dearer to him than his brother of the same blood, especially if he is a 'foster brother of the blanket, cup and bed'; in other words, where they are reared together from infancy.

If a man is killed, not only must his nearest male relation be compensated, but a fine named an airer, *consisting of one-seventh of his honour price, is paid to his foster brother.*

Mara glanced up at the sun. She had noted its position when Fachtnan left and it would be, she reckoned, a good hour before he and Nuala came back. No time should be lost with the investigation into the murder. She looked again at the naked body on the limestone slab, noticing that it still had potential to shock even someone as used to violent death as she was. And she nodded her head. Shock was often a useful weapon when looking to uncover the truth.

'Fetch me my satchel from the mare, Finbar,' she said, and seated herself on a nearby boulder, directing him to open it and hold the inkhorn in his hand while she took a small scrap of vellum and a well-trimmed quill. 'The advantage of living on the Burren, Finbar, is that you can always find a stone exactly of the size and shape that you need,' she said as she picked up a small, flat piece from the ground. She talked on as she wrote a few lines. She was sorry for the boy. He was immature and not too clever; neither Domhnall nor Slevin, friends for the last six years when they entered the law school together, had too much time for him. Now they were busy looking into the gorse bushes, methodically searching them inch by inch. If she asked, Domhnall would give Finbar something to do also, but they did not naturally include him.

'Take this to the priest's house at Kilnaboy and give it to the O'Lochlainn,' she said, rolling up the note and tying it firmly with a piece of pink tape from her satchel. 'Make sure that you hand it to him and to no one else. If he is not there, go and find him, and if by chance he has returned to Lissylisheen, then bring this straight back to me. In any case, return as soon as you have handed over the note.'

'I'll run there and run back,' promised Finbar. He cast a smug glance at where Domhnall and Slevin were still searching the undergrowth and set off at a tearing pace. It would only take him a few minutes to arrive at the priest's house and after that she had to rely on Ardal's quick wits and his obedience to her as the representative of his king.

Of course, by now, she thought, with another quick glance at the sun, it was very possible that the absence of the false pilgrim from his place of sanctuary at the church might have been discovered and the hunt might be on. In fact, Ardal might even now be on the road to Cahermacnaghten Law School − though it would be more like him to send one of his men to fetch her and to lead the hunt for Hans Kaufmann himself. She was sure that he and his men had kept a good watch overnight on the boundaries of the sanctuary land.

And that meant that Hans Kaufmann, the German pilgrim, had been killed by someone from the inn, or from Father MacMahon's house, or from the house of the remaining *coarb*, or heir of the monks of Kilnaboy, Nechtan O'Quinn. No outsider could have easily got through the guard on the boundaries. Only one road led into and out of Kilnaboy.

'Do you feel sorry for him, Brehon?' That was Domhnall. Her grandson's shrewd eyes were fixed on her as she stood meditatively looking at the naked body.

'I think I do, Domhnall,' she said honestly. 'He didn't go about things the right way − it would have been better if he tried to persuade rather than to destroy, but he should not have been killed. That is a crime and a crime that was committed in our kingdom, so it is something that must be solved.' Yes, I do feel grief, she thought, looking at the magnificent specimen of manhood, stretched out as though on a butcher's slab.

'Yes,' she said aloud, 'yes, I am sorry for him − he had his life ahead of him – he is probably only in his late twenties and perhaps as he grew older he would grow more tolerant and allow people to have their own beliefs and not try to change them. It's sad when anyone doesn't get a choice to repent of the errors of their youth. He was a fanatic, I suppose, and he died because of that.' She wasn't sure whether Domhnall understood her or not, but he nodded in that sage, serious way of his and she did not insult him by explaining further.

Fanaticism – I was right to mistrust it, her thoughts went on, though who could have foreseen that this would have been the ending of the pomp and ceremony of yesterday?

'It's something that you should remember, both of you,' she said aloud, 'and it is especially important if you become Brehons; people's beliefs are important and should always be respected and listened to. Now,' she said, changing her tone, 'I have planned a shock for everyone at Kilnaboy. I've asked the O'Lochlainn to bring everyone here, but I haven't told him why. I would like to notice their reactions – where should we stand so that we are out of the way and can watch without them seeing us?'

'That's clever,' said Slevin with an admiring glance and then he gasped. 'But Brehon, what about the prioress, and the other two ladies, her sisters; won't they drop dead with shock when they see a naked man?' He giggled nervously and Domhnall clapped his hand over his mouth, his dark brown eyes wide with a mixture of shock and amusement.

'I didn't drop dead with shock,' said Mara with a shrug, but she knew that they regarded her as 'the Brehon', not as a delicately nurtured lady. 'Let's find a place to stand,' she went on.

'Over there,' said Slevin promptly, pointing to a large gorse bush on the south side of the small, grassy enclosure. 'They'll come up that path and they'll see the body on the tomb and that will keep them looking that way – in fact, you could say that they won't be able to tear their eyes away from it.' He gave another quick nervous giggle.

'Let's try,' said Domhnall. 'Brehon, you and Slevin go and stand by the gorse bush and I'll come along the path and see whether I notice you.'

'Better still, that sounds like Finbar coming – quick, let's get over there and see whether he notices,' said Slevin.

Finbar was running fast, judging by the pounding of his feet, and they barely had time to get over beside the exuberantly flowering gorse bush before he burst in, gasping, 'Brehon!'

Not something else! thought Mara, but Finbar didn't look distressed, just puzzled at their absence as he drew to a halt. Although he had already seen the marble-like figure on the slab, it drew his eye instantly and he stayed there for a long minute, eyeing it with an expression of uneasy fascination on his face. Yes, thought Mara, Slevin has chosen well. I'll be able to see as well as listen. Hopefully, Ardal, who was quick-witted, would lead them all well into the enclosure. She had not told him what they had found, but if the absence of Hans Kaufmann from his sanctuary had been discovered, then he would have a shrewd idea of why she had sent for him to bring everyone to this spot.

'Psst!' exclaimed Domhnall and Finbar jumped – much to the amusement of the other two.

'The *púca* are here,' wailed Slevin.

'That's enough,' said Mara. Her ear was caught by the sound of horse hoofs from Roughan Hill – someone was riding at breakneck speed towards them. It couldn't be Nuala already. In any case, Nuala was a cool, calm, collected young woman who would never ride like that. She listened with half an ear to Finbar telling her that he had given her note to Ardal O'Lochlainn and then assuring Domhnall and Slevin that he had known it was they all the time and that he didn't believe in ghosts or the *púca*, but her mind was on that horse getting nearer by the minute. She climbed on a tall boulder at the edge of the enclosure and then sighed with a mixture of annoyance and relief.

'Cormac,' she said with exasperation. 'What on earth are you doing back here?'

'Art didn't want to go back to Brigid; he wanted Mama. He said he was sick and he started to cry so Fachtnan dropped him off at *Dat's* place.'

'And you?' Fachtnan had probably made the right decision about Art, to bring him back to his mother, but she was surprised that he had allowed Cormac to come back. He would surely have guessed that she was only too pleased to get both nine-year-old boys away from this gruesome murder. She would have expected that Fachtnan would either have left him with his foster mother or else returned him to Brigid at the law school.

Cormac's eyes fell before hers. 'Well, I stayed with Art for a while, but then I told *Mam* that you . . . then I said that I had to get back . . . that you would need me.'

'I see,' said Mara, repressing strongly the slight feelings of jealousy that always arose when Cormac referred to his foster mother by the affectionate familiar name of *Mam* and his foster father as *Dat*. He had, after all, spent his first five years of life with them, she told herself. It was reasonable that he had a strong affection for them, but reason didn't always shut out jealousy.

'Stand over there, Cormac, behind me, and don't breathe a word,' said Domhnall sternly. Cormac was, in fact, Domhnall's uncle, but Domhnall kept an effortless authority over the younger boys and Cormac meekly did as he was told. Mara promised herself to have a stern word with her son afterwards, but in the meantime there were more important matters to be dealt with. This murder had to be solved and solved quickly. The pilgrims could not be detained for long. They had a right to be allowed to proceed on their pilgrimage to Aran and to celebrate the feast day of the saint that they had come to honour.

'They're coming,' said Domhnall in a low murmur.

It took a minute, but then Mara heard them – the high-pitched tones of the prioress, the sibilant Latin of Father Miguel, Father MacMahon agitated and appealing to Ardal to tell him why the church was empty, Sorley grumbling, Nechtan explaining that he, Ardal, Ardal's steward and his men had patrolled the boundaries of the *termon* all night and that the German's horse was still in the stable; there was a confused medley of voices and languages. She stayed very still and was pleased to note that the truant Cormac was solemn-faced and standing meekly behind Domhnall.

It was unfortunate, but perhaps inevitable that the prioress was first. The men had all conceded precedence to the ladies, and, just as Slevin had predicted, she threw a fit.

Mara made no move to step forward and allowed her two

sisters to console her and to block the terrible sight from her chaste eyes. The exclamations and broken sobs sounded overdone, but then she would have expected someone like the prioress to react like that and Mara did not think that it was significant. She did not really suspect the prioress or her sisters. She could not imagine how they could have stripped the man, killed him and then carried him to this spot and hoisted him on to the slab.

In any case, she thought, the most likely reason why Hans Kaufmann had been killed was to punish him for his sin of sacrilege – the sacrilege of burning the sacred relic. The women pilgrims had not struck her as particularly religious. Probably they enjoyed the travel, and visiting holy shrines gave a perfectly respectable reason for journeying from country to country.

Now Sorley, she thought, had an odd look – not too upset, almost glumly satisfied.

Blad, well, he crossed himself in the conventional manner of people seeing a dead body. But shocked? No, not really, she thought. More like a man putting on some show of sorrow when attending the traditional *wake* of a long-term enemy. Mór was very white, but had herself well in hand – not stunned by the nakedness of the corpse, just looking slightly to the left of it.

Nechtan – calm, dignified, not at all like the gossipy, friendly Nechtan that she had known for so long. Perhaps, she thought with interest, the revival of the old traditions had lent him this new gravity, a new solemnity. He was, after all, the *coarb*, the inheritor of the lands, possessions, and, to a certain extent, the revenues of those monks of old who had come to settle on the banks of the River Fergus, and who had built their magnificent stone church with its inlaid stone cross in the gable.

And Narait, Nechtan's wife? Bewildered . . . bewildered at first, amended Mara. And then? And then – well, terrified would be the only word for her expression. Terrified and eyeing her husband with fearful mistrust. After one frightened glance, her eyes avoided the figure of the naked man.

And the clerics? Well, Brother Cosimo had a look of grim satisfaction, almost as though he were thinking that the false pilgrim had been satisfactorily punished – or was it that he felt a satisfaction at the sight of his handiwork?

Father MacMahon was very pale, immediately and mechanic-ally crossing himself and muttering a prayer.

And Father Miguel. Now that was interesting, thought Mara. Father Miguel's fine Spanish profile, viewed in the light of the morning sun, silhouetted against the western sky, had a look of fury – lips compressed, two patches of red on the high cheekbones, dark brows slightly raised, black eyes burning. He had the appearance of a man baulked of his prey. Or was it just that the very sight of the German pilgrim reminded him of the terrible sin committed when the relic of the true cross had been destroyed?

Mara stepped forward. 'As you can see . . .' she said, pitching her voice to a level where it smothered the hysterical sobs of the prioress. 'As you see,' she repeated when there was a cessation in the frenzied noises, 'someone has desecrated the sacredness of the sanctuary evoked by Herr Hans Kaufmann. The man threw himself upon the mercy of the church and this God-given protection was profaned.'

And that, she thought, was a masterly way of putting things. The clerics of three countries – Ireland, Spain and Italy – were looking at her guiltily, and even old Sorley, dour and gruff from long years of gravedigging, eyed her with a certain measure of shame. Nechtan tightened his lips and looked straight ahead of him and his wife gazed up at him with that unusual air of timidity. Blad, the innkeeper, gave a quick, impatient snort, and Mór, his daughter, shook her head sadly and mopped her eyes with a snowy, well-laundered handkerchief. Only the prioress ignored her words and continued to shudder and sob artistically.

Mara gave them a minute to think about this and then changed her tone to a more business-like one. 'Who saw Hans Kaufmann since the hour when I left Kilnaboy yesterday?' she asked.

'I brought him supper at about an hour after sunset,' said Mór after a pause during which all looked at each other and then at the ground beneath their feet – anywhere except at the body on the slab.

'Yes, I remember it was agreed that the pilgrim should have supper,' said Mara with a nod. 'So just take us through it, Mór.'

'Well, I went over with some food in a basket, in a couple of baskets, Brehon,' said Mór. Her voice was hesitant. Mara waited. She could see that Mór was wondering whether to tell her something or not.

'And was all as you expected to find it?' she queried in a matter-of-fact way.

'Well, no, Brehon.' Mór seemed relieved to be asked that question. 'The church was locked, Brehon, and I didn't expect that. I thought that it had been agreed that the church would be left open.' She looked across at Nechtan and he frowned but said nothing.

'So you had to go over to Father MacMahon and fetch the key?' Mara wondered whether the Spaniard had locked the church. Father Miguel certainly looked pleased with himself when he heard Mór's words, but then perhaps that was his normal expression.

Mór and her father exchanged looks and Father MacMahon flushed a patchily red colour and stared so fixedly and with such a heavy frown at the gorse bush that Mara turned her head to see what he was looking at. Cormac, she noticed, had his right hand half-raised as though he were in the school room asking permission to speak and wore a slight grin on his face. The pale green eyes that he had inherited from his father were alight with amusement. Mara frowned slightly and Domhnall nudged him hard in the ribs. Mara turned her attention back to Father MacMahon and raised her black eyebrows at him. He continued to look uncomfortable and she waited.

'She fetched it herself,' he said eventually, the words spurting out. His eyes had an embarrassed look.

'Fetched it herself,' repeated Mara. She was beginning to understand. She should have guessed. Now she knew what Cormac wanted to tell her. He knew Kilnaboy far better than she did. His father, King Turlough, was a man who loved to linger over his food, and while he sipped a post-meal brandy with Blad, his youngest son was probably down by the river or climbing trees in the churchyard. Since no one else seemed about to volunteer any information, she turned to Cormac.

'You have some information for me, Cormac?' she queried.

'Just that the key is usually kept in a hollow behind the . . .

behind the statue above the south door,' he said, biting his lips while his eyes slid sideways to look at Slevin's flushed face.

Mara sighed. She knew what was amusing them. In fact, that statue that he spoke of – a *sheela-na-gig* it was called – she had always thought was an amazing thing to have above a church door, though Turlough had assured her that there were many of them in churches all over the kingdom of Thomond. It was a carved figure of a woman displaying her enormous genitals and was, according to Turlough, supposed to show that lust was a terrible thing. She was surprised that Father MacMahon would place the key above that figure.

'I suppose,' she said aloud, 'that from time immemorial, the church key has been placed in that spot.' That would, she thought, have been the only reason for such a bizarre choice. Custom, in the kingdom of the Burren, was a hallowed thing.

'That's right, Brehon,' said Blad, looking uncomfortable. He shot a quick glance at his daughter and then looked at the ground again.

'And you found the door locked, looked up, found the key, and then unlocked it. Is that right, Mór?'

'That's right, Brehon,' said Mór demurely.

'And replaced the key.'

'I thought it had probably been locked by mistake, Brehon,' explained Mór.

'Who would know that the key was placed there?' Mara addressed herself to Sorley and he answered readily.

'Everyone knows that, Brehon. Everyone in the parish.'

'And the pilgrims?' Mara switched quickly to Latin and her eyes went to the silent clerics. No one answered, but the *moue* of distaste on the prioress's lips, the slight smile on the widow's face, and the embarrassed blush on the cheeks of the youngest sister told her that the ladies, at least, had viewed this '*sheela-na-gig*'.

'We saw the church being locked after the service of Benediction on the eve of the Feast of the Holy Cross,' said Brother Cosimo eventually. Father Miguel, noted Mara, did not speak.

'They stood around waiting for you to store the key?' Mara switched back to Gaelic, addressing Sorley.

'The ladies were there,' he said. 'That one,' he nodded at the prioress with an annoyed air, 'she made a sort of clicking with her tongue and I think that the brother and the priest came across then. They had been looking at the tomb slab with the bell and the crosier in the churchyard – the grave of the pilgrim of time long gone by.'

'I did not notice where the key was placed,' said Brother Cosimo stiffly. So he has picked up a little Gaelic, thought Mara – interesting.

'Did you see it, Father Miguel?' Mara looked across at the Spanish priest, but translated the question into Latin.

'I think I may have. Yes, I did – an interesting old carving.' The words were dismissive but the eyes were keen. He was eyeing her with a look of dislike and Mara returned his gaze, holding it steadily until eventually he looked away.

No Spanish Inquisition here, Father, she thought triumphantly. No burning, no torture. Nevertheless, I am in charge and everything, from now until the moment when the murderer is convicted and punished, must go according to my word and my directions.

'I apologise, Father MacMahon,' she said, looking towards the priest, 'but even the church is under my authority until the crime is solved.'

'But, Brehon,' stuttered Father MacMahon, now speaking Gaelic, 'I wasn't the one that locked the church; I didn't go near the place.'

'It wasn't the Father,' confirmed Sorley. 'He didn't have a hand in it. It was that priest there, I guess. He was hanging around the churchyard and he seemed to be waiting until I went in for my supper.' He, of course, also spoke in Gaelic, but his finger pointing directly at the Spaniard made his meaning obvious to all.

'Did you lock the door, Father Miguel?' asked Mara in Latin.

There was a moment's silence, but then the Spanish priest nodded defiantly.

'Yes, I did,' he said. 'I was not satisfied that sufficient arrangements had been made to keep the guilty man safe.'

Mara was not sure whether Ardal and Nechtan understood the heavily accented Latin, but she thought it wasn't worth pursuing the point. Hans Kaufmann had been alive and well, and had eaten a good supper when Mór unlocked the door, so the locked door was not perhaps of significance at the moment.

Except so far as it showed the depths of Father Miguel's feelings towards the dead man and his abhorrence of the crime committed when the relic was burned.

'The question now,' she said aloud, 'is where are the clothes belonging to the dead man? They don't seem to be here so they must be at the church, I think. Will you follow me? Domhnall, translate, please.'

Domhnall, at ease with English, Latin and Irish, and having a working knowledge of Spanish from a very early age when he had accompanied his merchant father, Oisín, to the busy docks of Galway city, translated with ease as she led the way towards the church. There was no sign of the clothes anywhere in the church itself, but behind the altar were the German pilgrim's two leather satchels. Mara opened them and looked through the contents. Hans Kaufmann, she remembered, had been wearing a blue doublet, but only a green one was to be found and the linen was starched and the folds of ironing still sharply creased into the undergarments. Mara took out the small pile of shirts, shook them open and then handed them to Domhnall to refold. They had not been worn. The same with braies – they could never have been worn and still smelled of the laundry maid's soap. The mystery of the missing clothes had still to be solved. The second satchel held no clothes, but a leather bag filled to the brim with coins – at a quick glance, Mara could see a mixture of German, Italian and English coins. But still no sign of the clothes that Hans Kaufmann had been wearing yesterday.

Who had violated the sanctuary of the church? Who had killed the German pilgrim? And how had his clothes been stripped from him? And when his body had been taken to that screened-off spot, not far from the church, but also not far from the tower house where Nechtan and his wife lived, and from the small house which was the residence of the priest – well, what had happened next? One by one, Mara methodically tabulated the questions to be answered in a corner of her mind and then turned her attention to the people who had been present in the vicinity of the church during the night when the German pilgrim was killed.

No one, she noticed as she came out from behind the altar and eyed them keenly, had asked any of the normal questions. How did the body come to be in the open, out just beyond the churchyard? Why was it placed on the capstone of the ancient tomb? What is the significance of the missing clothes? She would have expected these questions to have come tumbling out, but there was a strange and uneasy silence.

'Can anyone suggest where the clothes of the dead man may be hidden?' she asked. 'My boys have already searched the ground around the tomb and the pathway that leads back to the church.'

A perfunctory effort was made by all to search the bare church, but no one seemed to be particularly interested and soon they were all back and gathered around her. The boys continued to root around the little loft where the choir would gather during a service, but they did so quietly and she allowed them to continue.

'Did anyone else see Hans Kaufmann alive yesterday evening?' she asked. 'You left the church unlocked, didn't you, Mór, once you had served him with his evening meal.' She waited for Mór's nod before continuing, 'Therefore anyone could have gone into the church after she left, perhaps,' she ended blandly, 'in order to convince him of his wrong-doing by the aid of argument.'

They all started and moved their eyes from the ground towards her face and then looked at one another. Even the prioress was now silent and defiant.

'I think that I was probably the last person to see him when I brought his supper,' said Mór bravely. 'He said that he was sleepy after he had eaten – he put his hands together like this and rested his head on them. He was teaching me some words in German.' The memory brought a flush to her cheek and a tear to her eye. Domhnall translated the Gaelic rapidly into Latin and then English for the sake of the foreign pilgrims. Time I started that clever boy on learning Greek, thought Mara, admiring his fluency in languages, and then dismissed the irrelevance.

'And what about breakfast?' she enquired innocently.

A cloud came across Mór's face. She put away her handkerchief and faced Mara defiantly. 'He told me not to bring breakfast, Brehon,' she said defiantly.

'In what language?' queried Mara with interest.

Mór's eyes fell before hers, but then she lifted them. 'In Latin, Brehon,' she said. 'I know something of the language – I have learned it so that I can talk with the pilgrims who come here.'

Easy to find out if that is true, thought Mara. I won't press her now. She looked at the other pilgrims.

'Have any of you, since the moment when he claimed sanctuary at this very spot, seen this man?' Dramatically she pointed across at the altar steps and noted how the twelve people who had crowded into the small space between the altar and the front row of seats seemed to shrink back on themselves and avoid looking at her.

'No one? No priest went to pray with him, to offer him spiritual guidance, to debate the precepts of Martin Luther with him? No one, except Mór, went to offer him hospitality – food, a drink, a blanket?' Her eyes wandered across the faces, but all heads were being firmly shaken.

'In that case,' she continued, 'I'd like you all to go back to where you are staying and to wait until I have time to question you all individually. I assure you that I will put everything into solving this murder as soon as possible and then only the guilty person will be detained.' She spoke slowly, leaving a pause after every sentence to allow Domhnall to translate.

'Guilty person!' exclaimed the prioress, suddenly deciding to take part. 'What can you mean, Madame?'

'"Brehon" is what I am called,' said Mara coldly. 'I am the king's representative in the kingdom of the Burren, just as a sergeant-at-law is in the kingdom of England. The guilty person will be the one that killed Hans Kaufmann.'

'But what if he was struck down by God?' The prioress asked the question shrilly.

Mara did not answer. She turned to Ardal and Nechtan. 'I shall rely on you both to keep a guard around the perimeter of Kilnaboy, its houses, church and inn. No one is to go in or out without my permission. Now all may go back to the inn.'

They went off, looking, to her eyes, more meditative than guilty. If she had to plump for someone at this moment, she thought, glad that her thoughts remained secret within her own head, she would plump for the Spaniard, Father Miguel. He was a fanatic and she distrusted fanatics. Someone killed Hans Kaufmann and she had little doubt that his death was due in some way to the burning of the relic of the true cross. Otherwise, why lay the corpse out like that in a ghastly simulacrum of the crucified Christ?

The four boys stayed still until the door shut behind them.

'Brehon,' said Finbar in her ear, and then more incessantly, 'Brehon! I wanted to tell you something.'

'Sorry, Finbar,' she said, immediately conscious of feelings of compunction. 'Weren't you saying something to me just before the others came?'

'I was just saying that I saw something funny when I was running back. I was going to tell you about it, but then you were all hiding and Domhnall—'

'Brehon,' said Cormac, 'I can see where he was killed.'

'What!' she exclaimed.

He did not answer but went and picked up a candelabrum from the side of the altar steps, holding it high and stepping down on to the tiled floor. There was a look of triumph on his face and in a moment she saw why.

The church was full of shadows and the carpet on the steps leading up to the altar had looked almost black until Cormac held the tall, thick candles of beeswax above his head. Now the carpet glowed in its pristine crimson shade, all except one step – the bottom step. And that was dark – almost black in colour.

Cormac handed the candelabrum to Finbar and bent down, touching the carpet with his finger.

'It's wet!' he said.

'With blood,' breathed Finbar, but he held the candles aloft and did not move. Domhnall pushed past him and he also bent down and touched the carpet.

'It's just wet,' he said in disappointed tones.

'Definitely not blood,' confirmed Slevin. 'It's not sticky.'

'Definitely wet,' said Cormac, feeling it again with a disappointed look on his face. And then he cheered up. 'Clever,' he said admiringly. 'That murderer washed the carpet.'

'Let me feel,' said Finbar, and Mara took the candelabrum from him.

'Just wet,' he repeated.

'But what would the murderer wash the carpet with?' Domhnall sounded puzzled.

'No water in a church,' said Slevin. 'When we kill the pigs,' he said with a swagger, 'we have to throw buckets and buckets of water over the yard. The smell – whew!'

'Yes, there is water in the church,' contradicted Cormac. 'There's holy water!'

'Holy water!' Finbar looked shocked, but the other three boys hurtled across the space towards the carved-out limestone basin near to the south door.

'Empty!' exclaimed Cormac. 'I'm right!'

'Carried it over in that silver ewer,' Domhnall nodded to himself.

'Should still be able to smell the blood,' asserted Slevin and knelt down, sniffing loudly.

'Can you smell anything?' asked Mara, still patiently holding the candles, but he shook his head.

'Nothing,' said Cormac.

Domhnall took a long time, smelling the carpet with concentrated care, but then shook his head. Finbar, copying him, took even longer, but in the end just volunteered that it smelled 'holy'. Mara handed the candle to Domhnall and knelt down, leaning over and almost touching the carpet with her nose, but she could not smell blood either. The whole church, she thought, was full of the highly perfumed smell of incense, beeswax and communion wine; it was no wonder that Finbar thought it smelled holy.

As for the holy water – that just came from the well and was blessed by Father MacMahon. She didn't suppose that it was any different to the water that they drank themselves. All of the water on the Burren was the same: bracingly astringent and tasting strongly of lime.

'Well done for spotting that wet patch, though, Cormac,' she said, noticing a look of disappointment on her son's face. He shrugged and said nothing and she wondered whether he thought that she was condescending to him as the youngest at the law school. He was very touchy about things like that. And then she forgot about him as she pictured the murderer scrubbing at the bloodstain with a stoup of holy water and one of those cloths that were in plentiful supply for the celebration of Mass.

'Brehon,' said Finbar insistently, and she realized that he had already spoken to her at least twice and had been telling her about 'something funny'.

'Sorry, Finbar, yes, what is it?'

'I saw something funny when I was running along the path to here from the churchyard, Brehon,' he repeated.

'Yes, Finbar, what was it?' she asked, bringing her whole attention to bear on him. She remembered his shout when he arrived, before he realized that there was no one to be seen.

'I saw something,' he repeated. 'Do you want to see it?' he invited.

'Yes.' Mara decided against inviting the other boys, who were amiably wrangling over the stain on the steps and poking around the church for bloodstained cloths. Finbar's 'something funny' might turn out to be nothing, in which case Domhnall and Slevin would be politely non-committal and privately contemptuous and Cormac would probably laugh. 'Come and show me,' she requested. 'Domhnall, when you are finished here, please lock the church and bring me the key.'

The object was not far down the path. It was surprising that it had been missed, but it lay slightly to the side of the path, almost hidden beneath a lichen-encrusted boulder, amongst a clump of the very pale flowers of the tall, pure-white, five-petalled marsh maidens. It was a triangular piece of cloth, about the size of a normal handkerchief, but thickly padded. She looked down at it in a puzzled way. What on earth was it? Certainly something that she had never seen before and she could not imagine what was its use. It had no blood on it, but it might be significant.

'Ask the others to come,' she said, 'perhaps they'll have some ideas.'

Domhnall and Slevin came instantly, tired of searching for bloodstained cloths, but it was Cormac, trailing behind them, who immediately identified the triangular piece of linen.

'That's a codpiece,' he said scornfully. 'Murrough has a pile of them. The King laughs at him about it. You wear it here under those tight hose.' He pointed between his legs with a grin. 'Makes you look b-i-g,' he said with a sidelong glance at Finbar, who giggled nervously.

'So that's it. Of course,' said Mara in matter-of-fact tones.

Turlough's second son Murrough, Cormac's stepbrother, was a young man who frequented the court in London. It was true that he always wore something that looked padded inside his hose, and Turlough had many a ribald laugh about his son's pretensions to manhood. The thing that Finbar had spotted, lying concealed among the oddly inappropriate white marsh maiden flowers, *was* called a codpiece, she remembered. It was something that would presumably be buttoned on to the hose around a man's groin. She had noticed the swelling between the legs of the young German and had wondered why young men like Hans Kaufmann and her stepson, Murrough, bothered to wear this obviously fake piece of padding.

But all that was of little interest now. What was of interest was that a piece of Hans Kaufmann's clothing had been dropped at the side of the path between the churchyard and the ancient tomb.

But it was not a handkerchief or a belt buckle that had been dropped. A living man could perhaps have mislaid something like that on a walk through the bushes. No, this article of clothing, this codpiece, could not have been dropped accident-ally – it would have been buttoned securely inside a man's hose.

That meant that Hans Kaufmann had been naked when his body travelled along the path either this morning or last night.

And his clothing had probably been carried by his murderer.

Seven

Bretha Nemed Toísech
(Laws of Noble Professions)

Three things confer nemed *status on a physician:*
1. *A complete cure.*
2. *Leaving no blemish.*
3. *A painless examination.*

The honour price of a physician is seven séts *or three-and-a-half ounces of silver.*

'Nuala's really slow,' commented Cormac. For the tenth time he climbed up on the low mound that held the tomb with the naked body and looked across the gorse bushes towards Roughan Hill. Nuala was his godmother, a great giver of presents – not just at birthdays and during the Christmas festival, but after each yearly trip which she took to the University of Padua to perfect her medical knowledge. Although still in her early twenties, Nuala was probably one of the most learned physicians in Ireland and her desire for more knowledge was insatiable.

'She'll come when she is ready,' said Mara. 'She's probably bringing a cart to take the body back to her hospital.'

'To open it up, is that right, Brehon?' said Domhnall.

Cormac's eyes widened. 'What for?'

'I'm not sure – it's a long time ago and I was young, but I think that she opens the stomach to tell when a person died. Something to do with his last meal, is that right, Brehon?'

'That's right, Domhnall,' said Mara, feeling thankful that the sensitive Art was not present. 'And, of course, to determine what actually killed the person.'

Cormac's eyes widened even more, but he prided himself on being tough so he just hoisted his shoulders with the air of a hardened soldier. It was interesting, thought Mara, that although Cormac had been studying at the law school for five years now, and really did not see a huge amount of his father, he was, nevertheless, far more of a warrior king than a scholarly lawyer like his mother, and her father before her. What would be his future? she wondered, and was seized with a sudden feeling of dread and vulnerability, almost as though she had foreseen an early death for this most beloved son of hers. He was clever and quick to learn, but not that interested in the law and without the drive and determination that characterized Domhnall. At the moment it seemed as though his whole life was devoted to having fun and playing pranks – and, of course, appearing tough. Now he wandered back to the corpse and stared intently at it.

'Here comes Nuala, I'd say; that sounds like a cart,' interrupted Domhnall. 'They're coming by the road.' Quick and neat in all of his movements, he climbed to the top of a young ash tree and then slid back down again. 'It's all right, Fachtnan is with her. She'll know where to go,' he said.

Marriage suited Nuala, thought Mara, as she watched the physician approach. She had been a pretty child – dark-haired and dark-eyed, but always with a slight air of sadness about her. Nuala's mother had died when she was quite young, and her father, the physician Malachy, had never acknowledged his daughter's brains and ambitions and continually frustrated her attempts to follow in the footsteps of her father, grandfather and other ancestors. This had cast a shadow over her girlhood. Now a successful and well-trained physician, married to Fachtnan, whom she had loved since childhood, owning her own hospital, the mother of two little girls, she was glowing with happiness.

'What'll she say when she sees the body crucified like that?' Cormac sounded excited and stood back so that the tomb and its terrible burden could have immediate impact.

Mara smiled to herself. She could guess what Nuala would say and was pleased to find herself right when Nuala, on her arrival, said nothing, just gazed on the corpse with the keen, steady gaze that she brought to all medical problems, whether they concerned a baby's rash or a man raving in a high fever.

She took her time, inspecting the five wounds and eventually said, 'The damage to the hands and feet appears to have been caused after death.'

Mara said nothing. She had guessed that. This was what she had expected. She saw Domhnall nod to himself and glance at Slevin as if to say, *Told you so!*

Then she forgot the boys when Nuala added, 'But some time after death,' and leaned over the puncture mark on the right hand with an air of interest.

'Some time after,' repeated Mara. That surprised her.

'Half an hour, at least, I'd say, but I can tell you more once I examine the body. We'll take it away now if there is nothing else that I can help you with.'

'We can't find the clothes anywhere, but we think that he was murdered in the church,' said Mara. She led the way to the place where the piece of linen still lay among the white flowers of the marsh maidens and nodded to Cormac to give his explanation when the triangular padded codpiece was unfolded. Fachtnan took the time to listen to Finbar's story of how he found it, and praised him for his cleverness.

'Bet I find the rest of the clothes,' boasted Finbar.

'And they are not in the church?' asked Nuala.

'Not a sign – so far as we could see.'

Nuala frowned over the codpiece.

'Could he have been wearing this when he was stabbed?' asked Mara.

Nuala's shake of the head was quick and decisive. 'Impossible,' she said. 'That knife in the ribs went straight into the man's heart. He would have poured blood.'

'No blood on him now,' said Fachtnan.

'Rained last night,' put in Slevin. 'I couldn't sleep – it was so hot and then I heard it rain. It cooled off a bit then.'

'Not last night, more the late evening – couple of hours after sunset,' contradicted Domhnall. 'I woke and went to the window and opened the shutters after it finished. The moon was only just up.'

Nuala went back to the body. 'Yes,' she said, 'it probably was the rain that washed the body clean. You can still see traces of blood in the roots of the hairs on the stomach. But,' she scrutinized the capstone on the left side of the body, testing a feathery piece of lichen with one fingernail and bringing her eyes close to the stone under the body, 'I'd almost be sure, Mara, that he was not killed here. Sure,' she amended, kneeling down and examining the grass by the stone. 'No shower of rain could have completely cleared traces of blood from this.'

'Someone hit him over the head, knifed him and carried him on to the slab,' said Cormac cheerfully.

'No.' Nuala wore a faint frown. 'No, no one hit him over the head.' She went back and made a complete examination of the head. 'Not a sign,' she said.

'Strangled him?' suggested Fachtnan.

Nuala shook her head again.

'He'd be blue in the face with his tongue sticking out if he was strangled,' said Cormac. 'The King was telling me . . .'

'That's enough, Cormac,' said Mara. Odd the way he always referred to his father as 'the king' – and to her as 'the Brehon'. We lost him when we gave him to Cliona and Setanta to foster, she thought sadly. And yet he is the world to me. But what am I to him? And then she took her mind back to the problem of the death of this German pilgrim.

'Not knocked unconscious, nor strangled,' she said with an effort. 'So how on earth did anyone get his clothes off? He's a big, heavy, strong-looking man.'

'I hadn't thought of that,' admitted Nuala. 'What do you think, Fachtnan?'

Fachtnan scratched his thick, curly hair. 'Strange,' he said. 'Why on earth should a man take off his clothes so that his murderer could stick a knife in his ribs?'

'What do you boys think?' asked Mara. It was the sort of odd problem that a young mind could solve.

'Went for a swim?' suggested Finbar.

'He was locked in the church, b—' pointed out Slevin, stopping himself just in time from calling Finbar a birdbrain. 'At least he was until Mór brought him his supper, and it's stupid to swim after supper – especially one of Mór's suppers. In any case, even if he was on his way to the river, he wouldn't run past the inn stark naked. He'd undress on the bank like everyone else.'

Mara explained to Nuala the arrangement about the church key at Kilnaboy and Nuala nodded. The majority of houses in the kingdom of the Burren had a favourite place where a key was supposedly hidden. The fact that usually all of their neighbours knew the hiding place was not considered to be of importance; Nuala herself, as a trusted physician, probably knew twenty or thirty such hiding places. In any event she showed no surprise that a church filled with treasures would have such relaxed security arrangements.

'There are absolutely no bruises on him,' said Nuala, examining the body again. 'I would be prepared to swear that no violence was used until the knife was slid in through his ribs, in here on the left side.'

'Perhaps someone dared him – you know – *you take off all your clothes and run up and down the church and see if God strikes you dead,*' said Cormac airily. 'Then, when he'd taken everything off, they stuck a knife in him, threw his body over a horse and took him out here – and then tried to pretend that he was crucified, by sticking a knife into his hands and feet.'

'I've got an idea,' said Domhnall suddenly. 'Could someone have put something in his food when he had his supper, something that would make him sleep and allow the murderer to take his clothes off; it would be someone who wanted to make it look as though God had taken vengeance on him for burning the piece of the true cross. It's just an idea,' he ended modestly.

'It's a very good idea,' said Mara warmly. 'What do you think, Nuala?'

'Some poppy syrup, perhaps,' said Nuala doubtfully. 'There are only two places that this could have been obtained – from my hospital, or from Caherconnell.'

Her face closed and her lips tightened as she said this. Nuala's father had left his physician's business at Caherconnell, the ancestral home of the O'Davoren physicians, to the son of his second wife, and Nuala had never forgiven this. If it had not been for the kindness of an elderly physician who had bequeathed to her his house and farm, thus providing her with an income to pay her fees as an apprentice to a famous physician in the kingdom of Thomond, she would never have achieved her dream. Mara could see now how she compressed her lips and passed her hand across her face before speaking.

'A man would have to be heavily drugged not to resist having his clothes removed, but I will certainly bear this in mind and examine the stomach contents carefully. Thank you, Domhnall, that was a good idea. I'll check our stores and send a message over to Caherconnell,' said Nuala with an effort.

'You forget,' said Mara quietly, and with a quick look along the path leading back to the churchyard, 'we do have five pilgrims here who may have been to lands where the poppy grows and where those drugs are readily available, or else they may have met other pilgrims who gave them some as a medicine – such things do happen, I think.'

'Or even the murdered man himself, he may have had something in his luggage,' said Fachtnan.

'Very possible; we must investigate everyone's belongings.' Mara was conscious that time was going by.

'Let's get the body into the cart,' said Nuala, and beckoned to her servant to bring the cart forward.

The driver of the cart was a big and strong fellow; Mara knew that he assisted Nuala in operations where, despite the soporific effects of the poppy syrup, patients had to be held down while an amputation or a deep incision had to be made. However, he still needed the help of Fachtnan in order to move the body on to the cart. As they were struggling, Mara's mind went to the murderer. It had to be a strong man, she thought, and then stopped herself from going any further. Facts first, she reminded herself, turning away and looking back towards the church of Kilnaboy.

How had anyone stripped the body and then killed the man? The other way around it would all make sense, but the witness of the clothes proved it wrong. No shower of rain could have washed the blood from that snowy-white codpiece, yet there was not a trace of blood on it.

'Brehon! Look!' shouted Cormac and Mara turned back quickly. Everyone was staring at the capstone. There, underneath where the body had lain, was a deep stain of blood.

'But it's on the right side – and he was stabbed on the left,' said Cormac.

'It's hard to tell,' said Nuala, inspecting the capstone with professional interest, 'but I would have thought there was not enough blood here. I still think that you are right to think that he was murdered in the church and then brought out here almost immediately. The blood would still be liquid when he was moved on to the stone and—'

'And he was lying on his face first of all,' shouted Cormac. 'That would be right, wouldn't it, Nuala? And some blood leaked out from the wound. And then the murderer turned him over on to his back, what do you think, Nuala?'

What a clever brain that child has, thought Mara proudly. Aloud she said judicially, 'That was well reasoned, Cormac.'

'And limestone does suck up moisture,' said Domhnall thoughtfully. 'I remember pouring out a cup of milk that Brigid was trying to make me drink when I came to the law school first – I poured it on to that big mounting block of limestone and it sucked it all up; she never noticed.'

'That's true,' said Nuala with a nod of approval at that piece of scientific observation. 'I think Cormac is right, though. This man was killed elsewhere, brought here, perhaps on the back of a horse – but after that heavy shower last night, it's no good looking for a bloodstain on a horse I would say – unless it was a white horse – so brought on the back of a horse, dragged on to the capstone, face down, and then – perhaps an hour or so later, after the horse had been returned to its field, arranged on his back.' Nuala looked up at the Roughan hillside where five dark brown horses grazed the clumps of grass between the gorse bushes. 'And that might have been the time that the murderer finished off the job – made a murder look like an act of God to the ignorant.'

'Marked the stigmata on hands and feet,' said Domhnall solemnly.

'Anything else?' asked Nuala after a minute. 'If not, I'll go now.'

Mara came out of her thoughts with a start. 'Yes,' she said. 'Yes, of course, you go on. I'll call down to Rathborney later in the day and see what you've managed to find out.'

She waited until the cart had trundled off and Nuala had followed, before turning to Fachtnan.

'But why were the clothes, bloodstained or not, so carefully hidden?' she asked, feeling quite exasperated by this minor puzzle. 'After all, the man is dead. There was no effort to hide the body – on the contrary. So why bother to hide the clothes?'

'I suppose,' said Fachtnan with his attractive grin, 'that if I asked you that question, you would tell me to think myself into the mind of the murderer.'

'So I would,' said Mara. 'And, do you know, boys, I am suddenly struck by the wisdom of my own words. Yes, of course. I ask myself what does the murderer hope that those finding the body will immediately think. Fachtnan, you and I have dealt with cases where the murder is made to look like an accident, or to look like suicide. But this case is neither of those. In the case of the killing of Hans Kaufmann, the murderer hopes that everyone will think that this man, this anti-Christ, this blasphemer, was struck dead by God himself – "*God is not mocked*" – that's what was written on his forehead.'

'And he wants us to think of the crucifixion,' said Domhnall.

'Where Christ had no clothes – though he did have sort of braies,' put in Slevin.

'And God is magic, so he could just whisk the clothes up to heaven, or so some people think,' was Cormac's contribution, showing, thought Mara, the effect of his religious upbringing in her household.

'That's what the murderer wants us to think,' put in Domhnall.

'But the Brehon is cleverer than the murderer so she knows that it wasn't God after all.' Finbar looked at her carefully to make sure that he had said the right thing – trying to ingratiate himself, as usual. He was, she thought worriedly, one of the most insecure children she had ever had in her law school.

'But where would I be without my scholars?' she said lightly. 'Now run on ahead, all of you, and wait for me by the church door.'

Eight

Bretha Nemed Déinenach
(Last Book of Judgements)

*'Folomrad do mairb' (to strip clothes from a corpse) is deemed to be
a very serious offence unless the act takes place on a battlefield.*

*Anyone who composes a satire about a dead person, or dishonours
their dead body in any way, will have to pay that person's honour
price to the nearest living relative.*

The five boys were standing in the sunlight beside the church
door when Mara and Fachtnan arrived there. Sorley was
digging a grave a short distance away – she assumed for the
German pilgrim. There had been, to the best of her knowledge,
no local death – certainly none had been announced at yesterday's
service. And presumably once Nuala was finished with the body,
it would be coffined and buried. She handed the key of the church
to Fachtnan and went over towards Sorley, who straightened
as she approached and stood leaning on his shovel.

'We thought that we would put him here, Brehon,' he said.
'He should be got below ground as soon as possible. There's
another pilgrim already buried there – so they say – it was
before my time, and before the time of my father – there
under that slab with the tau cross and the bell engraved on it.'

He must have seen some surprise on her face because he went
on, 'Father MacMahon thinks that he should be buried here,
poor man, beside his fellow pilgrim. He thinks it might have
been just a temporary madness that made him do an evil deed
like that, so we should give him a decent, Christian burial – that's
what the Father says. "Sorley," he says to me, "Mark my words;
even if God struck him down for blasphemy, it's not for us to
judge. Let God deal with him – let God put him in hell or in
purgatory – let the flames burn the sin from his soul – we will
put his body in the ground," so that's what I am doing, Brehon.'

It was an unexpected flow of words from one who was not normally so garrulous. And the phrase 'poor man' struck her as sounding particularly false.

'A very Christian-like gesture,' said Mara solemnly.

Interesting, she thought, that Father MacMahon should show himself so forgiving to a man who had desecrated the sacred relic of the true cross and ruined the lucrative business of pilgrims arriving and leaving donations. She would have expected him to direct that the German, as a blasphemer, should be buried outside the churchyard, in the scrap of nettle-infested ground that was kept for unfortunates who had committed suicide. Unbaptized babies should also be buried in that spot, but families usually kept the tiny bodies hidden and buried them secretly by dead of night in the ancient burial places of their pagan forefathers.

'So does Father MacMahon think that he should have a burial slab also?' she asked after a minute and was surprised when he nodded vigorously.

'Yes,' he said. 'The good Father is composing something just this very minute; he'll get the mason to carve it out on a stone.' And then he closed his lips firmly and went back to his digging with a muttered excuse.

'Father MacMahon is composing an epitaph for the dead man,' she said to Fachtnan when she joined them in the church. She shut her ears firmly to Cormac's mutters to Finbar. As far as she could hear it was a rather ribald verse about the dead man's state of undress – no doubt something Cormac had picked up from his kingly father. However, it was, she thought, rather good to see how happy Finbar was with Cormac as a temporary friend. Five was a bad number of boys to have at the law school; she wondered whether she could recruit another twelve-year-old to be a companion for Finbar, though twelve was rather too late to start on law studies. The task of memorizing the hundreds and hundreds of triads – pithy, three-part summaries of complicated laws – was so much easier when done before the age of nine when the memory is at its height. Still, perhaps a merchant's son from Galway who wanted to know a little native law – that might be ideal. Once Art was back at the law school, Cormac, she knew, would desert Finbar;

Cormac was intensely loyal to Art. In any case, Cormac and Art were not just foster brothers; their very different temperaments made them ideal companions, in the same way as Slevin and Domhnall got on so well and always had done.

'Let's look at Hans Kaufmann's satchel again. We've already looked at it to check that the murderer had not put his clothes in it, but he hadn't. You'll remember that he was wearing a blue doublet and that is missing – the underwear and shirts in the satchel are newly laundered. But let's look to make sure that there is nothing else before we question the other pilgrims.'

She went briskly up to the dim space behind the altar, noting, as she passed, that the various gold, silver and bejewelled crucifixes and holy figures all seemed to be in place and untouched. Of course, she thought, Martin Luther may not have been against such things, only relics and indulgences. She regretted that she had not made more time to talk with the German pilgrim yesterday. It would have been interesting for herself and for her scholars to have joined in the debate that seemed to be going on in Europe at the moment about certain aspects of the Roman church.

'Put the bag over here on this table near the door, Fachtnan,' she said aloud. The light was very dim in the church, but she did not want to go outside in case Sorley came near and tried to pick up some tit-bits of information in order to relay them to Father MacMahon.

The clothes were of good quality, she noticed, as, one by one, Fachtnan took the garments out and laid them on a stool. He had three spare tunics as well as a pile of shirts and braies, all neatly and carefully laundered and none darned or frayed in any way. There was also a travelling ink horn made from pewter, such as she had herself, and a smart leather wallet enclosed a set of quills and a small notebook, with a separate pocket for some small leaves of vellum.

'Neat,' said Domhnall admiringly. 'There's a leather worker in Galway could make you something like that, Brehon, if you would like one. My father would see to it for you.'

'That would be kind,' said Mara absent-mindedly.

The small leather notebook was filled with an elegant Teutonic script. Mara turned over the pages rapidly, mentally translating the enigmatic entries. There was a long list of places with initials after them, each probably signifying some scandal or abuse – R, she thought, probably stood for robbery, *raub*, and then there was a capital K in various places, including that of the convent of St Winifred at Holywell. *Kind*, of course, was the German word for child. For a moment she felt a spasm of dislike for the dead man. Why go around rooting through people's lives, discovering carefully kept secrets, just because they differed from you in religious matters?

However, that was not her business. A murder had been committed in her territory and she had to solve that, make sure that the guilty person was accused of the crime before the people of the kingdom and the appointed retribution paid. She turned her attention back to the leather folder.

One of the leaves of vellum had something written on it – not a prayer, more like a letter. She read it in silence, thinking hard.

'May we know what it says, Brehon?' asked Domhnall after a moment.

'Yes, of course,' said Mara. It was always a conviction of hers that her scholars were being trained, not just in the law, but in how to understand human nature, how to deal tactfully and sensibly with people, how to investigate a crime – all of these lessons they could only learn if they were admitted to all stages of her enquiry. She would read the letter to them; it certainly explained one of the entries in the notebook.

'You do remember your oath?' she said, and listened as Domhnall fluently recited the traditional promise to keep silent in public about all matters discussed at the law school. The scholars swore this at the beginning of each Michaelmas Term, and from time to time throughout the year she reminded them of that. Emphatic nods greeted his recitation.

'Shut the door, Cormac, and Finbar, bring over that candle from the altar,' she said when Domhnall had finished. When they were all standing in front of her she showed the writing to Fachtnan and then read aloud:

> Brother Cosimo:
> *The good lady, known as a* Brehon, *the King's representative*
> *in this strange land, has told me that I will have to pay a fine*

as retribution for what is deemed my crime in burning that piece of wood in the round tower, wrongly designated as a piece of the true cross.

I find myself a little short of silver at this moment and am sure that you will be happy to supply me. If not, then it would be interesting to see what Father Miguel thinks about that cross which I saw in your satchel and which I know that you stole from the Shrine of the Virgin near Bern in Switzerland.

I appreciate that you have already paid me for my silence on this matter, but I now realize that the thirty pieces of silver was not enough. Expect further demands from me, but for the moment five ounces of silver may suffice − I will see what the lady says tomorrow.

I am, dear Brother Cosimo, yours in the bosom of Christ, Hans Kaufmann.

Mara finished. She looked towards Cormac, the youngest member of her law school, but he was nodding happily, eyebrows raised, so she guessed that he understood the Latin. She did not look at Finbar; he would not admit to being bewildered once he saw Cormac nod, and she would only shame him in front of the other boys.

'So Brother Cosimo has already paid blackmail,' said Fachtnan quietly. He looked towards the boys expectantly.

'But this letter hasn't been delivered yet, has it?' was Slevin's comment.

'But he had already blackmailed him and blackmail could provide a motive for murder.' Domhnall's voice was meditative. 'And he could have guessed that Hans Kaufmann would come back to him for more money − after all, he was present when you explained about Brehon law and about fines. Even if he hadn't received this letter, then he might well be expecting it and might have decided to quickly get rid of the German pilgrim, the follower of Luther, and hope that everyone would think that God had struck him down.'

'Who was going to give it to Brother Cosimo, Brehon, do you think?' asked Cormac, and then, hardly drawing breath, 'Mór,' he said triumphantly. 'She was sweet on him − I could see that, couldn't you, Domhnall?'

He was probably right, thought Mara, and then while Fachtnan took the boys through the various motives for murder, her mind went to Mór. There was something that puzzled her, something that Mór had said that had not made sense at the time. Her mind had picked it up and put it on a shelf in the background until she had time to think of it. Now she revisited that shelf, took out the incongruity and examined it.

Mór had said that Hans Kaufmann had not wanted breakfast. And that did not make sense.

Why did he not want breakfast? He was a big man with, no doubt, the appetite of a big man. In any case, the arrival of breakfast would break the monotony of the night in the church with nothing but sacred objects to keep him company, and he could enjoy a quick flirtation with Mór as well.

So Mór had lied, thought Mara. But why?

'Do you remember what Mór looked like when I asked her whether she'd arranged to bring some breakfast to the German pilgrim?' She put the problem to her young scholars. At that age their eyes were keen and their memories excellent.

'Embarrassed,' said Domhnall and the others nodded agreement.

'Could it have been true that he didn't want any breakfast?' wondered Mara, carefully sticking to her rule that all facets of a problem had to be examined before any conclusion were drawn.

'No way, not one of Mór's breakfasts – no one would turn one of them down,' said Cormac emphatically.

'So did she lie?' asked Domhnall, and then, as he often did, answered his own question. 'She looked like she was lying. She was embarrassed; I do remember that. And I saw the innkeeper, the man who is her father, I saw him look at her, just like he was surprised or something like that.'

'Perhaps she murdered the German,' said Finbar hopefully, and Cormac frowned.

'Mór wouldn't murder him; why should she? She liked him. He was cuddling her in the kitchen.'

Fachtnan's eyes went towards Mara and she gave a slight nod. Neither said anything, though. This was a chance for the boys to think things out for themselves. They seemed puzzled, though, so after a minute Mara said, 'Do you think that Mór was sorry for Hans Kaufmann? And if so, what might she have done about it?'

'I know,' said Cormac triumphantly. 'She might have given him a chance to escape during the night.'

'That's clever,' said Domhnall. He took his duties as head boy of the law school very seriously, and although he would reprove the younger boys, he was quick to give praise when praise was due.

'She gave him the key,' said Slevin.

'But he wasn't locked in,' said Cormac.

'Or just told him a time to go,' amended Domhnall. 'Told him to wait until after midnight or something.'

'Perhaps she was going to help him to escape by the river,' said Slevin suddenly. 'Blad has a boat, isn't that right, Cormac?'

'That's right,' confirmed Cormac.

'She would have made an arrangement to sneak back for him when no one was around; perhaps when Ardal and Danann were handing over the guard duties to Nechtan and his steward.' Domhnall nodded his head with satisfaction at the neatness of the explanation.

'And then got a terrible shock when she saw him lying out there on the tomb with no clothes on,' finished Cormac.

'I remember that I thought she looked very pale,' said Mara, 'and, of course, that could have been just shock, as you say, Cormac. I think it is quite possible that she was sorry for him and that he persuaded her that he was afraid of Father Miguel.'

It would have been, she considered, a valid fear. There was a large network of Dominican abbeys in Ireland, and doubtless Father Miguel would have found fellow countrymen who were willing to assist him.

'Who shall we question first – Mór or Brother Cosimo, Brehon?' Slevin was a boy who liked action.

'Brother Cosimo,' said Mara. 'Fachtnan, would you fetch him and all of his baggage, whatever he has with him? And I think it might be best if the boys go with you and bring back the baggage of the other four pilgrims, the three women and Father Miguel. I'm doing that,' she explained, 'because if anyone has anything to hide they might get rid of it before we get a chance to talk to them.'

'The women wouldn't be guilty, would they? After all, they couldn't have lifted him up on to that slab. Women aren't strong like us men,' said Cormac with a swagger.

'Still, if they were all three in it, well, that would be three times the strength,' pointed out Slevin. 'They could be suspects, you know. That prioress is very holy and she might have said to her sisters: *this man deserves to die! Let's see to it, sisters,* and so they did,' he finished, reverting to his own voice after giving the prioress's words in a high-pitched tone which was a particularly good imitation of the lady's voice.

'And the widow is quite a strong-looking woman, though the prioress is a bit dainty. And the other sister, the one with the scars on her face, she mightn't look too strong, she's very thin, but she is quite tall.' Domhnall backed up his friend.

'But in the meantime,' said Fachtnan gently, 'we must investigate all of the pilgrims, so we'll go over now and collect their baggage, and, who knows, we may pick up some clues from it.'

'Don't forget to be extremely polite to everyone,' said Mara as Fachtnan gathered them up and ushered them from the church. She spoke automatically and knew that she sounded absent-minded. Her whole attention was focused on Brother Cosimo, remembering his fury when he heard that the man who had been blackmailing him was the one who now was, in his eyes, guilty of a greater crime. Did he take the opportunity of getting rid of Hans when the man was alone in the unlocked church? And did he really think that everyone would believe that the death was an act of vengeance by God – that God, who in the words of St Paul, was '*not mocked*'?

Nine

Brecha Crólige
(Judgements of Bloodlettings)

There are two fines to be paid by a person who murders another. The first is called the éraic, *or body fine, and this is paid to the nearest kin of a murdered person. It is forty-two* séts, *or twenty-one milch cows, or twenty-one ounces of silver. Added to this is the second fine, also paid to the nearest kin, and this is based on the victim's honour price.*

In the case of duinetháide, *(a secret killing), the* éraic *is doubled.*

Fachtnan, side by side with Brother Cosimo, led the little procession back to the church. He was chatting about the Aran Islands and the many churches there. Mara could hear the Italian monk asking some question about the age of the church of St Enda and she half-smiled to herself. Fachtnan was very good at this sort of thing. He carried the monk's satchel as if he were performing a normal courtesy to a guest, not as though he were a lawyer taking possession of possible evidence. The young scholars trooped behind him at a respectable distance and each had a bag to carry: Domhnall with a rather battered bag which probably belonged to Father Miguel, and the three other boys carrying the more ornate bags of the women pilgrims.

'Perhaps you would be good enough to unpack your bag,' said Mara gravely to the monk. 'Please put all of your clothes in one pile, here on this bench, and then everything else on this bench beside me.' It was only right, she thought, that some privacy should be afforded to the pilgrims and she had no wish to be fingering through the man's undergarments.

Mara was uneasily aware that it would be hard to justify a search, but then remembered that she could be looking for a weapon. Nuala had made no comment on the size or shape of the death-dealing instrument – and, knowing Nuala's cautious nature, Mara had not wasted time asking her before the complete examination of the body had taken place – however, Brother Cosimo and the other pilgrims were not to know that. To her, the stab wound in the left side of the pilgrim had looked like a knife wound, and every one of the pilgrims had a serviceable knife – she had seen each produce one during the meal yesterday, and even those belonging to the women had a long blade and sturdy handle.

Brother Cosimo was surprisingly willing to obey her. He picked out the garments one by one, and one by one he stacked them on the bench that she had indicated. Fachtnan, without being told, had taken up position near to it and, in the background, four sharp-eyed boys had their whole attention glued to his movements.

Finally everything was removed from the bag, the clothes on the one bench, and on the other, near to her, were his rosary beads, his prayer book, his small travelling lamp, a package containing ginger, figs and some lozenges – 'for my health,' he said, when she picked up the small cloth bag that contained the large-sized medical potions.

Mara nodded at his explanation, sniffed the lozenges and handed them ceremoniously to Fachtnan, who also sniffed at them in a non-committal fashion and then retained the bag in his hand.

'You will get them back before you depart,' said Mara curtly as she saw the very black eyebrows of the Benedictine monk draw together in a frown. All such medicines, she had determined, unless instantly recognizable, should be retained to be tested by Nuala. The guess that Hans Kaufmann must have been drugged heavily before his clothes were stripped from him seemed, in the complete absence of any bruises or blows to the head, to be the only possible theory at the moment. And there was, she thought, an unusual smell from the medicine.

'Anything else?' she asked as Brother Cosimo stood back and thrust his hands into the large sleeves.

'Nothing, my lady – Brehon, I mean,' he said in a voice which he strove to make sound ingratiating. He picked up his leather satchel, pulled it open and showed her the inside. It was completely empty. Mara's eyes met Fachtnan's and instantly he left the church.

'What do you think happened to the dead man, Brother Cosimo?' she asked quickly, hoping to cover the sound of Fachtnan's departing footsteps. 'You must have some guesses, you and the other pilgrims – it seems such an extraordinary thing to happen. I'm sure that you must have some theory, an intelligent man like you,' she continued.

He shrugged. 'I have no knowledge of the working of the mind of God,' he said.

'So you think that God struck him down, or did God work, in mysterious ways, through a good servant of his – perhaps God put it into the mind of one who loved him well to avenge the desecration of a relic. Do you think that was what happened?'

Her scholars, Mara was amused to notice, were staring at her wide-eyed, Finbar looking confused, Slevin interested, Cormac slightly scornful, and Domhnall, eyes narrowed, mouth compressed, his face full of thought. Brother Cosimo did not answer for a moment. She could see him wavering, uncertain whether to encourage her in this idea, or to stick to the original theory that this murder was an action by the Almighty himself.

'It is written,' he said eventually: '"*Vengeance is mine; I will repay, saith the Lord*".'

'I see,' said Mara. 'So you would have left revenge to God and would not have killed the man to punish him for what could perhaps be an act of sacrilege?'

'No, I would not.' His voice was curt and he stared at her resentfully and then looked around the church, and seemed to notice for the first time that Fachtnan was missing.

'I hope that young man of yours is being careful with my lozenges. They are very important to me.'

'Why?' Mara asked the question in a careless way, glancing idly around the church, but very quickly she brought her eyes back to his face. He did not look disconcerted, she thought, and he answered quickly and readily.

'I sleep badly when I am in strange places. The herbalist in our monastery in Rome gave me those lozenges. I take one at night in order to help me to sleep.'

'I see,' she said, her eyes on the fat purse which lay beneath the prayer book on the pile before her. 'Could you take out your coins and stack them here,' she said.

He was more hesitant about that, but eventually took them out. 'You have a rather small amount of Italian coins,' she remarked. 'You may be interested to know that we found coins like these in Hans Kaufmann's purse. How do you think that he came by them? Was he planning a pilgrimage to Italy?'

'It is possible.' He shrugged and then swung around as the door to the church opened and Fachtnan came in, breathless and panting. Held in his hand was an elaborately carved and jewel-encrusted crucifix.

'Where did you get that?' The fury was barely contained. A man of a savage and ungoverned temper, thought Mara – possibly a temper which, if provoked, might lead to murder.

'Does it belong to you?' she countered quickly.

That made him stop and think.

'No,' he said after a minute.

'I found it in Brother Cosimo's room; Blad had a spare key.' Fachtnan addressed himself to Mara.

'But, of course, you are right, it does not belong to you, although it was found in your room,' said Mara affably to the monk. 'I understand that it belongs to the Shrine of the Holy Virgin at Bern in Switzerland. I was curious to see it when I read what Hans Kaufmann had written,' she continued. She took the letter from her pouch and read it aloud to him.

'Of course,' she said when she had finished it, 'you never got that letter; before it could be delivered to you, the man was dead. In fact, he may not have sent it even if he had lived. However, he had, as he mentions, already extracted blackmail from you about this matter and that accounts for the Italian coins in his bag.'

If Mór had offered to assist the German to escape, then Hans would probably have thought twice about bringing his flight to the attention of Brother Cosimo. In any case, if he had departed in the middle of the night then there would have been no trial, no fine to be paid. He had plenty of coins in his pouch and would easily have been able to purchase a horse once he was in Thomond. From there he would have gone to Limerick, English-owned and dominated and may well have reached that city before his absence at Kilnaboy had been noted. That letter would not have been sent and Brother Cosimo left in possession of a valuable crucifix which he had stolen.

But, of course, if the theft was reported to Martin Luther or to any of his followers who were pouring out leaflets about the corruption of the Roman church – well, then Brother Cosimo's crime would have been made public and that may have meant the loss of his position in his monastery, of his means of living, or perhaps even of his life if someone like Father Miguel of the Spanish Inquisition had got hold of him. There was, thought Mara, ample motive for Brother Cosimo to get rid of Hans Kaufmann if he thought that he could do it safely under the guise of the vengeful God.

It would be interesting, once she got an approximate time of death from Nuala, to find out what Brother Cosimo had been doing at that time – and to find out what his lozenges were made from and whether they would have been enough to drug Hans Kaufmann to the extent that he did not struggle when his clothes were removed, allowing himself to be arranged in ghastly semblance of the crucified Christ.

'One last matter,' she said. 'I see that you have no knife here. Presumably it is on your belt. Could I please see it now?' She held out her hand, giving him no chance to deny possession of a knife. No traveller ever omitted to carry a knife on a voyage. Even the genteel prioress had produced hers when the food was brought to table at the inn.

It was an ordinary knife and she took it from him and brought it to the door, inspecting it keenly, then called her scholars to her.

'Any trace of blood?' she queried, and handed it first of all to Domhnall, who took it to the light outside the church. He inspected it keenly and then passed it on to Slevin. Nothing would be found, she was almost sure of that. The knife was a plain one, the steel shining and polished, the leather of the cross-guard and of the handle also well polished, soft and supple – treated with oil, she imagined. Suspiciously well cleaned, but then how could one fault a man for keeping his knife clean and in good condition? She looked along the row of faces, but each boy shook his head in turn, and then she took it back from Cormac, who was reluctant to let it go, and returned it to the clergyman.

Brother Cosimo had a faintly scornful smile on his lips and there was a confident air about him.

There was, of course, the possibility that a man might have two daggers.

'Fachtnan,' she said when she returned to the church, 'could you escort Brother Cosimo back to the inn – return his lozenges, but retain one for testing. And bring me Father Miguel so that I may question him.'

She waited until the two had departed before turning to her scholars.

'If you had committed a murder and held a blood-soaked knife – and you had two knives in your possession – and there was a corpse in front of you, well, how would you get rid of it?' she enquired.

'Throw it into the bushes,' suggested Finbar.

'Climb a tree and stick it into the bark so high that no one would notice it,' was Cormac's imaginative response.

'Dig a hole and bury it,' said Slevin.

'Three good ideas,' said Mara with a nod of approval. 'What do you think, Domhnall?'

He didn't answer for a moment. A thoughtful boy, he considered all possibilities before speaking. And when he did speak, she thought, rather sadly, that he was probably correct.

'I think that I would throw it into the centre of the River Fergus, Brehon,' he said, and she sighed.

'I hope you are not right, Domhnall,' she said. 'We'll never find it there.' But even as she spoke she acknowledged that it was probably the most likely place that any murderer would have thrown the knife. The River Fergus, after all, ran deep and wide, just on the south side of the inn. It would have been an ideal place in which to consign the murder weapon – once at the bottom of the water it might never be found again.

Ten

Bretha Comaithchesa
(Judgements about Neighbourhoods)

In all neighbourhoods there are common rights to seaweed if it is required
as a fertilizer, and it has been thrown up on to the high tide line.

Duilsc (edible seaweed) which grows on rocks also is common
property.

But grazing rights for cattle belong to the owners of the land that
adjoins the shore.

Father Miguel was in a very different mood to Brother Cosimo.
He was suave, at ease and outwardly very co-operative. He
asked several interested questions about Brehon law, immediately
emptied his bag, efficiently sorting out the clothes and the
personal belongings from the holy objects such as his beads,
his tiny relic of a bone from St Eustace's foot, which he
explained had preserved him on many occasions from death
at sea during storms. There was no sign of any medicines –
lozenges or powders of any kind.

But, thought Mara, was that an inevitable sign of innocence?
After all, the River Fergus flowed outside the windows of the
pilgrims' bedrooms. It would have been as easy to dispose of
some poppy syrup, or even some lozenges, as to throw a knife
into its depths.

Mara, busy with her thoughts, allowed Father Miguel to
talk on and ignored the fact that the four boys had drawn nearer
to see this miraculous relic and its sacred powers. Cormac, the
foster son of Setanta the fisherman, was particularly interested
in the bone and asked many searching questions on how it
actually performed its miraculous duties – whether it was a
matter of calming the storm from the heavens above, or whether
it instructed the master of the boat, in some secret way, of the
correct way of proceeding. Did it tell when to lower or raise

the sail or anything useful like that? And if so, did it actually talk, or else just put an idea into your head? The questions poured out from him and he looked furious when Father Miguel adopted a lofty air of preserving a secret about the holy powers.

'*Dat*,' said Cormac to Mara, in explanation, 'always says that a man is master of his own fate when he is in a boat during a storm.' He turned back to Father Miguel with the self-assurance which seemed to have been bred into him by his princely birth and enhanced by his frequent stays at King Turlough's tower house at Bunratty in the kingdom of the Burren.

'My foster father, Setanta, says, "*You must work with sea, not against it*,"' he quoted, adding, 'that's what he's always told me, and he is a fisherman, so he probably knows more about it.' He left it unsaid whether he meant Setanta was superior in knowledge to God or to Father Miguel, and for the first time the Spanish priest began to lose his urbane charm and self-possession.

'You are too young to understand,' he said shortly. 'The relics of our blessed Christ and of his followers have powers over the sea which have nothing to do with men's rules and customs. You know what the Bible says, don't you? "*The Lord on high is mightier than the noise of many waters, yea, than the mighty waves of the sea*."'

'*Dat* says that the waves in Aran Sound are mightier than any other waves in the world, but he's able to manage his boat in them with no help from anyone; he never calls on God,' said Cormac, stubborn as always.

'Thank you, Cormac, that is enough. This Spanish Inquisition, Father Miguel,' said Mara, intervening on the nautical discussion, 'could you explain a little bit to me about this. How does it work? What is the justification for burning someone whose view of God differs from your view?'

'There is only true faith, and any man who does not believe as the Pope directs is a heretic,' he said sternly. 'It's difficult to explain it to a woman but I will try. You see, dear lady, heretics destroy the bonds of society by weakening the basic authority on which all institutions rest; their mere existence brings down the vengeance of heaven on the regions in which they live or where the acts of heresy have been committed – such as here at Kilnaboy. I have told Father MacMahon that the round tower, the place where the sin against God was committed, must be cleansed from top to bottom and must then be reconsecrated. I must remind him of this.' He stayed silent for a moment and she watched his face carefully. There was an intense and brooding expression on it and she was reminded of her words about a fanatic. This Father Miguel was a fanatic – but was he insane? That she could not tell. So far there was little evidence. She could see that his eyes, burning with fervour a few minutes ago, now seemed as though shutters had been drawn over them. He obviously decided that he would say no more about the Spanish Inquisition and so turned to her with a false smile.

'Now what is it that you wish to look at among my poor belongings, Brehon? You are welcome to see all that I possess, with the exception of one thing. The documents of the Holy Inquisition are not open to profane eyes.'

'Very well,' said Mara quietly. 'But I wish to be assured that the name of the dead man, the name of Hans Kaufmann, does not appear in them. I know Spanish, but my assistant, Fachtnan, does not. You may show him the individual pages with confidence that he will not be able to read any secrets and let him check that the name does not appear.'

She waited until Fachtnan stepped forward and then watched carefully to make sure that all of the pages were displayed in front of him.

It was a very cursory glance that was permitted to Fachtnan, but after his nod Mara felt reasonably satisfied that nothing was written down in these which dictated the murder of the German pilgrim. That, of course, did not mean that Father Miguel had not decided to do the deed after the destruction of the relic. He was a big man, much older than Hans Kaufmann, of course, but he might have been able to move the dead body. But how did he manage to strip the clothing, leaving no marks or bruises, unless, of course, the German pilgrim was unconscious after the administration of some drug?

There was nothing of great significance among the Spanish priest's possessions – his clothes were of a poorer quality than those of the Italian, there were no jewelled crosses, but there was a big batch of prayers. Yet nothing about '*God is not mocked*'. Could he have had that prayer, and if so, could it have been placed on the brow of the corpse on the ancient tombstone?

One by one, Mara turned over his belongings and then asked to see his knife. While she was carefully inspecting this, and checking, by the light of the candle, for any sign of blood-stains, a voice from behind suddenly piped up.

'I think that the Inquisition is abominable. Imagine burning someone to death because he did not share your view about God,' said Cormac O'Brien, the youngest of a long line of the kings of Ireland; the voice of his ancestors – of Turlough of the Triumphs, Brian of the Battles and of Teige the Bonesplitter – gave to his childish tones a confidence which made his words ring to the rafters.

Father Miguel wheeled around, fury inflaming the skin over his cheekbones, and causing him to clench his fists. 'What did you say?' he growled.

'Cormac, go and wait outside,' said Mara coolly. 'Wait until I come out to you.'

'I might as well help Sorley with replacing the thatch on the roof of the round tower while I am waiting for you; that'll be interesting, at least,' said Cormac defiantly as he strolled to the door. To Mara's fury she saw him exchange a wink with Finbar, who sniggered. Domhnall moved a little nearer and glared at Finbar so Mara said nothing. There was, she thought, some excuse for the twelve-year-old, who was so lacking in confidence and who now hoped to have his first real friend during his time at the Burren; for her son, Cormac, there was no excuse. He had been a member of the law school since he was five years old and knew that he had to keep silent while accompanying the Brehon on legal business.

'What is your opinion, Father Miguel, about the death of Hans Kaufmann?' she enquired, deciding to ignore Cormac's intervention. He was a hard, cruel man, and to apologise to him for her son's behaviour might make him feel that he had the upper hand.

He paused for a moment before answering; it seemed as though the question took him aback. She could see the denial, the assertion of ignorance trembling on his lips, but she kept her eyes fixed on him, and after a minute he gave her an answer which in turn took her slightly aback.

'*God is not mocked,*' he said defiantly. '*Be not deceived; God is not mocked: for whatsoever a man soweth, that shall he also reap.*'

Mara looked at him steadily. 'I find that an interesting quotation,' she said sternly. 'Were you the person who placed that quotation from St Paul on the forehead of the murdered man?'

She waited for a moment for the answer, raising an eyebrow when none was forthcoming.

'Come now,' she said. 'The question is an easy one. Surely you can answer it.'

The silence in the church was intense and it seemed to last several minutes. Glancing momentarily across at her scholars, she could sense that Domhnall seemed to be holding his breath. But almost immediately her eyes returned to Father Miguel. There seemed to be a struggle going on in the dark-skinned, dark-eyed face before her. For a few moments she almost thought that he might be going to confess to the murder. But then he glared at her.

'I must be about God's business. The devil may still be present in that tower,' he said wrathfully. With hands that seemed to shake, he crammed his belongings back into the satchel, picked it up, turned on his heel and left the church without answering her question. Her scholars stared after him, wide-eyed with surprise. They were so used to the deference with which everyone on the Burren treated their Brehon, so used to the fact that, as the king's representative every courtesy was due to her, and her verdicts instantly obeyed, that this defiance by a Spanish priest shocked them.

'Do you think that he is guilty, Brehon?' asked Fachtnan after a moment.

Mara thought hard. 'It is possible,' she said. 'What do you all think?' she asked, looking around at her scholars.

'What did he have to gain from the murder?' asked Slevin.

'Nothing, really,' said Finbar tentatively. 'All that money was left in Hans Kaufmann's pouch. You'd think that the murderer would have stolen it from the satchel – though perhaps he had intended to do that, but didn't have time to visit the church since we came so early in the morning and we discovered the body . . .'

His words tailed off. He was looking at Domhnall, whose face showed that he was deep in thought.

'Well reasoned,' praised Mara, but she also looked at Domhnall.

'You can get satisfaction from doing something that is nothing to do with any monetary gain,' said Domhnall slowly. 'Like scoring a goal in hurling, or climbing to the top of a wall of rock.' He looked, not at his fellow scholars, but at Mara, and she could see that he was considering the matter carefully. When he spoke again his voice was full of confidence. 'I think that Father Miguel is the type that might get satisfaction from what he saw as his duty to God. He wouldn't need to steal. He probably did believe that Hans Kaufmann was possessed by the devil and killing him might have given him . . . a sort of inward glow,' he finished, and Mara burned with pride in him.

Domhnall O'Davoren, the son of her blue-eyed and fair-skinned daughter Sorcha – a girl who had no interest in the law, and who, though artistic, and talented in anything to do with the hands, had found difficulty with what Brigid called 'book learning'. Sorcha had given birth to this boy who had inherited the brains and passion for the law from Mara's father, his great-grandfather, the Brehon of the Burren. He had also inherited the dark eyes and black hair of the O'Davorens – not just through Mara and her father, but from his father Oisín, also an O'Davoren and a distant cousin of Mara. He had come to the law school at the age of eight, and from his first days in the schoolroom she had been sure that he would be a worthy heir to the position that his ancestors had held.

Cormac, her son by her second marriage, probably had a different future ahead of him, she thought sadly. He had plenty of brains, but so far didn't appear to have a lawyer's temperament.

'You may well be right, Domhnall,' she said aloud and looked across at Fachtnan, waiting to hear what he would say.

'Revenge is probably only a valid motive if there is some-thing slightly insane about a man – in my opinion, anyway,' he said carefully. 'The question is whether Father Miguel appears to be unbalanced.'

'Yes!' said Slevin fervently.

'I agree,' said Finbar quickly.

'He could be unbalanced,' said Domhnall after a short pause. 'He talks rather wildly, doesn't he? All this stuff about scrubbing the marks of the devil out of the round tower – hard to clean stone at the best of times,' he added judicially, and Mara concealed a smile. Her grandson had a practical and analytical mind and looked at all aspects of a problem.

'Well, now,' she said with a sigh. 'We'd better see the prioress and her sisters. Would you fetch them, Fachtnan?'

'The prioress is having a hysterical fit and her two sisters are tending her. They say that she is quite unable to rise from her bed.'

'Well, I'll have to go across to the inn then,' said Mara. 'Blad won't mind.' She thought for a moment. 'I think, Fachtnan, I will interview the three women on my own, so it might be best if you took the scholars back to school now. The prioress may object to men and boys being present and I would not like to offend her needlessly. In any case, I feel that everyone should do some work today – I've promised Cumhal that we will all come to the bog tomorrow to help him load up the turf. Bring back their bags to the inn, boys, will you, and then collect your ponies and ride back to the school.'

There were broad smiles at that reminder. It was an annual treat going to the bog on the tableland between the mountains to the west of the law school. It was always an immensely sociable day where the whole neighbourhood helped each other to get the dried sods of peat loaded on to the carts. Nechtan, she had noticed when going into the church, had already drawn his turf and his men were busy unloading it from the huge, high-sided cart and wheeling the sods into the barn where they were stacked to a cottage-sized heap so that they would dry over the next four seasons.

Sorley had left his gravedigging – all was ready for the body – and he was now busy putting another layer of thatch on to the roof of the round tower. The renewing of the top layer of thatch on houses, barns, sheds, dovecotes and other farm buildings was an annual early autumn task throughout the Burren. On the whole, unless there had been damage by storm winds or by rodents, the bottom two layers of the thatch – measuring up to two feet in thickness – were left untouched, and neatly-tied bundles of freshly dried reeds were pegged on top, using hazel sticks to pin them in place, just as hairpins fastened braids to the head. When it was finished the thatch would be immensely thick and completely rainproof.

Cormac was dashing to and fro from the cart and handing up the sheaves to Sorley. Father MacMahon and Father Miguel, grim-faced, were deep in conversation at the bottom of the short ladder that led up to the doorway to the desecrated shrine. While she watched them, a couple of maidservants came out from Father MacMahon's house, bearing long-handled brooms and carrying buckets of water. As they drew near, Mara could smell the odour of a strong solution of the lye soap and see the flat grey bubbles on the top of the buckets. She suppressed a smile and accosted the priests politely.

'I see that you are about to purify the place,' she said to Father MacMahon.

He nodded gloomily. 'Though we will never be able to afford a relic like that again,' he said. He raised his voice slightly as Nechtan drew near. 'Kilnaboy Church has held the relic of the true cross for almost three hundred years,' he said clearly and distinctly. 'The O'Quinn family presented it. Ah, Nechtan, I was just telling the Brehon that it was your great ancestor, Cathal O'Quinn, who brought the relic back from the Holy Land and presented it to the church of his ancestors.'

Mara looked at Nechtan with sympathy. How would he answer that? Would he turn it aside with a jest? He was not, she reckoned, a particularly rich man; Cumhal, her farm manager, had hinted that he had a poor steward for his lands, and that Nechtan himself did not properly supervise the work. Certainly Roughan Hill, behind the church, appeared to be almost covered with gorse bushes and brambles. There would be meagre grazing on that. And the turf that his men were stacking appeared, by its very black colour, to be poorly dried. He said nothing in reply to the priest, but the slight flush of shame and his lowered eyes gave him a guilty look.

'How does one go about obtaining a relic?' asked Mara in an interested tone. 'Do they all have to come from the Holy

Land, or do we have any relics here in Ireland? After all, we have plenty of Irish saints and also plenty of holy wells, don't we? There's one over there, associated with the daughter of Baoith, a very holy woman,' she informed the Spanish priest, adding her contribution to the discussion in order to give Nechtan time to recover.

'A well,' said Father Miguel, and in his voice was a note of derision.

These wells, thought Mara, feeling annoyed by his scorn, were venerated by people from ancient times, venerated with various ceremonies. The well of the daughter of Baoith was decorated throughout the year with tiny scraps of cloth which were tied to the branches of a thorn tree that grew beside it. She would not be surprised to learn that the custom was an extremely ancient one, and she guessed that the ceremonies of going around it 'sunwise' fifty times when asking for a favour might well have distant druidic roots. In any case, it was probably very soothing to a worried or despairing person and certainly did no harm, nor caused needless expense, as did those pilgrimages to far-flung lands. However, she said nothing, just inclined her head.

'There is, of course,' said Father Miguel to his fellow priest, disdaining to address Mara on the subject, 'a big difference between the relics of the first class and relics of the second class. Pilgrims want to see relics that are associated with Jesus and his holy mother – relics of the first class – not just relics of obscure saints – second- or even third-class relics.'

Mara felt a surge of partisanship for the obscure native saint of Kilnaboy – daughter of Baoith, she was known as; her own name had not come down through the centuries – but nevertheless, she held her peace. Her business was to solve the murder that had occurred on her territory, not to engage in religious disputes. In the meantime, she would speak to her son. Discourtesy from a scholar of her law school could not be tolerated.

'Cormac,' she called. 'Come here, please.'

He came reluctantly and there was a challenging look in the pale green eyes which he turned on his mother.

'Yes, Brehon?' he said haughtily.

'I think you owe Father Miguel an apology,' she said firmly. 'What you said was rude, impertinent and, actually, none of your business.' She spoke in Gaelic, but then added, 'And in Latin, please. And do make sure that I won't have to feel ashamed of you again.'

She listened critically as the apology flowed fluently from Cormac's lips. Certainly she need not blush for the nine-year-old boy's prowess in Latin; he bore the air of one reciting a lesson and she knew this was deliberate. There was nothing penitent about him as he stood very straight and fixed his eyes on a spot just slightly above the priest's left shoulder.

'Now go back over to the stable and collect your pony. You will return to school with the others,' she said when he had finished. The Spaniard had listened, scowled and then turned to talk with Father MacMahon again. For a moment she was almost as angry with him as with her son – after all, the boy was only nine years old – he could at least have acknowledged the apology. And then she sensibly decided that the manners of the priest were not her business, whereas her son's manners were. She would not let this matter rest, she decided. Cormac was behaving in a spoilt and arrogant manner and he could not be allowed to go on like this. He was, after all, the most junior member of the law school. She watched him cross over towards where Fachtnan was standing, and every inch of that straight back seemed to show that he was deeply offended.

Father Miguel was now haranguing the rather exhausted Father MacMahon about the advisability of sprinkling holy water on the walls and floors of the round door so as to make it fit for the relic that some kind person would present to the church in place of that which had been destroyed. Nechtan looked embarrassed and frustrated as the glances of the two priests continually slid in his direction, so she invited him to walk across to the inn with her.

'I must see the prioress and her two sisters,' she said to him as they went through the gate and into the river meadow that surrounded the inn. 'Isn't everything looking beautiful here,' she said cheerfully as they walked on the well-trodden path through the grass.

Blad had no use for hay so the grass had been allowed to

grow after its summer cropping and the field was like a woven tapestry, where the seedheads of foxtail, yellow oat grass and long-haired grasses formed a beautiful background for the clumps of creamy froth from the meadowsweet, the jewel bright purple knotweed, and the dramatic spires of crimson loosestrife. A slight wind had sprung up causing the flowers and grasses to ripple almost like the waves of some exotic sea. Mara pointed out its beauties to Nechtan and was relieved to see his depressed expression lighten as they moved further away from the gloomy priests and the desecrated tower.

'I'm sorry that you have such a long ride to and fro from the other side of the Burren, Brehon,' he said with his usual friendly good manners. 'And I suppose that you will be coming over again tomorrow morning?'

'Not tomorrow morning,' she said. 'Tomorrow is "bringing home the turf day" and my scholars will not wish to miss that. They always have that treat at the beginning of the Michaelmas term, and this year it's lucky that they've started back early because the turf has dried out well enough to be moved in early September due to the fine weather.'

She had thought briefly of not going to the bog, of abandoning the scholars to the care of Fachtnan and returning herself to Kilnaboy first thing in the morning, but so far she felt herself completely puzzled by this almost inexplicable murder. Perhaps a morning spent away from everything would clarify matters for her.

It was such a puzzling case. Mara frowned to herself. At this stage it was completely understandable that she had little idea of who the murderer was. But not to know how the crime could possibly have been accomplished – well, that was strange. If the German pilgrim had been found murdered on the steps of the altar, wearing his ornate and colourful clothes, then it would have just involved a careful sifting of evidence, times, alibis, motives.

But that large, heavy body, stripped of all clothing and yet not bearing a single bruise, moved a distance of about 150 yards from the church, then spreadeagled in the shape of the crucified Christ on the capstone of an ancient tomb – that, so far, seemed inexplicable.

'I'll be back in the afternoon tomorrow,' she said aloud. By then Nuala would have found out the time of death and the real questioning could begin.

'Stay tomorrow night with us,' he said immediately. 'And your scholars, too. It will be lovely to have young voices in the castle again. When myself and my brothers were growing up the place rang from morning to evening. We were outside every day, no matter what the weather, and then when darkness came we would be up in the old room under the roof and playing with bows and arrows and having sword fights and making up plays. What energy we had, all four of us. Poor fellows – I still can hardly realize that they are dead. That terrible shipwreck . . .' He paused for a moment, his face full of sorrow, and then said more cheerfully, 'We'll give you supper, Brehon; your boys will find plenty to eat. The company will be good for Narait, too.' He paused for a minute and said quietly, 'We have almost given up hope of a child of our own. It will take a miracle now, I think. And Narait is in no mood to wait for a miracle.'

Mara nodded sympathetically, but there was nothing that she could say. This was Nechtan's second marriage and no child had resulted from either of them. It looked as though he were barren. And his brothers with two cousins had been killed in a shipwreck so now he was the last of the ancient family of Quinn – *coarbs* to the ancient lands of the Kilnaboy monastery. Under Brehon law, Narait could now leave him, be impregnated by another man and then return to him. Nechtan would have to rear the child as his own. Mara felt intensely sorry for him, but there would be little that she could do if Narait wished to avail herself of the provision within the law – after all, why should she remain barren and not know the delight of giving birth to a child and rearing it? Mara thought back to her own joys and deep delight in her son Cormac, and although there were moments of worry and anxiety, overall was this feeling of huge triumph and achievement. – *this is my beloved son*, she thought, and knew that nothing that Cormac would ever do would rob her of this feeling. No, she thought, if Narait had left the barren marriage bed and had sought the love of a lusty stranger, then she had nothing to expiate under Brehon law.

But Nechtan, her husband, was the descendent of an ancient line; he could not be expected to welcome this. And if the stranger who had impregnated, or had wished to impregnate his wife, was one who had already desecrated the church of his ancestors . . . what then?

'Yes,' said Mara to Nechtan. 'Thank you very much – we would love to do that. The boys and I will enjoy it and it will save me a lot of time.' She had half thought of leaving the boys behind, thinking they might be tired after their early rising and hard, back-breaking work at the bog, but they would be excited to stay overnight with Nechtan.

Eleven

Bretha Crólinge
(Judgements on Blood Lettings)

When blood has been shed, it is the responsibility of the culprit to maintain his victim in a hospital, or in a house appointed by the physician, until a full recovery has been made.

A physician's house or hospital should be placed in a quiet spot and if possible should have flowing water nearby so as to calm the spirit of the sick person.

It should always have a garden where herbs may be grown. A good physician will have more than a hundred herbs within the enclosure so that all illnesses can be treated.

'She's feeling quite ill,' said the widow firmly. She waited until Mara had glanced through their belongings and then she took the three bags into her powerful-looking hands and dismissed the boys with a nod. They took formal leave of the Brehon and went across to the stable. The widow waited until they were out of earshot before hissing, 'She cannot possibly see you. That was a terrible shock, this morning. You should have warned us. In any case it was quite unnecessary to subject us to such a sight.'

Yet there was a certain edge of amusement to her statements. Mara eyed her tolerantly and said: 'Nonsense!'

The widow began to laugh. She was a plain-looking woman in comparison with her delicately-made elder sister, but there was a spark of humour in her sharp grey eyes and a twist to her mouth which amused Mara.

'She thinks you are quite uncivilized,' she warned. 'She wants to see a sergeant-at-arms.'

'She's out of luck and in the wrong place,' said Mara crisply. 'This kingdom is ruled by the law of the king and through him by his Brehons. I am the Brehon of the Burren and I am the law. Now, tell me, when was the last time that you saw Herr Hans Kaufmann?'

'Same time as yourself,' said the widow readily. 'I saw him when he claimed sanctuary at the church – quite exciting it all was, made Madame almost suffer a spasm.'

'The prioress's name is Eglantine, I understand,' said Mara.

'Can't get used to it,' said the widow frankly. 'Can't get my tongue around Eglantine. She was christened plain Margaret – Meg – and I was Bess, and the youngest of us,' her face changed and softened, 'poor thing, she was christened Grace because she was so beautiful – she was the loveliest little girl. We all adored her.'

'I can see the traces of beauty,' said Mara gently. 'She has a lovely mouth, lovely hair. Grace is a pretty name.'

Bess heaved a sigh. 'We don't know what is to become of her,' she said. 'My mother is dead; my father died a long time ago; my brother has a large family – his wife doesn't like Grace. I'm to be married again. I know I'm a bit on the old side, but Lord bless us, my new husband is on the old side too – captain to a trading ship, so I'll be off on voyages with him. Meg has her convent and her nuns, and Grace refuses to become a nun – come what may, she will not abide to be shut up in one of those places, she says.'

'Very much younger than you and your sister.' The prioress, thought Mara, must be in her late fifties and her sister, the widow, was even older – or perhaps that was her weather-beaten complexion. Grace, on the other hand, seemed more like an eighteen-year-old.

'A big family,' said the widow firmly, 'and, of course, as usual in big families, the eldest has to look after the youngest. But I cannot take her on the ship with me.'

'So this pilgrimage . . .' hinted Mara.

'It was Meg's idea,' said the widow frankly. 'She thought that the girl might pick up a husband – you'd be surprised who goes on these pilgrimages. There was very merry company at Canterbury. Lord bless you, there were a few lusty fellows there staying at the same inn as we. I could have fancied one or two of them myself if I didn't have my own Ned, of course.'

'Of course,' said Mara with a smile. 'But Grace . . .'

'Oh, she . . . yes, well, she is fussy.' The widow shut her mouth firmly.

'And Hans Kaufmann, did you meet him at Canterbury?'

The widow's face lit up with amusement. 'Now, he was a bit of luck!' And then her expression changed. 'Poor fellow. No, we didn't meet him at Canterbury. We went there at the beginning of our pilgrimage and then crossed over to France to see the relic of the true cross in St Germain des Prés, then we went to Mont St Michel in Normandy to see the relic of the skull pierced by the Archangel's forefinger, then crossed back to Wales and then . . .'

'As a last resort . . .' prompted Mara mischievously, and the widow laughed uproariously, throwing her head back in genuine amusement.

'That's right,' she agreed. 'I never thought that I would go to Ireland – I've heard such strange things about this place, but we did make up our minds to it and there, waiting for the boat, was the German. Well, you must admit, Brehon, he was a fine figure of a man – even finer when you saw all of him, wasn't he?'

'He was indeed,' agreed Mara coolly, taking one step back so as to avoid being nudged in the ribs. She began to change her mind about Bess and to feel sorry for Grace. One sister was a pious hypocrite and the other coarse and vulgar. She wondered how the exchange had gone between the scarred woman and the handsome young German while both sisters were eyeing him and summing up his possible matrimonial intentions.

'And they got on well, the two of them; talked together during the journey?'

'They did indeed,' said Bess emphatically. 'He was a cloth merchant and Grace is very clever with her fingers, always making something – spins, dyes, weaves the wool from my brother's sheep. Pity she can't have some land of her own and her own sheep, somewhere in the mountains, but she falls into terrible depression if she is on her own. She has no friends, never goes out, only wants to be with me. And now I'm off and she can't come with me. And there is no money in the family to provide for her.'

'But this pilgrimage, surely that must have been costly for you, was it not?' hinted Mara.

Ardal O'Lochlainn had told her once how much a pilgrimage cost; she couldn't remember the exact sum, something like twenty gold pounds was in her mind, but whatever it was, the expenses must be huge – the hire of horses, the stabling, the cost of overnight stays in inns, food, fees for ship passages. It all amounted to a sum that only the very rich could possibly afford.

'Oh, that's all taken care of by the convent,' said Bess carelessly. 'They get these young girls entering with big dowries and, of course, pilgrims come to the shrine at Meg's convent and leave big donations. But she can't do another pilgrimage next year, or even the year after, that stands to reason, so you can see that we were desperate to get matters settled for Grace before we finished.'

'And so you came to Ireland.'

'That's right,' said Bess with a heavy sigh. 'We had no sooner reached Holyhead, got off the ship from Normandy, than we saw him there, outside the inn, waiting for a ship to Ireland. He could see that Grace was tired, poor thing. Her leg was paining her. He spoke to her very kindly and invited us into the inn for a drink, bespoke a private parlour and everything, put a footstool for Grace so that she could rest her leg.'

'What is wrong with her leg?' asked Mara sympathetically. 'Was it the fire?'

'That's right. There's nothing wrong with the leg itself; it's the scars pull when she walks. She's got in the habit of limping because of the pain – she can run as fast as anyone of her age if she forgets the tug of the scars. We scold her about it, tell her she'll never get a husband if she walks as though she were an old woman.'

'Tell me about Hans Kaufmann,' put in Mara, feeling even sorrier for Grace. No wonder the girl was so ill-at-ease.

'Meg was very taken by him, and so, I could see, was Grace, though she was shy of him. So I whispered in Meg's ear to say that we, too, were going to Ireland to see this relic of the Holy Cross – he was telling us that the one in Germany had been burned and that he had heard such tales from other countries also. So Meg said to me afterwards that it was our duty to go.'

'And it was all for nothing,' said Mara.

'That's true!' Bess sighed, then brightened up. 'Still, who knows what we might meet at Aran. They say that the world visits the shrines at Aran. It's the end of the world, and if you go further you will fall off the end of the world into hell, or else ascend into heaven.'

'Yes, I've heard such stories,' said Mara absent-mindedly. She glanced at the position of the sun and wondered whether it was worth trying to insist on seeing the other two sisters, but decided that it was probably more important to go back across the Burren. She had to see Nuala and find out the approximate hour of death and whether the dead man had been drugged. She should also, she thought, call in at the farm belonging to Cormac's foster parents and enquire about Art.

'Will you tell your sisters that I shall see them tomorrow afternoon,' she said, rising to her feet.

'The prioress will want to know when the funeral will take place,' said the widow. 'She wishes to say a prayer at it.'

'Not until I am satisfied that the body of Herr Kaufmann can give me no further information,' said Mara cryptically, and was interested to see a look of alarm jump into the woman's face. Puzzlement she could understand, but why alarm? Something more to think about, she decided, and glanced out through the tall window that gave such a splendid view of the Fergus.

Mór was out in the small vegetable garden that filled the space between the kitchen and the river. She had already filled her basket with cabbage leaves, but, unusually for her, was doing nothing at that moment, just standing gazing out over the river.

Mara made her farewells to the widow, then left the hall and went out through the busy kitchen and into the vegetable garden. There was, she noticed, a boat tied to a post at the far end of the little garden.

'How beautifully you keep everything,' she said enthusiastically, eyeing the neat rows of peas, all tied to their sticks, and the tall stalks of *cainnen*, each one bearing its cluster of tiny garlic-tasting cloves. Mór, on her arrival, had begun quickly picking these and pressing the individual cloves into an empty row of well-dug soil. She worked fast and neatly, keeping her eyes fixed on the soil.

'Let me hand them down to you; they are so wonderful in cooking, aren't they?' said Mara. And then as Mór looked up to receive the next clove, she continued quickly, 'What did you arrange with Hans Kaufmann when you brought him his supper, Mór?'

There was a definite look of alarm in Mór's eyes when they met Mara's and she quickly lowered them, but this time she took a long moment to insert the tiny clove into the well-prepared soil. Mara waited for a moment and then said gently, 'Did you promise to let him escape, perhaps to row him over to Thomond and let him find his way back to Wexford?'

There was no mistaking Mór's expression now. She raised her head, her eyes wide and her lips parted in an amused smile.

'No, Brehon, I didn't arrange anything of the sort. He was quite happy, you know. He said to me in German: "*Brehon eine gute Frau ist*" – a good woman, isn't that right?'

'So nothing was fixed up about an escape?' Mara watched Mór's face carefully, but could see nothing but amusement in her dancing eyes. And then suddenly that amusement was overlaid by a look of sorrow and her eyes filled with tears.

'Excuse me, Brehon,' she said hastily. 'I think I smell that sauce burning. These girls are so careless.' And with that she snatched up her basket of cabbage leaves and fled towards the kitchen, leaving Mara to make her own way out, around the side of the building and across the yard.

On her way out she noticed Blad was needlessly pulling up a few tiny weeds on the cobbled ground in front of the stables. He did not ask any questions when she greeted him, but she could see from the worried look in his eyes that he was deeply concerned about the future of his inn.

'You know, Blad,' she said impulsively, though with a quick look over her shoulder to ensure that no cleric was listening, 'things may not be as bad as you fear. There is a new movement in Europe, new religious ideas. It could be that relics will become as out-of-fashion as if you, in this year of 1519, were wearing a houpelande – you know, like the effigy of Nechtan O'Quinn's great ancestor wears on his tomb. It would be good, wouldn't it, if wells became the new fashion? We have plenty of these on the Burren – three, isn't it, in Kilnaboy? People might journey across the world to see them and purchase water from them.'

Just as sensible as praying to a piece of wood which might, or might not, be 1,500 years old and part of the cross of Jesus, she thought, watching his face light up.

'Or else,' she went on, 'this new religion will have its own saints and martyrs and Hans Kaufmann will be the first of them. The world might be beating a path to Kilnaboy if that is the way. You'll be as famous here as Canterbury was after the murder of Thomas à Becket.'

'I'll tell Father MacMahon about that,' said Blad, growing more cheerful by the minute.

'Best not,' said Mara hastily. 'He wouldn't like to think of a new religion – tell him about the holy well, though. It might be nice to have some more ceremonies connected with it.' She herself liked the present ceremony of tying little bits of cloth to the thorn bush beside it and loved to imagine the saint looking down at them, as though at a patchwork quilt, and picking out the owner of each piece and dealing with their troubles. However, that might be too domestic a ceremony to bring pilgrims from across the world. 'Perhaps someone might be healed at the shrine or perhaps Father MacMahon could devote a special day to the saint every year – or a couple of special days – talk to old people of the parish about ceremonies when their grandparents were young. I'm sure that Brigid was telling me something one day; I'll ask her about it. Kilnaboy people are very attached to that well.'

Mara felt rather pleased with that idea and congratulated herself on steering his thoughts in such an optimistic direction. And then she remembered that for the sake of the law and for her responsibilities as Brehon this murder had to be solved and the murderer brought to justice. Shrines could wait – murder and its effect on the community could not.

'Tell me, Blad,' she went on, 'did Mór say anything after she came back from bringing supper to the German?'

'I didn't see her then, Brehon. It was early – still bright – so I was trying my luck down at the river doing a bit of fishing. She'll tell you herself. I saw her later on in the evening – must have been just after that heavy rainstorm when I was serving a last cup of brandy to Brother Cosimo and Father Miguel. Father MacMahon came around to have a drink too – said he needed a nightcap and nothing in his own house. God bless him, he had had a bad day! They were all talking about the German, saying terrible things about him, but in the pantry Mór told me that he had been in good spirits when she brought him his supper and that he had thanked his lucky stars that he was in Ireland and going to be tried under Brehon law and just pay a fine, rather than Spain and be burned to death in one of their nasty . . . inquisitions, I think she said that he called it. Do you want to talk to Mór, Brehon?'

'No, Blad, I must be off now,' said Mara, climbing up on the mounting block in his yard and waiting until one of the stable lads brought across her elderly mare. Brig had been the first present that King Turlough Donn had given to Mara ten years previously, and it would be a sad day when the horse grew too old to carry her mistress on her legal affairs throughout the length and breadth of the 100-square-mile kingdom of the Burren. Her old dog Bran had died a few years ago and she had not really been able to face replacing him yet. Brig, named by Mara after a female Brehon who was able to show a young male judge where he went wrong in his judgements, was now twenty years old and next year would probably have to be turned out to grass. I'll keep her in the orchard, thought Mara, planning a new stable for her old friend, but her heart was sore at the thought of the inevitable loss.

As she rode meditatively down the road towards the west, her mind speculated upon the information which had poured out so freely from the widowed woman called Bess. Was any of it of any use to her, she wondered? She noted Hans Kaufmann's reported comment about the loss of other relics of the true cross and guessed that he might have been involved in their destruction. He had been kind to the terribly scarred Grace, but there probably was no more to it than that. She thought it unlikely that he would offer marriage.

And it was even more unlikely that any one of the three women would have had anything to do with his death. Even heavily drugged, he would have been a great weight to lift. She reckoned that Slevin was correct; in life the German pilgrim would have tipped the scales at a couple of hundredweight.

There was no sign of Art when she arrived at Cliona's farm, but Cliona herself was busy in the barn with a couple of sick sheep and came out when she heard the mare's hoofs on the cobbled surface of the yard.

'How is Art?' asked Mara. She did not dismount. Once on the ground it would be hard to get away quickly. Cliona was very hospitable and would be disappointed if her offer of refreshments were refused.

For once, however, Cliona was not thinking of proposals of hospitality. There was a frown of anxiety on her forehead.

'He seems to have a bit of a fever,' she said with a worried air. 'At first I thought that he was still a bit upset – Fachtnan told me all about it, said that all the boys were shocked but that Art vomited so you said to take him home – so I took him out with me to tend the sheep, but then he started shivering and when I felt him he was burning with fever. He's asleep now and he seems cooler – just one of those things that children get, perhaps. How is Cormac?' she finished.

'Badly behaved,' said Mara with a slight grimace.

'Perhaps it's the shock,' said Cormac's foster mother comfortably. 'He's like that, Cormac. You can never get him to admit that he's upset. He just gets bad-tempered or cheeky. What did he do?'

'Rude to one of the pilgrims – not that he said anything that I was not thinking myself,' admitted Mara, 'but he's going to have to learn that he has to keep his thoughts to himself and to behave properly when he is on legal business. And then when I made him apologise, he was very – well, you know what he's like, he made a bit of a mockery out of it. We're all going to the bog tomorrow and I was half thinking of saying that Cormac shouldn't go.'

'I wouldn't deny him of that, if I were you.' The words came impulsively from Cliona, though she added hastily, 'You know your own child best, of course, but I think that it would upset him badly – he's very proud and that would shame him in front of his friends.'

'I won't then,' said Mara. 'But I hate him being badly behaved when I'm working – it doesn't matter so much around the law school.'

'Perhaps you might be expecting too much of him,' said Cliona gently, looking up at her anxiously. 'He's only nine, you know. He acts big, but he's still a little boy inside.'

'You're probably right. I think, perhaps, that I might be a bit hard on him because he is my son,' said Mara with an effort. It cost her something to say it, but she knew that Cliona would not have disagreed with her unless she was very sure of herself. 'You see, everyone around the place spoils him a bit – Brigid is his slave and you know how sensible she normally is with the boys and how she makes sure that they mind what she says. Well, she just seems to laugh at Cormac, and all the men around the farm encourage him to think that he is clever and are just amused when he shows off. I feel that I have to be stern with him . . .'

'It's difficult for you, but I suppose it's difficult for him, too,' said Cliona sympathetically. She said no more, but didn't go back on what she had said and Mara admired her for that. In Cliona's creed, the child came first.

'Well, I must go. I'm going down to the physician's place so I'll tell her about Art and his fever. She might send something up by one of the apprentices. In any case, she will know if there is some sickness around, or whether the shock upset Art. He's a sensitive boy. Keep him until you think he is back to himself again, Cliona.' Mara raised her hand in farewell and rode off, resolutely keeping her mind away from Cormac and fixed on the murder that needed solving as quickly as possible.

The farm of Rathborney was at the bottom of a steeply spiralling road, and Mara dismounted from her mare and led her carefully on the soft grass at the side of the worn limestone surface of the road until they reached the flat ground of the valley. Nuala had inherited this land and house and had made very good use of it, building a small hospital beside the fast-flowing stream and adding a building to house her apprentices.

Nuala herself was taking a break from her work, walking with her two little girls in the herb garden. The elder of the two, four-year-old Saoirse, was picking off the heads of the lavender flowers and popping them into a basket, while the two-year-old Orla chased butterflies around the sweet-smelling enclosure. Mara watched from the shelter of an elderberry bush at the gate for a moment. She knew that the instant she appeared Nuala would switch from being a mother to being a professional physician − concentrated, precise and totally focussed. Mara wanted to go on watching her being a mother for a change. It was lovely to see the girl who was almost a daughter to her so happy and relaxed, enjoying a few moments of utter pleasure with her children. Should I have kept Cormac at home with me, just as Nuala kept her two, she wondered? Would that have been better for both of us? Brigid would have looked after him, and I could have enjoyed odd moments with him throughout the day, just as Nuala is doing now, moments when we became close. I love him so intensely, she thought, just as intensely as Nuala loves her little girls . . . but he? These days Cormac seemed to have grown up and grown away from her. Their relationship seemed to be of teacher and pupil, rather than mother and son. And his relationship with his father, of whom he saw relatively little, was more of a benevolent grandfather and over-indulged grandson. There was no doubt, she had to admit, that Cormac's real parents were those who had fostered him: Cliona and Setanta. And yet, thought Mara, I made the decision for his own good. Cliona had been his nurse, had fed him and Art at the same time. The boys had a close relationship, and a decision had to be made whether to part Cormac from his foster brother as well as his foster mother when Cliona decided to marry the fisherman Setanta and move out of Mara's household and back on to her own farm. Mara sighed to herself. It was stupid, she knew, to worry about what was past and gone. The decision had been made eight years ago and probably the same decision would be made again if she were given the opportunity of going back into time.

'Mara!' Nuala had spotted her, and almost as if she were waiting in the background the children's nurse appeared and took the two little girls away, the elder carefully carrying her basket of herbs.

'Training up Saoirse to be a physician?' asked Mara, smiling.

'I've given her a mortar and pestle and she loves squashing the lavender flowers and making medicine for headaches,' said Nuala, and then instantly banished her daughters from her mind and said promptly: 'You've come for the report of the autopsy.'

'That's right.' Mara sank down on to the bench and hoped that Nuala would not insist on her viewing the dead body – or even worse, the innards. She felt tired and discouraged. This murder seemed insoluble, yet it did need to be solved quickly. How on earth was Hans Kaufmann stripped of his clothing, murdered and then carried from the church to the tomb? Still, she thought, one step at a time, that's the way that crimes are solved. She settled herself to listen and turned attentive eyes towards Nuala.

'I like to see you with the little girls,' she said with a smile. 'I hope you take lots of little breaks with them. Don't work too hard. Enjoy them. They'll grow up quickly and then things get more complicated. I could see that you were having a lovely time with them just now.'

'I needed it, I was depressed,' said Nuala. And then, before Mara could speak, she said hurriedly, 'Not the autopsy, I don't care about things like that. It's Aoife, Muiris and Áine's daughter. She's dead. Her ninth child in ten years – Rory called me too late and she died of blood loss – exhausted, poor thing. She almost died with the last one and I told her not to have another baby, taught her how to count out the days each month, but Rory was too selfish; of course a bard like him can't be expected to confine himself to twenty days in the month!'

'Poor Aoife,' said Mara compassionately. 'I remember her ten years ago – a beautiful girl, madly in love with her poet. What's going to happen to the children?'

'Muiris and Áine swooped down and took them home with them; one of his shepherds has a wife with a year-old son – she'll feed the baby for the moment. Rory,' said Nuala drily, 'feels that he has to go off to the mountains of Donegal and write a poem about Aoife. He thinks he might be away for a few months.'

'The children will be better off with their grandparents,' said

Mara consolingly. It hurt her to think about the sorrow that
they were all now undergoing. Aoife, the golden girl of ten
years ago, had been the darling of her parents, and Muiris
had been reluctant to agree to a marriage with a bard who
relied on selling his poems at the fairs and market places. They
would be heartbroken at her death. She looked at the dark
eyes of her young cousin and said gently, 'You don't blame
yourself, Nuala, do you?'

'Let's talk about the autopsy,' said Nuala, and Mara knew
that she would say no more about Aoife. Later on, though,
perhaps with Fachtnan, who would, as always, give a reasoned
and sensible judgement. Nuala could have done no more than
warn Aoife and give to her the benefit of all that she had
learned during her trips abroad and during her years of study.

'Tell me what you've found about this German pilgrim,' she
said aloud.

'He was killed about an hour after he had a heavy supper,'
said Nuala promptly. 'He had eaten venison, probably some
sort of rich pastries, very highly flavoured sweetmeats, and had
drunk quite a lot of alcohol as well. He was a big man, but I
would guess that he was quite inebriated at the time that he
was killed.'

'And drugged?' enquired Mara.

Nuala frowned impatiently and Mara recognized the expression. Even at twelve years old Nuala had frowned like that
when her knowledge could not satisfy her curiosity about the
human body.

'Unfortunately, that is not something that I can tell you,' she
said, shaking her head with a slightly exasperated air. 'You see,
we physicians have no ways – none that I know of anyway – of
testing what is in a person's blood; only what is in his stomach.
We are no better than butchers, really. We open up the dead
man's stomach and look, and smell . . .' She smiled at the
expression on Mara's face. 'You get used to it,' she said with a
half-smile. 'This is something that I learned to do in Italy. We
started with animals – pigs, usually – where we knew how long
it had been since the last meal, then progressed to criminals
who had been hanged, and then to suicides – drowned bodies
fished out of the river – and so on. Now I can make a fairly

good guess. So I can be confident when I tell you that diges-tion of the food had hardly begun so it was only about an hour after a heavy meal. I can tell you that he had wine and that he had brandy and that he had heavily flavoured food – there were spices and even scents, from the sweetmeats, I suppose; some of them were almost whole in his stomach. But there is no way that I can tell you whether he had opium from the poppies or not – all I can tell you is that I did not smell it.'

'But due to the rich, spicy, fragrant food and the wine and the brandy, you probably would not have smelled it even if it had been present, is that right?' Mara felt her heart sink. It didn't look as though the autopsy, to which she had pinned her hopes, was going to be too much help, except in pinpointing the time of death.

'That's right,' said Nuala, economical with words as usual.

'What does opium smell like – is it a strong smell?' persisted Mara. She tried to think back to the church – were there any particularly unusual smells there when she and the boys had gone in, probably about twelve hours after the death of Hans?

'Rather like the incense that the priest shakes from the thurible at High Mass.'

'I see,' said Mara with an impatient sigh. 'Just the sort of smell that you could really easily pick out in church!'

Nuala smiled. 'You're tired. You always get ironic when you're tired. Why is this business about a drug so important?'

'Well, you saw the body yourself, Nuala,' said Mara im-patiently. 'You saw how difficult he was to lift on to your own cart. How could he have been stripped of his clothes in the church, murdered, and then carried out and placed on the tomb? I know it's a very low one, but even so. He was a big, heavy man. And who did it? And there are so many questions attached to this death! Was burning a piece of the wood, supposed to come from a fifteen-hundred-year-old cross, enough of a motive to take a man's life? But if that was not the motive, what was the point of stretching him out on the tomb so that he looked like crucified Christ himself? Or did someone . . .' Suddenly Mara thought of the lozenge taken from Brother Cosimo.

'Did Fachtnan send down that lozenge we took from the Italian monk?'

'Not opium.' Nuala shook her head firmly. 'Mainly chamomile and a few other herbs – harmless and not particularly strong.'

'So no possibility of one of those lozenges drugging the young German to the degree that he could have been undressed without a struggle,' said Mara. 'That seemed to be the only possibility in the luggage of the pilgrims. There was nothing in the three women's bags, nor in the bag belonging to the Spanish priest. And their rooms have been searched also.'

'You're sure that he was murdered in the church?' It was just like Nuala not to speculate on names or motives. She dealt with proven facts.

'I can't be sure, but we did find a soaked spot on the carpet, bottom step of the altar. It was very wet.'

'Sticky?'

Mara shook her head. 'No, just wet. Soaking wet. And the holy water font was completely emptied. I know it was full earlier in the day – I did the usual dip and flick into it on my way out of the church. And the container below it was empty also.'

'Any stained cloths?'

Mara shook her head. 'The boys searched very thoroughly.'

'Any smell?'

'Finbar thought it smelled holy,' she said, and Nuala smiled for the first time.

'Shows the power of suggestion,' she said. 'So you think that he was stabbed there on the steps. The murderer scrubbed out the stain where he bled – would have been a lot of blood, of course, there was some still on the capstone of the tomb. And then, in some way, the body was carried – perhaps thrown across the back of a horse – right out to the tomb.'

Mara sighed and got to her feet. 'I must go back,' she said. 'It's getting late; you'll need your supper. And I must see that the boys get to bed early. We're going to the bog tomorrow morning. Cumhal wants to set off at about five o'clock in the morning so that the main work is done before it gets too hot. We'll be back about noon, and then go across to Kilnaboy again. Nechtan O'Quinn has asked us all to stay for the night and I think that the boys will enjoy that and perhaps I'll get more inspiration when I am on the spot. I'll walk around the church a couple of hours after sunset and sit there and try to reconstruct what happened.'

Twelve

Cáin Iarraith
(Law of Children)

The relationship between a felmacc, pupil, and his master is similar to that of a foster father and his dalta, foster son. The felmacc must be taught board games, such as fidchell, chess, and must be instructed in all aspects of the profession of his master. The master is responsible for the safety of the felmacc.

When the party from the law school set out to go to the bog the following morning, only three boys, Domhnall, Slevin and Finbar, accompanied Mara.

Art had not yet returned. With a pang of guilt Mara had remembered as soon as she got back that she had forgotten to ask Nuala about possible feverish and stomach complaints. But her mind was fully occupied with another matter.

Fachtnan had been a student teacher and then a full teacher at her law school for over seven years. During all of that time he had managed the pupils, even those not too much younger than himself, with a mixture of common sense, tact and quiet, firm authority. He very seldom complained of a scholar, but usually preferred to deal with matters himself.

But when Mara arrived back from her talk with Nuala she found him in an exasperated state. Cormac had been in one of his wild, silly moods and had translated a piece of Caesar's wars in France into stupid schoolboy nonsense. Fachtnan did not offer to show it to her and said, when she enquired, that he had told Cormac to put it into the fire. She guessed that it might have had something about her in it because Fachtnan pretended that he had forgotten.

He was, however, quite adamant that Cormac should repeat the work, and Cormac was equally adamant that he had done his best and that the translation was too hard for him. Mara glanced at the Latin just to satisfy Fachtnan, but knew that his knowledge of what the boys could or could not achieve would be as accurate as her own. If anything, he was inclined to be a little more lenient.

No, there was no getting away from it, Cormac had to be punished, and as there was no corporal punishment in her school, then he had to be deprived of a treat. Cliona's words – '*I suppose it's difficult for him, too*' – were in her mind, but she could not help it. Fachtnan's authority had to be backed up; Cormac had to be disciplined for his insolence and bad behaviour, as well as for his idleness.

There was an odd look of almost satisfaction from him when she told him that he would have to stay behind tomorrow and do the work that he had failed to do the day before. He said nothing, just bowed in a formal way, almost as though aping Domhnall, and then went off to bed in the scholars' house.

'Ah, poor little fellow,' said Brigid. 'Sure, he's only young. Likes to have a joke, doesn't he? He's like the King, God bless him. He's going to be sorry afterwards, but he won't admit it. Not he, he's too proud! Still, I'll get him something nice for his lunch and Cumhal thinks that you'll all be back by midday. He's taking everyone on the farm, just leaving young Seánie with me in case there's any problem with the cows. With that crowd the turf will be soon loaded on the carts. You enjoy yourself, Brehon. You have enough to worry you at the moment. You always did love the bog – even when you were only two or three years old. I can remember myself and Cumhal taking you and you insisted on serving the food to all of the workers. You had your little basket full of cakes and you walked up and down the line of them when they sat on the wall for their lunch. Shame Cormac has to miss it.'

Mara concealed her exasperation. Brigid had looked after her when she was little, and then afterwards had been nurse to Sorcha, her daughter, was devoted to both of them, but now Cormac was the darling and could do no wrong.

'What do you think about this murder, Brigid?' She said the words in an effort to avoid an argument about Cormac's punishment, but then found herself interested in Brigid's ideas about the affair at Kilnaboy.

'Struck down by God, they say; not that I believe that. Why would God give the satisfaction to that pagan of appearing like his beloved son? I ask you, Brehon, would that be right? No, you mark my words, Brehon, God didn't do that. Some godless man did it and took the name of the Lord in vain,' was Brigid's viewpoint, and it interested Mara. Brigid had a great fund of common sense and could see to the heart of the matter very quickly.

And, of course, she was right. It was, the ancient saints thought, a privilege and a sign of sanctity to have the marks of the crucifixion on your body. Would Father Miguel, whose knowledge of biblical matters must be as good as Brigid's, have given the honour of − what was the name for it? − the stigmata, that was it, bearing the five marks of the crucified Christ to a man whom he described as an anti-Christ? The answer to that, in the case of a very literate priest, was, she thought, in the negative.

But when it came to a man like Sorley, well, then she was not sure. And what about a lay person − might that not have occurred to him, or to her?

'You put it out of your head for the moment and have a good day at the bog tomorrow morning, Brehon,' said Brigid firmly. 'You'll come up with a name in a day or so. I was saying that to Eileen from Kilnaboy − came out here to know did I want to borrow her new cream skimmer; just to gossip, though, I'd say myself. So I said to her; "You don't need to worry, Eileen; not you, nor anyone else in the parish. The Brehon, God bless her, she'll know all about it in a couple of days. She puts all the facts into her brain, just like you and me put the cream into the churn. She gives them all a good stir, and out she comes with the solution." That's what I said to her, Brehon, and not a word of a lie!' finished Brigid triumphantly.

'I hope you are right,' said Mara lightly, but she was touched by Brigid's faith in her. Perhaps the air on the bog would work like the paddle in her brain, and the solution to this puzzling murder would surface just like a pound of the best butter.

'I suppose that the people of Kilnaboy are very upset about the loss of the relic of the true cross, are they?' she enquired.

It was that more than the death of an unknown man which had sent Eileen over to garner some information from Brigid, she guessed.

Brigid sniffed. 'Very puffed up they were about that; Kilnaboy people always think that they are something special. And of course they've got that wishing hole – you've heard about that hole – you put your arm in if you have rheumatics or anything like that, or else you put your leg in, you say three Our Fathers and three Hail Marys and you wouldn't credit it, but within a week, or a month or so, well, you'd be as good as new. Well, that's what the people of Kilnaboy say, and it would be a brave person would give them the lie.'

'I'm not sure that I've heard about that hole,' said Mara idly, half-listening and half-meditating on her problems.

But then she stiffened as Brigid said: 'It's a long time since I've been over there, but it was outside the church – at the side of one of these old tombs. There was a loose stone – a stone that fitted into another stone – Cumhal will remember – but it was just beyond the churchyard. Funny little circular place – they used to gather the sheep there.'

'I know where you mean, Brigid,' said Mara. She was ominously still. Then she moved towards the stable yard and without a word, and avoiding the gaze of her dear old mare, Brig, but giving her an apologetic pat on the shoulder, she took the cob – the cob who was everyone's horse and who was used for all of the odd jobs and errands on a busy farm like her own. Quickly she saddled it herself and rode out of the law school yard.

She was not going to be able to sleep until she verified her suspicions that this ancient hole, suddenly recollected by Brigid, was hiding a recent secret.

The sun had sunken down behind the mountain range to the west of the Burren by the time she reached Kilnaboy. The lights were on in the priest's house and a couple of candles from within the church cast pools of light and shade on to the path around it. The tower house where Nechtan and his wife Narait lived in childless misery was illuminated in every window. The inn also had a cheerful blaze.

Mara did not go near to the stables, but rode the placid cob into the churchyard and urged him along the path that led to the gorse-enclosed circle. It was getting dark now, but luckily the moon was waxing and its light fell along the path. Mara went steadily ahead, noting how the tall white flowers of the marsh maidens reflected and enhanced the light, whereas the crimson cranesbills were almost black.

This reminded her of the altar carpet and the blood that had been spilled on it, and she set her lips and went steadily on until she reached the tomb.

Without its deadly burden of the corpse of the false pilgrim, the tomb was just part of the landscape, one of the many hundreds that were dotted all over the kingdom of the Burren. But did it still hold a secret? Mara went first to one side and then to the other. And on the eastern flank she glimpsed what Brigid had reminded her of.

The large stone that formed the side of the wedge tomb had a flaw. Somehow the porous limestone had crumbled away with the acidity of the rainwater and had left a large, irregular oval-shaped hole in its side. And someone, in the dim and distant past, someone with infinite patience and skill, had carved a stone, a lump of limestone, so that it fitted almost exactly into the boulder.

And that was what was removed when the people of the parish, crippled with rheumatism, or possessing a withered arm, or broken leg, or an ankle that refused to heal, came here to this enclosed spot, took out the stone and thrust a limb into the gap left exposed.

Mara went down on her knees and carefully worked the limestone plug loose from its socket. Yes, there was the hole. And within the hole there was a gleam of white. Mara glanced back at the moon in the eastern sky and then leaned forward and reached in. Her fingers met fibre – soft, fine, well-woven wool. She drew the article from its hiding place. It was a doublet woven from the finest weavings. She put it aside and reached in again. This time she found linen, a shirt – full sleeves, but crumpled and smelling slightly of sweat – a pair of hose, braies and last of all two sturdy leather boots.

Mara held up to the light of the moon the braies and then the shirt – both were gleaming white and there was not a drop of blood on them. So whosoever murdered Hans Kaufmann in the church had murdered him when he was naked and had then carried his clothes out and hidden them inside this place sacred to the people of Kilnaboy when suffering from strains and aches of the limbs. But on their way they had dropped the codpiece worn by this fashionable young man.

Carefully Mara replaced all of the articles within their hiding place and then she picked up the stone. It took a little effort, but after some twisting and manoeuvring it fitted back into its hole. After it was replaced Mara sat very still for a moment.

That morning the five remaining pilgrims; Nechtan O'Quinn, who had lived here at Kilnaboy Castle all of his life, and his wife Narait who had been with him for two years; Father MacMahon; his sexton, Sorley; Blad; his daughter Mór – all had stood there while she showed them the naked body of the murdered man and not one of them had drawn her attention to the fact that there was a gap in the side stone of the tomb.

Did they think it didn't matter?

Was the sight of the dead body so overwhelming that they forgot?

Or was there another more sinister reason?

Thirteen

Cis Lir Foðla Cire?
(How Many Kinds of Land Are There?)

1. Best arable land suitable for corn, milk, flax, woad, honey, madder and fruit. It should be weed-free and not require manure.
2. Hill arable land. Can grow good ash trees and has water nearby.
3. Woodland that can be cleared by the axe and turned into arable land.
4. Rough land covered with a mixture of rushes and grasses — suitable for the grazing of young bullocks.
5. Mountain pasture — only suitable for sheep and goats.
6. Wet land: marsh and bog land.

The sun was a dark red ball above the mountains to the east when the party from the law school set out for the bog. The night had been much cooler and the air felt more like September than had the preceding days when it seemed as though the sultriness of August would never come to an end. Mara's old mare whinnied energetically and surged out in front of the boys' ponies as though to show that she was as young as any of them.

The bog was part of common land for the inhabitants of the six townlands that lay around Cahermacnaghten. It was situated, oddly enough, halfway up the side of a mountain, apparently built up on one of those flat limestone tablelands — perhaps where an old lake had quickly filled with trees and other vegetation. Even now, huge, gnarled stone-hard tree trunks were dug out from time to time.

The sun was showing its rays by the time they arrived and the surface of the bog glistened a deep brown-black and smelled pungently of fresh peat. The view up there was extraordinary — to the west was the brilliantly sparkling pale blue sea, with its white-capped waves, on which seemed to float the Aran

Islands; to the north was the rounded summit of Slieve Elva, and behind and below them was the valley land. Mara drew in a breath of satisfaction looking at the fluffy white heads of the cotton flowers and the myriad of bees that haunted the purple ling. Overhead a hen harrier flew with great beats of her wings and in the centre of the bog small piles of dried sods were warmed by the early-morning sun into a golden brown.

Although the party from the law school arrived by six o'clock, dozens of people from the surrounding farms were already hard at work.

Mara walked around exchanging the traditional greeting of 'God bless the work', and somehow it felt very soothing to be greeted so warmly by all. It would have been tempting to have spent the morning at her desk, or even pursuing her enquiries in Kilnaboy, but she had always gone to the bog every September since she was a child, and if she had missed this year there would have been enquiries about her absence. It was in any case, she always felt, an important part of her work to be a member of the community. After all, Brehon law only worked if the community willed it to work. She had a friend who was a lawyer in the English tradition, working in the city of Galway, and he could never understand how they managed without the threat of prison or the hangman's noose, never could understand how pride in family and clan could ensure the good behaviour of each and every member of this close-knit society.

The turf on their patch was ready to be taken home – Mara could see instantly that the colour of their winter fuel was now a pale brown, very different from the rather black-looking sods that Nechtan's men had been stacking the day before. Cumhal was an excellent farm manager and Mara lived in fear that he and Brigid, both of whom had served her father before her, would decide to retire. With that in mind she continually insisted on them employing adequate staff. If only Cumhal would go on supervising she would not ask any work of him, but, as usual, despite being a man in his sixties, he was the most active of all, effortlessly swinging himself up on to the back of the cart and unloading the turf barrows that were heaped up there and handing them over to his workers with many instructions about how to stack the turf and avoid breaking the sods.

Finbar shot past her with one of the turf barrows, narrowly missing entangling her gown and shouting out, 'Sorry, Brehon, did I hit your knee?' And suddenly Mara realized something.

Knee-high! she said to herself. The turf barrows were all knee-high, light and long – broad enough and long enough to carry the body of a man. She had been considering Sorley, whose muscles were toughened by forty years of gravedigging, when thinking about Nuala's suggestion of lifting the corpse on to a horse, but a long, low, light, two-wheeled turf barrow was a different matter. A weight could be pushed on that with little effort – and it would certainly be narrow enough to be wheeled in through the church door to the lowest step that led up to the altar.

She gazed at the clumps of rushes and tufts of purple moor grass beside the path, but her mind was seeing the churchyard at Kilnaboy. Nechtan's men had been stacking the turf. There had been three or four turf barrows coming and going from the piled-up cart. No doubt, though this was something which she could check, they may have been left accessible during the night – the work was still going on the following morning. This meant that the murderer could have wheeled one into the church. With their handles and their two props at the back to keep them level during loading, these turf barrows were ideal for moving a heavy weight with relatively little effort.

Any able-bodied man – Father Miguel, Brother Cosimo, Father MacMahon, Blad or Sorley – could easily have rolled Hans Kaufmann from the altar steps to the barrow and from the barrow to the top of the wedge tomb. But what about women?

Mara went on mechanically greeting, admiring the quality of the turf, enquiring about family members – one very small portion of her mind was all that was needed for these familiar courtesies. The rest of her mind was furiously active – churning the evidence, she thought to herself with a small smile, as she remembered Brigid's words.

Hans Kaufmann was a man with a mission. He had not only

wanted to destroy the faith in relics and other such miracles, but also to expose corruption within the Roman Church. He had found out about Brother Cosimo's theft of a valuable crucifix. Had he found out some other guilty secrets? The reaction of the prioress, Mara thought, as she looked back, had been over-done – as good as a play, Slevin had said, and he was right. It had been a bit of play-acting. So had Hans Kaufmann known of a guilty secret of the prioress? Ardal had been talking to Father MacMahon about this Martin Luther and how he had loved to expose sins like sodomy, indecent living or illicit pregnancies among the priests and nuns, in their parishes, monasteries, abbeys and convents.

An illegitimate daughter! Perhaps the prioress had an illegitimate daughter. Mara's mind went to the letter K – K for *kind* – the German word for child. It might have referred to one of the other nuns, but could have meant the prioress herself. The huge age difference between the girl Grace and her supposed sisters – what if the prioress had slipped, had a secret love affair, had given birth to a daughter and then her family had rallied around; her mother had taken the baby, and with the help of Bess, had reared her. But if Grace herself knew the secret, she might have betrayed it to Hans Kaufmann. There was little doubt in Mara's mind that the girl had been attracted to the handsome young pilgrim.

Hans Kaufmann was a fanatic, Mara told herself. Fanatics always feel that the end justifies the means. The young girl's murmured confession of her secret and illegitimate birth would only be grist to his mill. What would he have done? Well, he would have confronted the prioress, possibly taken money from her, threatened to expose her, certainly left her anxious and vulnerable. She would have confided in Bess.

Together they could have disposed of this false pilgrim.

Was the girl Grace involved?

Mara thought not. Her sensitivity, and her fondness for the German pilgrim might have caused trouble for the other two more practical ladies.

The prioress and her sister the widow could have visited the church after Mór had brought supper to the pilgrim. Hans would, according to Nuala, have been quite drunk at the time, might have mocked their request for clemency, for silence. And then one of them, the delicate-minded prioress or the tough-minded widow, stuck a knife in him.

So far, so good.

But before the knife was stuck into him, he had been stripped. The evidence of the clothes was quite unmistakable. These garments which she had discovered in the wishing hole bore not even a drop of blood, and they had definitely been those worn by Hans Kaufmann when he had sought sanctuary in the church earlier that day.

So how had he been stripped? Mara's mind went back to Cormac's suggestion that he might have done it for a dare. Or perhaps out of fear. What if a man or a woman held a knife to his throat, or to another part of his anatomy – and Mara's mind went to the earthy Bess – and threatened to kill him if he did not strip?

But how could they have stabbed the man to death? He was far too strong for one to hold while the other killed. It just didn't make sense.

Or was it Sorley, a man whose whole life was bound up in his worship of the relic entrusted to his care, in the round tower that he and his father had built, in the round tower which had been desecrated by the German pilgrim?

Or could it have been a group of people? If that was the way, then the whole ghastly simulation of a crucified Christ had been planned from the beginning. And that meant, thought Mara, her eyes fixed intently on a grey furry butterfly quivering on the tiny pink cups of the heather flowers, that meant that some sort of perverted religious motive must have been at the back of the murder. '*God is not mocked*' were the words on the scroll inserted into the crown of thorns, and perhaps that was a message to others that might come to this sacred place at Kilnaboy, where the double-armed cross built into the gable of the stone church proclaimed the resting place of the venerated relic of the Holy Cross. She stared for a moment at the four round eyes marked on the butterfly wings, giving the insect an owl-like look of wisdom. There is something in this case that I am not seeing, she thought impatiently. Perhaps now that I am forty-six years old my brain is not as keen as it used to be. The thought was a depressing one.

'Thinking about the case, are you, Brehon?' Fachtnan came over and stood beside her.

'An excuse for idleness,' said Mara, watching the busy figures everywhere, backs bent, and hands busily picking up and tossing the light, well-dried sods. 'Still, coming to the bog has triggered some ideas in me,' she added. 'It suddenly occurred to me that Nechtan's men were using a couple of turf barrows to unload the cart on the day that the German was killed. They would have been ideal for taking the body from the church to the tomb – long enough and broad enough for the body, but narrow enough and light enough to take into the church – the weather was so dry up to then that they could have left no marks.'

'You're sure that he was murdered in the church?'

'Not sure about anything,' said Mara honestly. 'And now I've found the clothes and they were neatly under the body – inside the tomb. Would you believe that—'

'The wishing hole!' he interrupted. 'Of course, I'd forgotten that. It's under the capstone, isn't it? There's a stone that fits into the hole at the side of one of the upright slabs. I remember one of the young O'Lochlainns, one of Ardal O'Lochlainn's nephews, telling me about that. His dogs followed a fox and the fox got himself into the churchyard – some old woman had just taken her sore arm out of the sacred wishing hole and the fox jumped in and lay down. She said that he had found sanctuary, that he was God's creature, and she put the stone back and there he was as snug as anything and the hounds raging outside and going around and around the tomb until they were dizzy. The O'Lochlainn lads were furious about it but she wouldn't let them touch the stone. She was as old as the hills, old Brídín, you know – must have been about eighty at least – but she stood up to them and told them they should be ashamed of themselves and to take themselves and their dogs out of God's acre. So off they all went with their tails between their legs, men and hounds!'

Mara smiled at the story. Forty-six years old, she thought – that's nothing! Think of Brídín, as sharp as a knife. I'm at the height of my powers, she told herself firmly. Hard work and careful step-by-step thinking will solve this problem.

'This finding of the clothes there was strange, though,' she said aloud. 'I didn't know about the wishing hole, though Brigid did, and so do you, now that I have recalled it to your mind. But who else, other than the people of the parish know of it? And it doesn't sound the sort of thing that Father MacMahon would approve of. After all, the tomb is a pagan object, not a Christian one. I doubt that he would boast of it to any visitors. It almost puts all of the pilgrims out of my mind,' said Mara. 'I don't think that any of them could have known that story, do you?'

'I'm not sure,' said Fachtnan. Conscious of being idle among a mountainside of busy people, he went and secured an empty turf barrow and began to throw the dried sods into it, bending and swinging with the rhythm and vigour of a young man. Mara decided against helping him, though she wondered if the physical exertion would clear her mind. The people of the Burren had a strong notion of what was due to her status as the King's wife as well as his representative, and would be shocked at her doing such heavy work.

'Remember, the pilgrims arrived a couple of days before the feast of the Holy Cross,' said Fachtnan, continuing to load with such rapidity that the barrow was now a quarter full. 'They could have been speaking to someone in the churchyard – could even have seen someone put an arm or a leg in through the wishing hole.'

'That's true,' said Mara. 'And, of course, they had been to supper with Nechtan and his wife the evening before – they could have heard the story there. I'll ask him about that. We are going to visit him today and to stay with him overnight – it will save my poor old mare a double journey. He's asked the boys too, but you won't want to come. Nuala needs your company. She's upset about Aoife's death. You ride over in the morning.'

'I know,' said Fachtnan thoughtfully. He threw a few more sods in and then paused in his loading, straightened his back and moved a step nearer to her. 'This is a strange case, Brehon,' he said meditatively. 'Usually there is some real reason for murder, some intense fear, some intense greed; this time it seems as though this murder has most likely been committed as a religious protest or some form of revenge and that does not seem to be a strong enough motive.'

'You're forgetting Brother Cosimo.'

'He could always deny it. Once Hans Kaufmann accepted money from him, Brother Cosimo probably thought that he could silence him easily enough.'

'True,' said Mara. 'In any case, according to Ardal O'Lochlainn, the followers of Luther are saying such terrible things about the Church of Rome, and the followers of the Church of Rome are saying such terrible things about the followers of Luther, that in the end sensible people may start to shrug their shoulders and believe little of what they hear.'

'So we come back to religious revenge.' Fachtnan fastened up the sides of the turf barrow and continued to lob the light sods over the top of the nearest one.

'And a burning belief in being God's agent – like the angel in the Bible, the one with a flaming sword.'

'You are thinking of Father Miguel; I could imagine him with a flaming sword,' said Fachtnan, pausing in his work to wave a greeting to a man leading a donkey heavily burdened with a basket full of turf suspended from each shoulder. 'How's the leg, Micheál?' he shouted.

'Never better, thanks be to God,' came the reply and Fachtnan grinned.

'Thanks to Nuala,' he said in a low voice. 'That's a man that could tell you all about the wishing hole of Kilnaboy, Brehon. He was sticking his leg in there for years and nothing happened. Then he came to see Nuala and she found that when he broke his leg years earlier, a bit of bone was left in the flesh and that was causing the ulcers. She dug it out and he hasn't known himself since.'

'That's another thing!' exclaimed Mara. 'I was talking to Blad, the innkeeper, about how pilgrims might still come to Kilnaboy even if the relic of the true cross no longer existed. I was trying to cheer him up and I was saying that they might come to see the sacred well of the daughter of Baoith – so why didn't he say that Kilnaboy has a wishing hole? After all, that must be fairly unusual. I've never heard of one before now.'

'You don't suspect Blad, do you?' Fachtnan stopped his work for an instant and looked at her with surprise. 'I don't see Blad murdering anyone,' he said, resuming the rhythmic tossing of the sods. 'He's a fisherman and fishermen don't do anything on impulse. There would be no point in murdering Hans Kaufmann. The deed was done and the piece of the cross was burned. Nothing could be done about that. If the German was murdered because of that, he was murdered for revenge and that would hardly be worth it – that wouldn't give a man back his livelihood.'

That was an interesting idea about fishermen, thought Mara. She supposed that it might be correct. Fishermen had to be quiet, slow-moving, meditative, and above all optimistic. The person who killed Hans Kaufmann was probably impulsive, quick-thinking, filled with self-righteous anger – someone who felt that they were the instrument of God, *the angel with the flaming sword*.

'Father Miguel,' said Fachtnan, echoing her thoughts. He moved to another small mound of turf sods. Using both hands he began firing them two at a time into the barrow. 'What would you think of him, Brehon?'

'He has the anger, the courage, probably the ability to think fast.' Mara spoke slowly and judiciously, but she could hear a note of doubt in her own voice.

'And the desire to let the world know about what happened to a man who questioned the sanctity of relics – to an anti-Christ and a blasphemer,' queried Fachtnan, and Mara nodded with approval.

'That's a very important point, Fachtnan,' she said. 'After all, if Hans Kaufmann had been killed and his body left in the church, that would be enough for someone like Brother Cosimo to silence a man who could do him harm. By dragging the body from the church, wheeling it out to the tomb, laying it out there, spreadeagled on the capstone, in the shape of the crucifix and sticking a knife into the hands and the feet – as well as the knife thrust into the left side – all that seems to show a man who was willing to run the risk of being seen in order that the world should hear about this death and should regard it as miraculous. I wouldn't be surprised if the name of Hans Kaufmann were to be known throughout the world as the man who was struck down by the wrath of God.'

'So we tentatively cross Brother Cosimo from our list,' said Fachtnan.

'I think so,' said Mara. And the same applies to the prioress, she thought. If it were true that Grace was the prioress's daughter, and if Hans Kaufmann had discovered the secret and was threatening to reveal the truth, well, the prioress, just like Brother Cosimo, would have been interested solely in silencing the man, not in making a public show of his dead and naked body or in marking hands and feet with the stigmata – all of which added hugely to the risk of the murder being uncovered.

'And Blad,' she said aloud. 'He might have been fearful that his livelihood would be threatened by the loss of the relic, but I'm not sure that he had anything to gain by murdering him in that strange way, stripping the man before death and then wheeling the dead and naked body through the churchyard, up the path and then positioning it on the tomb with the clothes hidden underneath it. Surely nobody would go to that trouble just in order to dispose of a man who was a threat to your security of office – or even who had perhaps ruined your business? Though I suppose it might be a sort of double bluff – make the murder look as though it were done for religious reasons . . .'

Fachtnan nodded. 'I think that seems to be complicated, given that it added so much to the danger of the proceedings.' Mara nodded. He had echoed her thoughts.

'So we are left with a motive of revenge for religious reasons. And that leaves Father Miguel, Father MacMahon, and, I think, Sorley. Though I had discounted that, your notion of it warning others not to do such a thing has made me change my mind.'

'And what's the next step?' Fachtnan dusted his hands and stood back from the barrow.

'The next step is to find out where everyone was at the time of death – about an hour after his supper, according to Nuala.'

'Will everyone remember?'

'I think,' said Mara, 'this might be quite easy to remember. That heavy shower of rain came at about nine o'clock in the evening. It lasted less than an hour and I was thinking that might be a time when our murderer might have been able to dispose of the body and rely on the downpour to wash away a lot of the blood.'

'Yes, you're right – I remember it. And it didn't last too long, did it? Nuala and I went out into the herb garden for a few minutes after the rain stopped, just before going to bed. Everything smelled very sweet there. It seems terrible to think that at that time, on the other side of the Burren, someone was being murdered for a stupid reason like disagreeing about relics and their significance.'

Mara glanced across the bog; the workers from Cahermacnaghten law school had worked with immense rapidity and energy. Their two high-sided carts on the road were virtually full, and one of Cumhal's men was walking the horses over to be harnessed to the shafts. Cumhal himself was wreathed with smiles. This was the successful ending to a process that had begun last May when Cumhal and his farm workers, armed with those long-bladed spades known as *sléans*, would have sliced the mud-like sods from the wet bog and heaved them on to the bank above. Slice, lop . . . thud. Slice, lop . . . thud. Mara had often watched the process when she was a child. It would have gone on for hours, and then later on the sods would have been stacked, five or six leaning against each other and then a final sod placed on the top to hold all in place. Two or three times during the summer the piles would have been undone and then rebuilt again. There was heartbreak, some wet summers, when rain fell almost continuously and thick mists swept in, day after day, from the Atlantic – summers when natives said to visitors: '*If you can see the Aran Islands, it's a sign that it is going to rain; and if you can't see them, well, it's already raining.*' On years like that the small stacks of soft, wet, slimy sods might just have to be abandoned to sink back into the bog again. But this summer there had been lots of fine days and strong drying winds; this year the crop looked good.

No wonder Cumhal was smiling – now all of the hard work

had come to a successful conclusion. Tonight there would be a special supper for the Cahermacnaghten workers to celebrate what was known as 'the drawing home'. *Hay is carried; turf is drawn* – Mara remembered Cumhal teaching her that when she was a small child; it was something to commit solemnly to memory at the same time that, in the schoolroom, she was chanting the value of different types of land and its significance for inheritance.

Mara bent down and picked up the last two sods of turf lying on the ground, feeling their dry, uneven surface and noting the small traces of hardened twigs and desiccated tree knots in their structure. She waited until the contents of Fachtnan's barrow had been unloaded on to the second cart. Then she walked over, placed the last two sods, one on the top of each cart, and said in clear, loud tones: 'Thanks be to God; the turf is saved.'

And then she forgot about murder for the moment as her scholars and workers cheered this successful conclusion of an annual task. The turf would be drawn home and then built up into an enormous stack, thatched and allowed to dry still further. They would be burning this harvest in the year of 1520 or even 1521.

Would the memory of the dead man, stretched out in a ghastly imitation of the crucified Christ, have faded from the memories of the people of Kilnaboy by then?

Fourteen

Liability for the offences of a child under the age of seventeen is normally borne by his father, or by his foster father during fosterage.

Heptad 34

There are seven fathers who are not considered to be liable for their children's offences:

1. *A king.*
2. *A bishop.*
3. *A poet.*
4. *A hermit.*
5. *A man without property.*
6. *A person of unsound mind.*
7. *A slave.*

Cormac was very cold with his mother. He presented a beautifully written, excellently worded translation of the Latin that he had declared to Fachtnan that he could not understand, looked indifferent when she praised it, fixed his eyes on a spot above her head when she explained why courteous behaviour was important for all of the scholars at the law school, and then slid out of the room as soon as possible.

On the ride across the Burren to Kilnaboy, he and Finbar were noisy and silly, exchanging jokes and laughing immoderately at them. Cliona had sent over a message to Brigid to say that Art's fever had gone, but that she would keep him for another couple of days to make sure that he did not pass on any illness to the other boys. Mara had sent back a message saying to tell Art that they were all missing him. However, Finbar, although more than three years the elder, seemed to be enjoying Cormac's company and that, thought Mara, was good.

She moved her mare up to ride beside the two older boys and was amused to find that they were discussing religion.

'It makes you do some extraordinary things, like fasting until you are almost dead, or whipping yourself with a scourge, or allowing yourself to be killed,' said Slevin.

'And do extraordinary things to people who don't agree with you,' pointed out Domhnall in the judicial tones of an elderly judge. 'Look at what happened to the poor old Jews and Muslims out in Spain. My father has a friend, a Jew, a merchant from Normandy, and he gets the shakes when he sees a Spanish ship and he'll run a mile from the Dominicans.'

'Like Father Miguel; he's a Dominican priest,' said Slevin. He looked across at Mara. 'Domhnall and I think that he is the most likely person to have committed the murder, Brehon,' he said. 'We were talking about it when we were riding home from the bog.'

'We were thinking, Brehon,' said Domhnall, 'that no one stole anything from Hans Kaufmann – so it wasn't greed that caused his death – no one benefitted financially by his death. I think that is significant; religion-mad people don't think about money and goods like normal people,' said the son of a successful Galway merchant.

'So we think that it must have been some crazy, religious freak who killed him,' put in Slevin.

'Going to all that trouble, putting on a sort of show,' supplemented Domhnall.

'That's interesting,' said Mara, feeling proud of them both. 'Fachtnan and I were thinking along much the same lines when we were talking together this morning up at the bog.' She wished that her son would join in with the discussion instead of singing to Finbar a silly song that he had learned on his last visit to Turlough's court, but then remembered Cliona's words. *He is only nine years old*, she told herself; Domhnall was five years old and had a younger sister and brother when Cormac was born. The thought of the frail baby that her son had been just over nine years ago filled her with a sudden gush of love, and she wished that she could stop and draw him to her and kiss him – and then smiled to herself at the thought of his horrified expression if she dared do such a thing in front of the other boys.

'The O'Lochlainn is coming, Brehon,' said Domhnall. His tone was respectful and he immediately reined in his pony. All of the boys had a deep reverence for Ardal – not only was he the chieftain of his clan, *the* O'Lochlainn, but he was the breeder of fine horses and her scholars admired him immensely.

'How is everything going, Brehon? I suppose you are off over to Kilnaboy again?' Ardal politely turned his stallion's head so that he could ride beside her and not delay her on her journey.

'I'm glad to see you, Ardal,' said Mara. 'I was thinking that I should drop in to Lissylisheen and thank you for your help the other night at Kilnaboy. It was good of you to offer to patrol the church boundaries when the unfortunate man claimed sanctuary.'

It had been in her mind to double check whether there could have been any stranger around the church that night, but that was something that she felt she could not ask outright of either Ardal or Nechtan. Yet this opportunity was too good to pass up.

'No trouble, Brehon,' he said lightly. 'I'm a man that sleeps very little and my steward, Danann, and I had some plans that we wanted to discuss. It so happened that recently every time we settled down to discuss them, we were interrupted. That night gave us plenty of time. We each walked the boundaries every fifteen minutes or so and then came together for another ten minutes near to the road, and continually checked the stables. Of course, Brehon,' he said looking at her keenly, 'we were making sure that the man did not leave sanctuary, but I would be fairly certain that no stranger came in during that night. Danann and I watched until about the hour of midnight and then Nechtan's men took over until dawn. We saw Mór going and then coming back with her basket from the church, but otherwise no one went near to it as far as we know.'

'And during the heavy thunder shower?'

Ardal smiled. 'Neither Danann nor I mind the rain much. We had our cloaks and pulled the hoods over our heads and we sheltered under that thick old oak tree in the *Crooked Moher.*'

Mara suppressed a sigh. The *Crooked Moher* was an oddly shaped small field beside the road leading west from Kilnaboy Church. It was named '*Moher*' because that was the old word for an enclosed field or meadow, and it had high stone walls all around it. The ancient oak tree was just next to the gate leading on to the road. It was a good place to choose if you wanted to make sure that no one escaped from sanctuary – and the old tree would have provided good shelter – but there would have been no chance of Ardal, deep in conversation with his steward, seeing anyone going into the church. They would have been facing in the opposite direction.

'Well, I'm glad to have had the opportunity of meeting you, Ardal, and thanking you for what you did,' she said, and he immediately took the hint.

'Call on me whenever you need me, Brehon. I'll leave you now and let you get on with your ride to Kilnaboy.'

Father Miguel was standing in front of the inn when they arrived at Kilnaboy. He did not greet her, but stood impassively, sliding the beads of his rosary through his fingers, his eyes fixed on the impressive double cross outlined in stone against the gable of the church. She gave him a quick glance, but decided that Slevin's words '*crazy, religious freak*' could be taken to apply to the priest and that excused him from ordinary good manners. She didn't like the unpleasant expression in his eyes, though, when they rested on Cormac's grinning face. Father Miguel, it appeared, was not one to forgive and forget easily.

'Brehon, welcome, welcome,' Blad bustled out, greeting the boys and summoning the stable boys.

'We're staying the night with Nechtan, Blad,' said Mara, 'but perhaps you could house the mare and the ponies for us.' She would not offer to pay him now, she decided, but Turlough, after a fleeting visit to the law school, would be on his way back to Thomond soon. She would make sure that he stayed overnight with Blad at Kilnaboy and Blad would be delighted to have the king and his follower. Turlough, as always, would be extremely generous.

'You are very good, Blad,' she said. 'Now could I trespass a little further on your kindness? Have you a small parlour where I can talk in private to the people who were present within the church boundaries on the night that the German was killed?'

She half listened as he assured her of privacy, made plans for light refreshments, and then left Domhnall to organize the bringing of the overnight bags to Kilnaboy Castle. She herself walked over to the church and sat down by the altar and gazed at the carpet on the steps.

It had been expensively woven, she thought. And dyed with some stuff from the east – no dye from the Irish hedgerows could have made that deep, strong crimson – almost purple, but with a glow of red illuminating the rich colour. She reached out and touched the stain. It was still slightly damp, but where it was starting to dry at the edges an ominous blackish shade was beginning to mar the brightness of the original dye. The stain could probably never be completely eradicated – another grief to poor Father MacMahon, another loss to the church of Kilnaboy.

She enumerated those she would see mentally. Five pilgrims; Father MacMahon and Sorley, that was seven; and then there were the two from the inn, Blad and Mór – their testimony about times and the whereabouts of their guests would be useful; and then, thinking of whoever was within the inner boundary around the church, she would also have to count in Nechtan and his wife. That meant that eleven people had to be questioned.

And what to ask them? In her mind she sifted through the questions. The rainstorm, she knew, had begun about two hours after sunset. A couple of years ago Mara had purchased in Galway a small clock for her house – it had come all the way from Nuremberg, her son-in-law, Domhnall's father, told her, and ever since possessing it she had become very aware of the time. The heavy rainstorm had begun, she knew, at nine o'clock. Mór's testimony was that the dead man had eaten his supper an hour after sunset – that would have been about half-past seven to eight o'clock. Nuala had not only stated that death occurred about an hour after the meal, but had pointed out that the blood had been washed from the body by the heavy downpour, which had lasted about an hour. All the evidence pinpointed the time of death to about two hours after sunset. In other words, thought Mara, about half-past eight to nine o'clock in the evening. The church bell would have been rung every three hours by Sorley, so at nine o'clock he would have pulled the bell, which, at Kilnaboy, was situated in the top of the round tower – only a few yards from the church.

I'll see Sorley first of all, she thought, and got to her feet decisively.

Fachtnan had arrived by the time she emerged from the church. He was standing by the round tower, talking with the boys, and Mara was glad to see that Cormac appeared to be animated and at ease with him. So it was only his mother that he blamed for being deprived of the fun of going to the bog. She wondered whether to say something else to him, but then decided that she had not got the time for tactfulness. Better to ignore his stiff, aggrieved behaviour.

'Blad has very kindly given us the use of his parlour,' she said to Fachtnan and led the way across to the inn. She said no more until they were all inside the room and Blad had retreated after being assured that they needed no refreshments.

He had set out a small table with an ink horn and a supply of parchment leaves and an ornate chair behind it. There were a couple of benches and a few stools also in the room. Fachtnan put a stool in front of the table then brought up another stool for himself and sat beside her chair.

'Put the benches along in front of the window, Domhnall,' directed Mara. 'You boys can sit there and you will be able to observe the faces very clearly with the light pouring in on them. Of course,' she said the words casually, 'you all know that you must not speak unless I ask you something. Your role is to listen and watch.' She carefully looked only at Domhnall when she said that and he nodded solemnly. She hoped that Cormac had taken in her words also. Finbar did not have much judgement, but he was tentative and unsure of himself and most unlikely to speak without authority. Domhnall and Slevin, she knew, could be relied on, but both were too sensible and balanced to take umbrage at her words.

Sorley was disconcerted to be first. It was against his sense of fitness to be summoned before Father MacMahon or the pilgrims. He knew nothing, could not remember seeing anyone – yes, he did remember the rain, kept a three-hour glass filled

with sand which reminded him of the bell; had certainly gone
out in the downpour, and put on his cloak, thrown an old
turf sack over his head, dashed out from his house to the round
tower, pulled the bell nine times, then dashed back again.

'And the turf barrow?' asked Mara innocently.

He glared at her. 'What turf barrow?' he asked.

'I wondered whether you fell over it – someone mentioned
it to me.'

He shook his head decisively. 'Didn't see anything of the
sort,' he said. 'The O'Quinn barrows were all under cover
inside the barn. That barn was locked.'

'I understood that one of them had been left out,' persisted
Mara, hoping to be forgiven for the lie.

He shrugged. 'Not my business – all I can say is that I didn't
see one.' His voice was harsh and belligerent. Mara noted the
fact without comment, glad to have an excuse to leave him
waiting for a moment. People often rushed in to fill a silence
with speech, but Sorley didn't.

'And who did you see on your way out and on your way
back?' she asked after a minute.

'Not a person. In rain like that? And there was good warning
for it. The sky had been black ten minutes before.'

That had been true, of course, but it didn't mean that no one
would have been out. After all, Ardal and his steward were out.

Aloud she asked, 'Did you take a lamp with you?'

He shook his head, giving her the information that she
wanted. 'No, there was no need for a lamp. Every blessed
candle in the church was burning. There was light streaming
from every window of it. If that's all, Brehon . . .' He had
begun to stand up as he finished and Mara could see no reason
to detain him, so she nodded a dismissal and Fachtnan escorted
him to the door, and then when Sorley's footsteps began to
echo down the passageway, he raised an eyebrow in query and
asked, 'Father MacMahon?'

Mara nodded and smiled. Fachtnan had been at her law
school since he was five years old; by now he could almost
read her mind. It would be good to see Father MacMahon
before he and Sorley could have a talk together.

But Father MacMahon also had little to say. He had been

in his house, had heard the bell, had seen no one, had noticed the prolific waste of his candles, but had decided not to go across to the church and challenge the pilgrim – 'given as he would only be one night there,' he said sagely, though Mara suspected that the elderly priest was probably a bit afraid of the burly and irreverent young German. But he had not noticed a turf barrow either, and confirmed what Sorley said by spontaneously giving his opinion that Nechtan's steward would have checked that they were all locked into the barn.

'Blad next, Fachtnan,' said Mara when she had finished with Father MacMahon.

Supper, according to Blad, was at sunset. The guests had lingered a long time over it, had eaten and drunk well, all of them, even including the three ladies. That supper had, of course, been paid for by the Brehon of the kingdom, and no doubt all of the pilgrims had been pleased to eat as much as possible, knowing that the bill would be the responsibility of the person who had halted their voyage to Aran of the Saints. They would, according to Blad, have spent about an hour and a half over it.

'They had plenty to talk about – all the places that they had been to,' was his comment. 'Talking about relics, they were.'

After supper the ladies had gone up to their bedrooms, according to Blad. 'Don't know whether they stayed there or not, Brehon, but I didn't see them down in the hall or in the parlour from then until the next morning at breakfast time.'

He couldn't, of course, be sure whether any or all of the ladies had gone for a walk. Mara clearly recollected how each of those bedrooms had two doors, one of which led to the gallery on the north side of the inn, leading towards the cobbled yard between the inn and the stables; the other led to a gallery facing on to the River Fergus and allowing the inhabitants to steal down on to the grass and walk back towards the church.

But, said Blad, just as she was thinking about the prioress, Father Miguel and Brother Cosimo *had* gone for a walk – to say their prayers, according to them; to walk off their huge meal, according to Blad, with a wink. They had come down for a cup of brandy later on, after the storm had blown itself away. They had come down together, but then their rooms were beside each other and one would have heard the other stirring. They had both got wet, he thought. He had sent the boy up to their rooms to make up the fire while they were busy drinking, and the boy had reported that their cloaks were steaming in front of the hearths.

'And yourself, Blad, did you go out towards the church? Or did you bring any comforts to the pilgrim in sanctuary? No? And did you see anyone at any stage? I've been wondering whether there was any stranger hanging around. You would have noticed a stranger, wouldn't you?' Mara asked the question in an indifferent manner, but he looked astonished and puzzled.

'Someone from Thomond, do you mean, Brehon?'

'Perhaps someone on the way back from Aran – someone who was going to spend the night in Thomond,' she improvised quickly, but he shook his head. 'I wouldn't know, Brehon. You're thinking perhaps someone called to see Father MacMahon. But I didn't stir from the river until the rain drove me indoors. It was a good night for the fish.'

'You can't catch river fish when the rain is heavy,' burst out Cormac, and then he turned a dark red and muttered an apology.

'That's right,' said Blad, beaming at him. 'Ah, you're a great little fisherman. You're right, of course. I stopped when the rain came down heavily. You should have seen the water, Cormac, when the rain came down. After ten or fifteen minutes the whole river was just filled with mud – stirred up the bottom, it did – no sense in fishing any more for the night, or yesterday either. It takes a few days for the mud to settle.'

So he didn't go straight indoors once the rain began if he knew what the river was like a quarter of an hour later, thought Mara, and forgave her son his impulsive interruption.

'I suppose Nechtan's turf got soaked,' she said innocently. 'I saw that he hadn't had time to thatch it – and, of course, all of the barrows were out in the rain.'

'Don't think they were,' said Blad. He sounded puzzled at her interest. 'His steward was telling me that they heaped as much turf from the carts as possible and pushed them all into the barn so that at least some of it didn't get wet. Not a good crop this year, he was telling me. They started a bit too late. Anyway, I shouldn't be gossiping – you've got your work to do, Brehon. I'll certainly ask all of the stable lads and the kitchen staff whether they saw anyone strange around the church that night.'

'Thank you, Blad, that would be very helpful. I'm sorry to be taking up your time. I know what a busy man you are.'

'Not at all, Brehon, I'm just sorry that I couldn't have been of more help to you.' Blad got to his feet with a relieved expression.

'You've been very helpful, Blad,' said Mara with sincerity, noting with approbation that Cormac was the one who got to his feet and went to open the door for the innkeeper. She gave her son a nod. Yes, she thought, Blad has been most helpful. There had been, it seemed, quite a few people out in the rain that night: Blad himself, Ardal and his steward, Father Miguel, Brother Cosimo, Nechtan and his steward frantically getting as much turf under cover as possible, and then there was Sorley ringing the bell in the round tower only about fifty yards from the church itself.

But ten minutes later, as the rain continued to lash down, in all probability only the murderer was left in the vicinity of the church. And within that church, relying on the ancient laws of sanctuary, was the pilgrim who had desecrated the relic of the true cross; the relic which was of great importance to the Church of Rome, as well as to the esteem, the wealth and the future prosperity of the small community of Kilnaboy.

Brother Cosimo was tight-lipped, arrogant and unwilling to say anything. Mutely he challenged Mara to find any facts against him, and she, with memory of his stolen treasure, stared back at him with a blank face and allowed him to wonder what evidence she might have garnered to convict him of the murder of the man who not only attacked his church, but who had threatened to expose him as a liar, a thief and a man who had desecrated sacred shrines.

'Fetch Father Miguel,' said Mara to Fachtnan. Brother Cosimo could, if necessary, be interrogated further and forced into saying more. But somehow she did not feel that he was guilty. It was very true what her scholars had said. A man who wished only for the death of his blackmailer would not have gone to the trouble and danger of setting up this elaborate simulacrum of a crucified Christ, would not have bothered stripping the live man, knifing him, conveying him to the ancient tomb, marking the stigmata on his hands and feet, hiding his clothes in a place that was unlikely to be discovered and, all in all, going to great trouble to give the impression that the death of Hans Kaufmann was the work of the vengeful God. This, she thought, was a crime of passion.

'*God is not mocked*' had said the script on the tiny scroll inserted into the crown of thorns.

And Father Miguel was the most likely person within the boundaries of Kilnaboy Church to have taken this statement seriously.

Fifteen

Che Law of Social Connections

How many kinds of social connections are there?
1. The chief with his tenants.
2. The Church with her tenants.
3. The father with his daughter.
4. A daughter with her brother.
5. A son with his mother.
6. A foster son with his foster mother.
7. A tutor with his pupil.
8. A man with a woman.

Father Miguel, to her surprise, came in eagerly, eyes wide, burning face full of impatience, hands outstretched.

'Madam,' he said, and then quickly amended it to 'Brehon. I do need your help,' he said eagerly. 'I'm sure that all is not right within that round tower – they have done their best, those maids with their buckets, their brooms and their cakes of soap, but I know that it is still not right. Something is wrong, but I cannot be sure. I need a young person, someone whose senses are still untainted by the world, someone who can smell . . .' and then he stopped, but after a moment said earnestly, 'The devil is still within the round tower. I know it deep down within my being, but I cannot smell him myself. I need a young person with young organs.'

His glance swept along the row of scholars, passed with indifference over Cormac's eager, *please-choose-me* face, went on to the end of the line, looked deep into Domhnall's earnest dark eyes and crooked a finger at him. Mara gave a sigh of relief. Cormac would have been unable to stop playing the fool, especially with Finbar's admiring eyes on him. Finbar himself was too unsure and might look to Cormac for a lead. Slevin was blunt and matter-of-fact and quite liable to ask awkward questions about the exact way that a devil should smell, but Domhnall was a diplomat and could be trusted to behave with discretion. His mouth was solemn, slightly compressed, and his eyes non-committal as he got to his feet.

Mara took one look at the three eager faces of the remaining scholars and melted to the appeal in their eyes. Once Father Miguel had ushered Domhnall out of the room, she beckoned to them, making sure to keep her own face very solemn and indicating to them that they should walk ahead of her where she could keep an eye on them. After all, she told herself, all of this is probably very good training for them, though she guessed that they would get a lot of fun out of it later on. So far, the west of Ireland was free of religious fanaticism; there was an easy tolerance of married priests and monks, and the weekly Mass was more of a social occasion than a time of heart-searching for sins committed during the week. But it was a rapidly changing world – the power of England over Ireland had waned during the last hundred years or so, but now it was waxing again. Who knew what these scholars of hers would have to face when they took office.

How would Domhnall handle this, she wondered, as she walked closely behind Cormac and Finbar, keeping her own face very serious? It was a tricky situation for a fourteen-year-old boy. Father Miguel, though a fanatic, was not a fool. He hesitated for a moment beside the ladder leading up to the door and then said to the boy: 'You go up on your own. That will be the best.'

Domhnall climbed the ladder instantly and was through the door without pausing. They heard his feet climbing up to the second floor and glimpsed his dark head through the narrow slit of the eastern window. He waited a few minutes and they all stood in silence looking up, waiting for his verdict. There was a strong smell of new thatch, thought Mara, but that was a wholesome smell – what was the devil supposed to smell like?

Domhnall reappeared eventually. He stood at the top of the steps for a moment, looking down at his friends, then reversed and came neatly backwards down the ladder. Without hesitation he turned and looked seriously into the face of Father Miguel.

'Well?' The Spanish priest's face was a dark red and his prominent eyes seemed about to burst from their sockets.

'There's a strange, bitter smell,' said Domhnall without hesitation.

Lye soap, thought Mara.

'Bitter!' The priest took a moment to think. 'Like wormwood?' he enquired.

'It could be,' said Domhnall cautiously, though his eyes, to Mara, seemed to say: *What does wormwood smell like?*

The priest's eyes glinted. 'And the Bible says: "*And the name of the star is called wormwood: and the third part of the waters became wormwood; and many men died of the waters, because they were made bitter.*" So you smelled wormwood, young man. Is that correct? It is as I thought: the devil may still be within. But why wormwood? Why not the fires of hell?'

He was addressing the two queries to himself, but Domhnall, trained to politeness, said helpfully, 'Perhaps the devil fears fire, Sir.'

'Because of the flaming sword,' put in Slevin.

'You may be right; I'll have to think about this.' Father Miguel was wide-eyed, full of thought. His gaze, fixed on the middle distance, was speculative.

'Perhaps in the meantime you would be willing to answer a few questions,' said Mara, falling into step beside him and firmly guiding him back towards the inn. 'You see, I, as the king's representative here, must determine what happened to Herr Hans Kaufmann. It is important to decide whether,' she said with a sudden flash of inspiration, 'he was taken from this world by divine or by human means – the truth must be established.'

'Indeed!' He turned to her eagerly, stopping so abruptly that Fachtnan, walking behind them, almost bumped into him. Mara heard a stifled giggle from the back of the line, but Father Miguel was deep in theological affairs.

'You are right!' He nodded his grey head. 'It will be of the utmost importance to make sure there was no human agency involved in this death and that it was God himself, as I do truly believe, who struck down the sinner and laid him out in all his nakedness.'

'Exactly,' said Mara emphatically. She opened the door to the parlour and urged him gently in. 'You, of course, can be of great use to us, as I understand that you were around the churchyard during the rainstorm. You remember, don't you, how wet you got? Did you see anyone near to the church – apart from Brother Cosimo, of course? I understand that he was with you.'

'No, Brother Cosimo had gone back to his room. But I did see someone; I saw the man who lives in that castle.'

'Yes.' Mara noticed that Fachtnan was making a note and that the boys had quietly resumed their seats. Their faces were excited and she was conscious of how keyed up she was herself. Perhaps they were coming near to the truth.

'Let me picture the scene,' she said thoughtfully. 'You were standing by the round tower, is that right?' She waited for his nod before continuing. 'And you saw Nechtan – your host of the other evening. I understand that Nechtan was anxious about his turf which had not yet been thatched.'

'I heard a lot of shouting. They were pushing those strange two-wheeled barrows into the barn. I'm not sure whether this man, Nechtan, was amongst them. I saw his wife, though. She was standing at the far side of the church. She had a basket in her hand.'

'Did Narait, Nechtan's wife, go into the church?'

Father Miguel shook his head. 'No, she went back towards the castle. I'm not surprised. The rain was getting heavier so that I decided to go back to the inn myself.'

'You must have been very wet by then; did Blad offer to dry your cloak?' asked Mara innocently.

'No, Brehon,' he said curtly. 'I did not see Blad. I went around the back and then straight up to my bedroom. There was a good fire there and my cloak was not too wet.'

That's not the story that Blad's serving boy told; he said that it was soaking, thought Mara, but she held her peace.

Her mind went to the picture of the pilgrims lined up in the courtyard, ready for their departure to Aran. She would check with the boys later on, but her impression was that all of them were wearing black cloaks. Black cloaks, she thought with irritation, not only hid the signs of a rain-soaking pretty well, but also hid the signs of blood. If the murderer had worn a black cloak, perhaps already wet, and then got thoroughly soaked in the downpour, there would be little or no evidence left on the cloaks.

'How do you think that Hans Kaufmann was killed, Father Miguel?' she asked.

His answer came rapidly, almost before she had finished speaking.

'He was struck down by God,' said the priest with great solemnity. 'There can be no other explanation. You are wasting your time, Brehon, if you are looking for a human agent. God is the God of Mercy, but he is also the God of Wrath; He will work His will with no help from man. Now, if there is nothing else that you wish to ask me, then I will leave you. I need to go and think about the purification of the tower where the sacred relic once lay.'

'Yes,' said Mara in as judicial a manner as she could muster. 'I think I have finished with you now, Father Miguel. I shall send my assistant with you up to your room to examine your cloak for bloodstains. This will be done for the eleven people who were present and who may have had reason to kill Hans Kaufmann, whether inspired by God or by the devil. As we agreed earlier, it is important to be able to assure the world that no human hand was involved in this murder – if that is the truth of the matter. Fachtnan, perhaps you will also examine the cloak belonging to Brother Cosimo.'

Mara waited until the footsteps of Fachtnan and the Spanish priest were heard going up the outside steps to the bedrooms and then she nodded to Domhnall.

'You did well,' she said. 'That was a difficult situation and you behaved with judgement and courtesy. I'm proud of you.'

And that, she thought, as she glimpsed a quick look of annoyance on Cormac's face, had to be said; Domhnall deserved the praise and she could not allow her son's feelings of jealousy to stop her from giving it. It's odd, she thought, but when Domhnall came to my law school six years ago I worried in case there might be problems with the other boys, since he was my grandson, and especially with Slevin who started the same day as Domhnall, but somehow it was never an issue for them, or for either of us. Perhaps, because of that, I hadn't expected so much trouble with Cormac. Yet it seems to be getting worse, not better.

'Cormac,' she said impulsively, 'would you go up to the prioress's room and ask her, very politely, could she come down and talk to me. Oh, and Cormac, ask her to bring her cloak, too. Don't give any reasons. Offer to carry it for her if she asks why.'

It was time, perhaps, to stop remembering all of the time that he was the youngest boy and to give him some responsibility and chances to use his judgement.

Fachtnan was back before Cormac and the prioress, and she knew from his face that nothing had appeared on the cloaks of Brother Cosimo and Father Miguel. He shook his head as soon as he closed the parlour door behind him.

'Nothing that I could see, or feel, on either cloak,' he said. 'You know what travellers' cloaks are like. These are the usual very thick wool, double cloaks – both of them are woven from the wool of black sheep, not dyed, so there are traces of grey here and there, but not a sign of a bloodstain on either of them.'

Mara nodded. The travellers' cloaks would have been made from unwashed sheep's wool, rich in lanolin and apt to shed water very easily. Even if some blood had splashed on them, a walk under the torrential rainstorm of the evening of the murder would have washed them clean. She sighed and wondered whether this case would ever be solved. There was still the huge problem of how the man, a big, strong man, probably the biggest and strongest man in the vicinity of Kilnaboy Church that night, had been murdered in that very strange way.

After a few minutes, Cormac slid into the room, looking a little embarrassed and slightly worried, but he held the door open in a very polite manner and said, in his best English, with the air of one making an announcement: 'Here are the ladies, Brehon.'

To Mara's dismay, not just the prioress but the lady's two sisters were with him. Still, they all had their cloaks – were wearing them, in fact, so that could be turned to an advantage.

She rose to her feet instantly and smiled as the prioress explained, slightly belligerently, that they had all been about to go for a walk. Mara waved the explanation aside.

'It was so kind of you all to come,' she said effusively. 'And how wonderful that you are wearing your cloaks; I promised Father Miguel that I would check everyone's cloak to make sure that there were no signs of blood on them. Father Miguel,' she said with great solemnity, 'is insistent that there should be no doubt as to the divine involvement in the death of the German pilgrim. I have promised to bear witness. Perhaps I could check your cloak first, Madame.'

By the time she had verified that there were no discernible traces of blood on the prioress's cloak, the other two had divested themselves and she could go through the same procedure while keeping up a flow of conversation about the terrible rainstorm of the night when the pilgrim had been killed.

Oddly enough, the three women wore what were known as 'Irish mantles'. Ardal O'Lochlainn, she knew, exported vast quantities of these through Galway to England, presumably by Wales, and they had been bought there by the sisters. These mantles were made from double wool, with honey combed through the nap until their surface was almost totally waterproof. If they were already running water from the heavy rain there would have been no chance of blood soaking into them. Nevertheless, Mara checked as thoroughly as she could, handing each garment back as soon as she had finished.

'What a shame to deny you of your walk,' she said. 'Cormac and Finbar, while I talk to the Lady Prioress, would you take Mistress Grace along by the river, show her the places where the fish rise; Slevin and Domhnall take Mistress Bess to the sacred well, she will be interested in that, I'm sure. And here, take this . . .' She produced a small, irregularly shaped piece of parchment and held it out to Bess with a smile.

'You can tie it to the thorn bush beside the well,' she said. 'Make a wish and then your wish will come true before the end of a year.'

Bess took the small piece of skin with a broad grin and a look of easy acquiescence. 'I'll wish for fortune, what do you think, boys? Will that work?'

'Sure to,' Slevin assured her, and they went off, Bess's loud, strident laugh sounding as they went through the door, Domhnall could speak English fluently and Slevin was good at the language also – they would keep her amused.

'Let's go to the river through the kitchen,' proposed Cormac to Grace. 'Mór generally gives you a cake or something as you pass through, and you can smell what's going to be cooking for dinner.' He did not seem to be embarrassed by her scarred face, but, Mara saw with pleasure, addressed her with more deference and courtesy than he usually showed towards adults.

'Mór's been a friend of mine all of my life,' he added with a note of conspiracy in his voice. Mara was pleased to see Grace's pale face gaining a little colour at the charm that, at unexpected times, emanated from her problem son.

'Yes, let's go and see what she can offer us,' she said, her face expanding into a smile and showing pretty, well-shaped teeth inside the twisted and scarred mouth. 'I'm very fond of cake myself.'

'I'll finish my task, Brehon,' said Fachtnan. Mara had given him a tiny sign, just the sliding of her eyes towards the door, but they had worked together in close harmony for so many years that Fachtnan knew instantly that this was an interview that the Brehon would wish to conduct without witnesses. He would, she knew, use the utmost tact while checking the cloaks of Sorley, Father MacMahon, Nechtan and his wife, Narait.

Left alone with the prioress, Mara did not rush into speech. This woman, she thought, looking across the table with interest, may have come from quite humble origins. She had probably entered the convent, less because of religious fervour, but rather through an ambition to make the most of herself – a belief that she had brains and ability and that she could do better than become the wife and slave of some doltish farmer. She had taken her vows, risen in the ranks, made a success of her profession, and then – who knows – on some moonlit night in a sultry June she may well have yielded to nature, have lain with someone: someone who, perhaps, was almost forgotten, but who had a delicate cast of feature and a blond hair of head, she thought, remembering that entry in the notebook belonging to Hans Kaufmann; someone just like the stricken Grace; someone who had seduced her senses and had led her away from the straight and narrow path.

And then, poor thing, the realization, the growing acceptance of the terrible truth; no doubt the confiding in her sister Bess and in the mother, now dead, and somehow or other a feigned illness, a secret birth and a resolute parting – the prioress returned to her convent and an extra baby was added to an obscure farm in north Wales.

'Was Herr Kaufmann blackmailing you about Grace?' Mara made her question purposefully blunt, but kept her tone of voice neutral and non-judgemental.

The woman whitened. 'What on earth do you mean?'

'My only interest,' said Mara, in tones that she made sound indifferent and uninterested, 'is in the death of this German pilgrim. Through long experience, and I have been Brehon – rather like your Sergeant-at-Law in England and Wales – here in the kingdom of the Burren for over twenty-five years now, I've found that the more I can learn about the dead person, the easier it is to solve the puzzle of the murder.'

'Twenty-five years,' said the prioress with a strained smile. 'You must have been a very young woman for such an important post.'

'Yes, I was probably too young,' admitted Mara. 'You see, my father had been Brehon before me. I had taken over his school and I suppose that made it easier for me to take over his position.' She smiled amiably at the prioress. 'I think I did everything too young. I had a daughter when I was only fifteen years old.' And then she stopped. If the woman were to imagine that Sorcha was born out of wedlock, then that was all to the good; one confidence might lead to another.

The prioress's expression was thoughtful. After a few minutes she said abruptly, 'How did you find out about Grace? Did Bess tell you?'

'Certainly not Bess, nor Grace either. Though I fancy,' said Mara cautiously, 'that she was the one that told Herr Kaufmann.'

'Stupid girl – trying to make herself important,' muttered the prioress.

'And he asked you for money – I saw the coins in his bag.'

The prioress pressed her lips together but said nothing.

'So you are telling me that he just threatened to reveal the truth about you and then left it at that?' queried Mara with a lift of an eyebrow, and when the woman just stared straight ahead, she went on smoothly, 'You can tell the truth to me and it will go no further. We are alone here. Your secret is as sacred to me as if it were told in confession. It will not be betrayed. Grace is a lovely girl and somehow, somewhere, sometime, a man will look beyond the scarred face and will value the spirit inside it. I don't think that Hans Kaufmann would have been such a man. He was someone who had a mission, he was a fanatic, he was looking for flaws within the Church of Rome, flaws that would give ammunition to his master, Martin Luther.' She paused and then said very softly, 'Only one thing interests me in this matter: did you have anything to do with the death of Hans Kaufmann?'

'Nothing!' There was a note of sincerity in the woman's voice which Mara recognized, and she nodded understandingly when the woman said, 'I thought it was all over and done with. I had given him the money that he demanded, and, to be honest, I thought he had a soft spot for Grace. He sought her out, talked with her and drew her out of herself.'

'Did you and your sisters go out that evening?'

'We got caught by the rain,' said the prioress. 'We ran back and raced up the back stairs to our rooms. This is a very good inn. There was a bright fire burning in my room and my cloak soon dried in front of it. My sisters, I'm sure, had the same. I saw neither of them until the following morning.'

'One more question,' said Mara. She got to her feet. She would stroll out and put the same questions to both Bess and Grace when they returned, but she was conscious that this woman was the leader of the little group and her word would be the most important of all three. 'One more question,' she repeated. 'Did you see Mór, the innkeeper's daughter, return from the church with her empty baskets?'

The prioress seemed surprised by the question, but she turned it over carefully in her mind. 'No,' she said, 'no, Brehon, no, we definitely did not see her. You see we went for a walk along the bank of the river – quite some distance – then the three of us came back the same way, by the river bank, and we were already soaking wet so we went up the outside stairs to the back gallery and wished each other good night, and each of us went straight into our bedrooms and did not come out again that night. You can ask my two sisters; they will tell you the same story.'

Sixteen

Irish Canon Law
De Canibus: Sinodus Sapientium
(Concerning Dogs: A Synod of Wise Men)

1. *Whatsoever mischief a chained dog is accused of doing in the night that shall not be paid for.*
2. *Whatsoever mischief a dog does during the day in his master's byres or pastures that shall not be paid for.*
3. *But if the dog goes beyond the boundaries of his master's land whatsoever mischief he does must be paid for.*

Nechtan and his wife were good hosts. They both seemed genuinely delighted to have the Brehon and the four boys as their guests. After supper they all went up to the big room at the top storey of the castle and found the toys and playthings that the four brothers had enjoyed. There were models of knights on horseback, siege weapons, a splendid castle with moat, a spectacular gate with towers on both sides, and a magnificent portcullis above the entrance; swords and shields, bows and arrows, even a painted target – the bottom of an old barrel – which the brothers had used for practice with throwing knives and arrows.

But Domhnall's eye was taken by the baskets of costumes for plays, and the other boys, as usual, followed his lead.

'We used to put on plays for the people of the parish,' explained Nechtan. 'Father MacMahon was a young man then, and he was full of zeal that everyone should understand the word of God. So me and my brothers, and my cousins, used to act out Bible stories. I remember them so well,' he said fondly. 'Here are the costumes. We would do the creation, and the fall of Lucifer, of course – here's the flaming sword.' Nechtan produced a wooden sword carefully painted in reds and blacks and finished off with yellow-edged scarlet-painted leather flames. Cormac gave it a few flourishes, and Mara thought secretly that with his handsome face and red-gold hair, he would make a wonderful angel. There was a devil's mask there also, made cleverly from leather, with curved horns and lines drawn with gold paint in straight slashes around the eye sockets and fanning out from the curved open mouth, but the angel costumes were spectacular with magnificent wings made from swans' feathers.

'And then there was "Cain and Abel",' continued Nechtan. 'And "Noah's Ark", of course. That was wonderful when we acted it. We brought all of the animals from the farmyard along to play their parts and you've never seen such a mess.' He laughed heartily at the memory, and Mara thought that she had never seen him look so happy.

'The costumes should all be here for the different stories,' he said, rummaging in the baskets. 'Father MacMahon used to get us to put on these plays for the pilgrims. This was before the inn was built, of course, but we used to act the plays amongst the ruins of the old monastery and the pilgrims used to sit on the stones and in the old blank windows. They would throw coins on to the stage, too, after the play was finished. Father MacMahon told us that the money was intended for the greater honour and glory of the church, but we used to retain some of it for our own uses.' He chuckled to himself, but Narait, Mara noticed, did not smile at her husband's boyhood recollections, as would most wives, but looked bored and wearied.

'I've seen the players act those plays in the courtyards of the inns in Galway,' said Domhnall, glowing with excitement. 'My father used to rent a place at a window of the inn and we all went. The little ones got tired after a while and my mother took them home. But I stayed to the end,' he finished, and Mara was sure that he spoke the truth. Domhnall, no matter how young, would always see matters to the end.

'Which was your favourite, Domhnall,' she asked.

'"The Shepherds' Play",' he answered immediately. 'That has such good jokes in it – I'd like to be the sheep stealer.'

'Why don't you put on a play for us all this evening?' said Mara impulsively. 'It's a shame to miss the opportunity of using these splendid costumes. Would you like to stay up here now and practise? Come down when you are ready. You won't need any play books or anything – choose something simple. You wouldn't mind, would you, Nechtan?'

'"Cain and Abel" would be your best chance; there are just four parts in that,' said Nechtan eagerly. 'Look, the costumes are there, just under the ones for Abraham and Isaac.'

'I'll be Cain and you'll be Abel,' said Slevin to Domhnall. 'The other two can be Adam and Eve.'

'I'm not being Eve,' said Cormac firmly. 'Not in a hundred years will I dress up as a woman.'

'Let's leave them to it,' said Mara hastily. Domhnall would work something out to soothe Cormac's dignity, she knew.

The conversation downstairs flagged a little after the boys had left. Fachtnan had checked the cloaks of both Nechtan and his wife and had found no traces of blood on either, though both had admitted to having been caught in the downpour. Nechtan had been checking that as much turf was moved under shelter as possible, and Narait had suffered a headache brought on by the sweltering heat and had gone for a walk. As soon as she could do so in a natural manner, Mara once again led the conversation around to the events of that evening.

'You see,' she said with the frank air of one putting all of her cards on the table, 'if only you could tell me, Nechtan, that one of your turf barrows was left out after you shut and locked the barn, that would make my task easier. I am persuaded that the murderer must have used something like one of these in order to move the body from the church to the capstone of the old tomb. It would be just about the right size and shape.'

Nechtan shook his head. 'No, I'm certain of this, Brehon, every one of my barrows was heaped with turf – and the turf was still there on them in the morning.'

'And the barn was locked, that's right, is it not?'

'That's right.' There was a slight hesitation in Nechtan's voice and Mara immediately understood.

'Don't tell me,' she said with a groan. 'You leave the key up on the eaves, or somewhere like that, and I suppose everyone knows about it?'

'Under the stone outside the door, actually,' said Nechtan sheepishly.

Mara thought for a moment. It was still possible for the murderer to have borrowed a turf barrow, even if they were locked up – the key could have been found easily and it would only have taken seconds to have thrown the load on to the floor, and not that long to have loaded it up again.

'Perhaps,' she said, 'it would be possible for me to have a look at your turf barrows while the light is still good enough to see. Will you come too, Narait?'

'No, I . . .' Narait gave a long look at Nechtan, and Mara saw him stare back. He said nothing, though, and did not help his wife in her search for an excuse. 'I think I'll go up and see how the boys are getting on,' she said eventually. 'They may need some help.' She got to her feet, looking uncertainly at her husband who had poured himself another cup of wine and did not seem ready to move until it had disappeared down his throat.

'Of course,' he said in conversational tones, looking straight at his wife, 'the German pilgrim was not the first strange death to occur in Kilnaboy Church. There was the case of that woman who stuck a knife into her faithless lover just as he walked into the church. That happened a couple of hundred years ago. There is something about it in the church history. It was the time of the monks and they held a service of cleansing afterwards so as to rid the church of the sin that had been committed.' The words came out fluently, too fluently, almost as though they had been committed to memory and practised beforehand. Nechtan had been drinking a lot of wine and it seemed to have altered his mood from genial host to a silent man who sat and stared ahead of him.

Mara cast a quick glance at him and then chatted easily with Narait about wolfhounds. A wolf had been sighted and several sheep found dead on the Roughan hillside. Nechtan, according to his wife, wanted to buy a fully grown wolfhound from Murrough who bred the animals, but Narait wanted a puppy. Murrough, she said, had a litter of four six-week-old puppies – two males and two females.

'Why not get two brothers from that litter and then they

would be company for each other at the puppy stage and would make a good pack to hunt wolves when they are a bit older?' Mara was thinking that Narait, frustrated in her maternal instincts, might find some sort of outlet in mothering a pair of puppies. Nechtan said nothing. Narait glanced uncertainly at him again and Mara decided it was time to separate husband and wife before something was said that might start a quarrel.

'It's very kind of you to help the boys with their play. Don't take any notice if they are all arguing,' she said to Narait as she rose to her feet and walked decisively towards the door without waiting for Nechtan to lead the way. 'Domhnall usually manages to sort them out, but there will be all sorts of disagreements first,' she said over her shoulder.

'I don't mind. I like children. What a handsome boy your son is, Brehon.' Narait's smile was genuine, but it quickly faded at her husband's expression as he got slowly to his feet. There was no doubt that this marriage was heading rapidly towards a divorce. A child would have united them, but now they had nothing to talk about, and even disagreed about what dog to get. Mara said nothing while they crossed the yard, but when she and Nechtan were almost at the doors of the barn, she thought that she would try to make him understand his young wife's loneliness.

'You would be much better off getting a couple of puppies if you want to keep the wolves away from your land, Nechtan. Murrough's adult dogs will give their loyalty to him; a puppy that grows up in the house will give its life for you, if necessary.' She hesitated a minute and then said, 'And I do think that Narait would find a purpose in life while caring for them – she seems a little depressed.'

'I'll think about it. Your advice is always valuable, Brehon.' His tone was polite, but she sensed little sympathy in him for his wife, and he immediately covered the awkward moment by shouting for one of his men to wheel out the turf barrows and to line them up in front of the barn.

'I'm looking for traces of blood,' said Mara bluntly once the barrows were in place, each one resting on its rear props as well as on the two wheels in the front. She addressed her remarks to the two men and the boy who had taken them out of the barn. The turf, she noticed, had still not been thatched, although her own farm manager, Cumhal, had already started on that task back at the farm in Cahermacnaghten. Once they had returned from the bog, Cumhal's workers had been given a meal, a short break and then had immediately got to work with the already prepared bundles of dried rushes. Still, Nechtan's farming practices were none of her business, she reminded herself, and asked the men to start searching the barrows.

'The Brehon thinks that the dead man's body might have been wheeled from the church on one of our barrows.' Nechtan's voice was neutral and she noticed that he did not, himself, take any part in the scrutiny.

'But I need your young eyes to look at them,' said Mara with an encouraging smile. 'What colour would bloodstains be on the wood?'

'Sort of dark brown,' said the boy enthusiastically.

'Brown – of course,' said Mara thoughtfully. She remembered her daughter Sorcha, who had many more housewifely skills than she, lecturing her on different types of stain and how each should be treated. Of course, blood turned brown after it was shed. She watched while they searched, all of them showing an enthusiasm that probably indicated that if they weren't doing this they would be undertaking a more unpleasant job. Her mind was not as engaged as theirs, though. A suspicion had occurred to her and she was glad that Nechtan had left her to explore her thoughts in peace.

And to think about blood.

No bloodstains were found, much to their disappointment, but Mara thanked the men profusely for their efforts.

'It would have been the rain, Brehon, washed everything down,' said one.

'Terrible it was,' said the other, glad to break off work for a chat. 'I swear to God, I thought the heavens were opening. And there was that strange heat all day. And then the rain came.'

'I was glad of it myself,' said the boy. 'After the work with the turf I was sweating so much that I went down to the river to have a swim. And then the heavens opened and I was so wet that I didn't bother jumping in. By then I was cooled off nicely, just went off up the road to my mother's place.'

'Did you see anyone by the river?' asked Mara casually.

'Saw the three pilgrim ladies coming back from their walk – they were climbing up the steps towards their rooms. Blad was putting his fishing rod into the stable. I heard Mór call out something about the church – don't know if she was going or coming. They say she brought him his last supper, so as to speak.'

The boy gave a nervous giggle and the older man said warningly, 'Don't let Father MacMahon hear you talk like that – sacrilegious, that is.'

'What do you think happened to the German pilgrim?' asked Mara, looking from one to the other encouragingly and hoping that Nechtan would keep out of the way for a while. This, she thought, had been an odd investigation; it had been centred on the pilgrims and she had not had the usual contact with the people of the area. The people of the Burren, she thought proudly, generally had a sensible outlook on life; there was, she reasoned, little chance of the involvement in the murder of anyone other than the pilgrims and those closely connected with the church of Kilnaboy and its famous relic. Nevertheless, those living in the neighbourhood must have some ideas about what had happened with this very strange death in their parish. Did they believe, also, that this murder was an act of the avenging God?

'Don't put any credit in angels and that like,' said the boy daringly.

'I told you to mind your mouth,' retorted the man.

'Father MacMahon believes that it was a divine punishment for the German pilgrim's sin, doesn't he?' said Mara lightly, and the older man nodded seriously.

'It was a judgement on him, Brehon. You can see for yourself. How else did he get from the church to the *gabhal* if it wasn't done by the power of God?'

'With no clothes on,' sniggered the irrepressible boy, but he muttered the words in an undertone and the others ignored him.

'Stands to reason,' affirmed the man.

Gabhal, thought Mara as she bowed her head in acceptance

of this irrefutable logic – now that was an interesting word. It was an old word, little used in her own time. She had heard Brigid, her housekeeper, use it; it meant a junction or a joining between two parts. So this ancient tomb of their pagan ancestors was known to the people of Kilnaboy as a junction, a joining place between this life and the next – a waiting place, perhaps. Whatever it was, the unfortunate German pilgrim who had waited there all night perhaps now knew whether Martin Luther or Pope Leo X was right about whether purgatory existed. Or indeed, thought Mara daringly, whether heaven or hell was as represented in the Bible – or did, in fact, exist.

'You've been very helpful,' she said to the men. 'I won't detain you any longer.'

Nechtan, she saw, was striding towards her, but she did not await his arrival. She went over to the church door and quickly paced out the distance between it and the tomb. Not far, she thought, when she reached the *gabhal*; ten paces to the end of the graveyard enclosure and then another three or four up through the bushes until the little circle, with its impressive stone monument, was reached. A man or a woman could traverse this distance quite quickly – though not, of course, if heavily burdened.

Mara stood for a while gazing down on the heavy capstone that spanned the tomb and imagining how the murder might have taken place. By nine o'clock that night, on 14 September, that day of the Feast of the Holy Cross, the sky had been dark, with thick clouds covering the moon – yet the church had been brightly lit and there would have been pools of light spilling out from the windows. No windows, of course, on the west-facing gable with its spectacular, double-armed cross, so that part of the pathway would have been obscured, but coming out of the south door, beneath the carving of the *sheela-na-gig* there would have been plenty of light from the windows; then a brief spell of darkness passing the west gable, and then some light, but not much, spilling across the churchyard from the windows on the north side of the church. Going the few paces up the bush-enclosed pathway to the *gabhal* – would that have had any light on it, or would it have been in complete darkness?

Mara gazed around her. This was a brighter day than the day of the murder, the day of the spectacular rainstorm, but the time must be about right. She could experiment and see whether that would confirm her suspicions.

A light suddenly showed from the small one-roomed cottage that stood beside Father MacMahon's more impressive residence. A door opened and the glow from the fire inside revealed the heavy figure of Sorley. He was holding a lantern in his hand and he went out towards the round tower. A minute later the bell sounded – nine strokes, as Sorley pulled the rope nine times. Nine o'clock. Hans Kaufmann had been given his supper about eight o'clock by Mór, so on that very hot night, anytime from nine o'clock onwards, if Nuala was correct, someone stuck a knife into his naked body.

Mara waited for a moment until Sorley climbed down the ladder again. He did not, she noticed, lock the door. Nothing there to be stolen now; the precious relic, the pride and joy of Kilnaboy, had been destroyed.

'Sorley,' she called. 'I'm sorry to trouble you, but would you go into the church and light all the candles that were lit the night that German pilgrim was in there.'

He faced her with a frown. 'All of them?'

'All of them,' confirmed Mara and waited, gazing at him steadily. He did not look well, she thought. A man of deep and sincere devotion to the church, he was, of course, of too lowly origin to have become a priest himself, but to serve a priest and to serve the church were the mainsprings of his existence. The destroying of the relic must have had a terrible effect on his life and his loyalties.

'Very well, Brehon,' he said abruptly and he went off with his lantern. A minute later the lights began to spring up, illuminating the windows. The unusual amount of light brought Father MacMahon to his doorway. He stared across at the church but made no sign. Had Father MacMahon come out that night, just as he had done tonight? Probably, but the candles had been lit earlier, perhaps while Hans was eating his supper. In any case, Father MacMahon had denied seeing anything untoward in the churchyard.

Mara ignored him now. She went to the south door of the

church, tapped on it and Sorley opened it immediately, allowing a blaze of light to fall on to the pathway. Mara nodded and thanked him, but then turned and strode off, counting under her breath.

Yes, it was as she thought. Pools of light and dark. She moved quickly and easily between them and then up the bush-enclosed path until she reached the ancient tomb and laid her hand on the capstone; it had taken her less than two minutes. Then she went back to thank Sorley once more and to reassure Father MacMahon that his precious candles were no longer needed.

The scene was set in the big hall for the play when Mara and Nechtan returned. Narait had organized the servants into putting up a screen – one of the many used to shield draughts from the badly fitting windows of the old castle. This hid the staircase leading out of the hall. In front of the screen was a square space marked out by benches, and to one side of this improvised stage, six of the servants sat as an audience. In the front were two cushioned chairs for Mara and Nechtan. Narait, one of the servants informed his master, was to be a player.

The play was surprisingly good for something that had been improvised so quickly. Narait made an excellent Eve, scolding her two sons for their jealousy and their quarrels and calling on her diminutive husband, Adam, to back up her threats of punishment. The part of Adam was acted with extreme embarrassment by Finbar, but Mara clapped him vigorously as his awkward endeavours to scold Cain and Abel reminded her strongly of King Turlough when he was ordered by her to reprimand his youngest son for some piece of bad behaviour. Once their father, Adam, and mother, Eve, had disappeared behind the screen, Slevin who was Cain and Cormac who was Abel had fun with a session of name-calling, which escalated until they each fetched a sword and shield neatly concealed under a couple of cushions. The temptation to show off became too much for both of them then, and they drew the jousting display out to such a degree that the voice of God hissed from behind the screen, '*That's long enough!*'

And then, once Abel dropped with an impressive thump

to the floor and rolled his eyes in a dramatic way, finishing with them fixed wide open on the ceiling above, God, arrayed in a priest-like garment, appeared shouting, 'Where is your brother?'

He made short work of the cheeky reply – 'Am I my brother's keeper?' – from Cain, and when he got the truth, lectured him for the murder of his brother and condemned him to be an outlaw forever. Slevin, in the character of Cain, tried some back-chat, but Domhnall, giving an insight into the dignity that he would hopefully bring to the office of Brehon later on in his life, dominated him, reduced him to a shivering wreck, then marked him on the forehead, using a rag dipped in ink, and dismissed him to be an exile and a wanderer for the rest of his life.

'Wonderful!' Nechtan was on his feet clapping as the cast, including the restored-to-life Abel, formed a line in front of the screen and bowed to their audience. His earlier bad temper seemed to be forgotten and he was generous in his praise for all of the actors and suggested that they might show it to Father MacMahon sometime – in happier times, he added quickly, remembering the unsolved death that still hung over the little community at Kilnaboy.

Seventeen

Brécha Crólige
(Judgements of Blood Letting)

Any offence committed against a child is punished with the greatest severity. No matter how lowly his father may be, the honour price of a young child is as great as that of the highest cleric in the land.

The fine for the murder of a child is an honour price of forty séts, or twenty ounces of silver or twenty milch cows added to the normal eraic or body fine of forty-two séts or twenty-one ounces of silver or twenty-one milch cows.

So the total fine would be either: Eighty-two séts, or forty-one ounces of silver or forty-one milch cows.

Or, in the case of secret killing: One hundred and twenty-four séts, or sixty-six ounces of silver or sixty-six milch cows.

Mara slept heavily that night – unusually heavily for her. The play had ended with a celebratory bowl of syllabub and a platter of sweetmeats. Nechtan had insisted on her drinking some mead with it and the creaminess of the sweet syllabub and the strongly alcoholic drink made her drop off to sleep almost as soon as her head touched the pillow.

When she heard her name whispered her first instinct was to turn over and bury her head under the blankets, but then she sat up and blinked sleepily at the candlelight in front of her eyes.

'Finbar!' she exclaimed. 'What on earth are you doing here? What's wrong?'

'It's Cormac,' he whimpered, and by the glow from the candle that he held unsteadily she could see that his face was very pale and that he had marks of tears on his face.

'What?' In an instant Mara had grabbed her nightgown and pulled it on over her shift and swung her legs out of the bed. 'Is he ill?' she demanded. It's only a fever and sickness, just as his foster brother Art had been suffering from, she told herself, but her heart thudded. Cormac was never ill.

And then she heard a quick sob from Finbar.

'It's not that, Brehon.' His voice was choked and she had difficulty in making out his words. 'The Spanish priest has got him.'

'Got him?' Mara grabbed her cloak from the nail on the back of the door and slung it over her shoulders. 'Got him where?' She bent down, pulled on her knee-high hose and then stuck her feet into her boots. Finbar was gulping hard and she could not make out what he was saying.

'Where is he?' she hissed.

'With Father Miguel – in the round tower.' Finbar seemed suddenly steadied by her fierce tone.

'Wait outside while I dress,' said Mara coldly.

I'm damned if I face that Spanish monk in my nightwear, she thought, as she rapidly pulled on a clean shift and her gown. She could guess what had happened. Cormac and Finbar were larking around in the round tower – probably with lights – and Father Miguel had caught hold of Cormac. *Serve the little wretch right*, she tried to say to herself, but she was filled with a cold anger that anyone would dare to lay a hand on her son.

'But Brehon, he's mad.' Finbar's mouth was at the keyhole.

'I'm sure he's furious,' said Mara, rapidly plaiting her hair and wishing that she had attended to it the night before.

'No, not furious!' Finbar's voice rose to a wail, but then he subdued it again. 'He's mad. He thinks Cormac is the devil – really the devil.'

'What did you say?' Mara drove a couple of hairpins into the back of her hair, picked up her cloak from the floor and pulled open the door. 'Speak quietly,' she said impatiently, 'don't wake the whole household. What have you two been doing?'

'Cormac told me to fetch Father Miguel.' He gulped hard and she swallowed her impatience with him.

'Come on,' she said, and went quietly down the stairs. 'Tell me as we go.'

'Cormac told me to get Father Miguel. He told me to say that . . .'

The front door was closed and bolted, but she slid the bolt

back and was outside in a moment, followed by Finbar. Only then did she notice that he was shivering and she reproached herself for her harshness.

'Told you to say what?' she asked more gently.

'That the devil was in the round tower. Cormac was pretending to be the devil. He sent me for Father Miguel.'

Mara sighed with exasperation. Now she knew what had happened. 'You took that mask of the devil from the players' chest, didn't you?'

He nodded. 'Cormac told me to tell Father Miguel that there was something strange in the round tower – that it might be a devil. He stood at the window, up on the top floor, and he held up a lantern so that he could be seen.'

And now, thought Mara, the priest is rightly furious to find that it was just a nine-year-old boy capering around, wearing an old leather mask. Still, she thought, it was fairly stupid of him to have believed that story. Did the man really think that the devil was in the round tower?

'Come on,' she said, touching Finbar on the shoulder. 'Let's find Cormac. Don't worry. I'll talk to Father Miguel.'

The boy was still trembling beneath her hand and she looked down at him with concern. There was not enough light in order to see his face, but she wondered whether he had a fever. Why should he be so very upset because Cormac was in the hands of the Spanish priest?

The night was dark with a sliver of a crescent moon and a few stars, but from behind the church the round tower glowed with light. That was good; it would light her way across to the inn if that was where Father Miguel had taken Cormac. She hastened her footsteps and then sniffed. There was a strange smoky smell in the air, a very familiar smell, the strong pungent odour of damp turf. Almost as though . . . No, she told herself. That's not possible. Not twice in two days. In any case, there was nothing of value in the tower now – no reason for a fire.

And then she noticed that Nechtan's stack of turf had collapsed on one side, just as though the sods had been pulled out of the carefully constructed wall. And that was definitely a smell of peat smoke filling the air. She turned back and grabbed the boy by the shoulder.

'Finbar, what's happening? What have you two been doing? Where's Cormac? Have you and he been lighting fires? Where is he? Is he in the inn?' She felt her heart thud, though she told herself that there was nothing that could happen to her son. Blad would soon interfere if Father Miguel got high-handed. But what had they been up to?

'Cormac told me to get the priest,' wailed Finbar. 'He told me to . . .' His voice faltered.

At that moment a glow lit up the east-facing window of the round tower. The silhouette was unmistakable: the gold gleamed around the huge eye sockets, large, coiled horns curved out from the domed forehead. Mara's heart thudded. It certainly looked realistic. Father Miguel had been summoned by Finbar out into the night. The devil was in the round tower, he had been told, but Cormac was still there – not pulled out and taken across to the inn by an indignant man who had been momentarily fooled by a pair of boys, but still up in the top storey, peering out through the narrow slit of the window.

So where was Father Miguel?

And then a shadowy figure pushed past them, almost knocking them over, and Mara felt the stiff, hard curve of a willow basket knock against her hip. There were footsteps on the ladder ahead of them and then a gleam of light as the door was pushed open, and a black-cloaked figure, hugging a basket of turf, was suddenly lit up. And then the door closed behind him.

But that half a minute was enough.

The ground floor of the round tower was on fire, with clouds of smoke rising up from the wet turf.

And on the floor above was the figure in the devil's mask.

'Get Nechtan, get Sorley, wake everyone!' screamed Mara, giving Finbar a push. She had little reliance on him but could not wait to see whether her orders were obeyed. She sprang up the ladder leading to the door and then realized that her shout had been heard. The figure was at the door, trying to close it against her. Her fingernails just touched it, and then she felt a blow. Her feet were still a couple of rungs from the top as he leaned forward, his black cloak flaring out. He bent down, his hands at her feet, fumbling. The ladder jerked abruptly, almost throwing her down, and the door flew back giving a sudden view of a smoking, smouldering fire in the centre of the wooden floor. Father Miguel looked over his shoulder. He stood up, abandoning the ladder, slipped back inside and then the door was pushed violently against her outstretched hands. She sprang forward. A second later her two hands were on the door and she was pressing it with every ounce of strength in her body.

'Get out of my way,' she said between gritted teeth. 'Get out of my way or I swear that I will kill you.' *My child is in there*, she screamed, but she did not know whether the words were said aloud or whether they just burned through her brain.

She pushed him vigorously, yet he hardly seemed aware of her now. He went to the door and dragged up the ladder from its place on the ground below, pulling it into the little circular room. Mara heard the door slam closed and the metallic click as the bolt was shot home. Now she was cut off from the ground, suspended halfway up the stone tower. She was closeted within the small room, locked into the company of a mad man. His eyes blazed but did not see her. With an enormous output of strength he crashed the ladder against the circular stone wall, smashing it into two pieces, holding them up, suspended in his arms.

The fire had been smoking in the centre of the room. Some sparks flickered but otherwise it seemed to just smoulder and she only spared it a cursory glance. She fumbled through the clouds of smoke, trying to find the ladder to the second floor. Surely it was there. Her memory was quite clear. It had been against the wall of the small round room, directly opposite to the entrance door at the top of the first ladder.

And then the Spaniard placed the two pieces of the ladder that he had just broken on top of the fire. A spark found the wood and the fire blazed up, clear flames adding to the clouds of yellow-white smoke. The whole room was lit up. Mara could see clearly the opening into the top room, the room that had held the sacred relic.

But that ladder had already been pulled down, and this time the man did not wait to break it. In a second it was placed on the fire. And this had not been outside in the rain and the mist, year after year; this ladder had been sheltered, had spent a lifetime under cover. It was as dry as tinder. Instantly the effect of it was seen. The first-floor ladder had begun to burn steadily, but once the second-floor ladder was added there was an immediate change. Flames leaped from the smouldering fire of wet turf and licked on to the wooden rungs and side pieces. The timber was old and dry and it flared up instantly. The room was small and the fire dominated it, bringing instant terror.

And now the way to the top storey was barred. Ten foot above, the opening yawned – now no longer an exit, an escape hatch, but a conduit, a chimney for the smoke that rushed up through it.

'Cormac!' Mara screamed, but there was no reply.

Suddenly the Spaniard seemed aware of her. 'Get back, get back,' he screamed in a strange high voice. 'Get back, woman. The devil must be burned. *"Depart from me, ye cursed, into everlasting fire."* Get back, go down.' He grabbed her by the shoulder and began to pull her towards the entrance door, trying to thrust her out.

Mara wasted no energy in argument. Why had Cormac not appeared at the opening? He was an active, athletic boy who would make nothing of dropping through from just ten foot above. She had seen him spring from tree branches higher than that. There was only one answer.

Cormac, her son, was unconscious. And the smoke rising up in an ominous column told her that there was no time to waste.

'"*Yea, though I walk through the valley of the shadow of death, I will fear no evil*",' muttered Father Miguel, but Mara ignored him. There was nothing worse that he could do now. She had sent her messenger for help, but Finbar was young and unreliable and help might arrive too late. Without hesitation, she grabbed the bell rope and pulled hard. The rope itself was hot, but it still held firm. The bell jangled once overhead, though she barely heard it.

Suddenly she had found a way to get into the top storey of the small round tower. The bell rope would be her stepladder.

The rope was rough on her hands, but she was an avid gardener and the skin had been toughened by her work with spade and shovel. Keep calm, she told herself, and made sure that the rope was gripped very firmly with one hand before moving the second hand above it. The muscles in her upper arms burned and her shoulders ached unbearably. She could hear more muttered verses from the Bible and, more ominously, the sound of wood crashing on to the fire. The Spaniard was still feeding the fire; he had, she guessed, moved more of the unburned section of the ladder to crown the flames. She felt the intense heat leap up and prayed that a stray spark would not lodge on the loose fibres of the rope. *Three times more*, she said to herself, *put hand above hand three times and I will be there.* She looked up at the wooden flooring above her – three more agonizing pulls. It seemed to take for ever, but the crackling flames from below distracted her from the pain in her arms and shoulders and drove her upwards.

By the time she got one hand firmly clasping the wooden boards of the floor above, the heat from below seemed to have died down, though it was replaced by an irritating cloud of smoke that got into her eyes and nose and prevented her from seeing anything beyond the glow of a lantern. Poor wet turf from the basket, she thought thankfully.

With a last tremendous effort she managed to heave herself up by her arms and get one knee on to the floor. Once the second knee was beside the first, she relaxed her tight grip on the rope and pulled it vigorously two or three times. She heard the bell jangle in a confused way, but then felt him seize the end of the rope from below and rip it from her hands and a voice shriek: *'"Be sober, be vigilant; because your adversary the devil, as a roaring lion, walketh about, seeking whom he may devour."'*

Mara abandoned the bell. Help would come – but would it come in time? She would have to rely on herself.

Now she could see her son. The lantern that he had brought with him was perched on top of the scorched wooden cupboard, that had formerly held the gold shrine. Its flame was sufficient to illuminate the small circular room. And wrapped in a black cloak, his face still covered by the devil mask, Cormac sprawled, face down, nose to the floorboards from which oozed up small wisps of smoke. Mara picked him up and felt the solid weight of him in her arms. He was completely unconscious and she knew that she had to get him into the air instantly. She tried to hold his face to the window slit, but very little air came through it. She wrapped her cloak around her hand and tried to knock the solid mullion that Ardal had broken when he had attacked the fire that burned the relic and the cushion, but it had been cemented back into place too securely and she could not move it. It was useless trying to break it, but the air coming through this tiny opening was not enough to bring back to his senses a boy overcome by smoke.

Not enough air, she thought rapidly, and was conscious that even her own mind seemed to be unusually confused. She pushed her chin under the neck fold of her hooded cloak and tried to breathe through the cloth. A glance at the opening of the floor showed that the flames were now snaking up the bell rope. Fire was a risk, but the choking clouds of smoke were worse. They could kill. She thought about trying to ring the bell once more, then discounted the idea. By now everyone within a mile of the church would already have heard the discordant peals.

But she could not afford to wait for rescue. Carefully she lowered Cormac to the floor again, winding a fold of his cloak over his nose and mouth. With a strength that she had not known she possessed she picked up the heavy wooden cupboard and thrust it with all her strength against the stone mullions. It thudded and bounced back against her hands. She tried again. There was a dent in the wood, but the stone held as firmly as ever.

Mara put down the cupboard and stared with a mixture of panic and frustration at the window. There was no time to waste: a column of spark-filled smoke was streaming up from the room below. She could no longer hear the Spaniard's voice, but there was a thundering at the door. Help was coming.

But it might be too late. One glance at Cormac's white face frightened her. She wanted to pick him up again, to feel the lovely weight in her arms, to touch his smooth skin, but she knew there was little time left. She had to get the boy into the air.

There was no point in trying the other windows; each was as solidly constructed as the one that she had been desperately hammering at. And there was no use in trying to go down. The burning of the two ladders had caused the fire to leap up through the opening in the floor.

The hammering at the door went on and then suddenly stopped. Why had it stopped? By now the brightness of the orange flames should have been visible through the crack around the doorway, perhaps even through the windows which allowed light in and out of the round tower. There were rescuers – shouts sounded from outside – they could be heard clearly from above. Why had they abandoned the door? Perhaps they feared to make the fire worse if they pushed it open. Yet there were plenty of rescuers out there; she could hear the voices coming down from above.

From above . . . coming down through the thatch above!

In a moment Mara had moved the small cupboard to a position just in front of one of the slit-like windows; the next moment she was on top of it – just four-foot high, but high enough. She dug her nails into the sides of the mullion and levered herself up. Standing on the solid wooden base, her arms reached up and almost without realizing what she had done she found that the knife which normally lived in her pouch was in her hand.

She had watched Cumhal at work often enough. She knew how thatch was constructed. First came the hazel slats and the twine that bound them together. On top of that came layer after layer of bundles of rushes, straw or reeds. By the time the last layer was laid, the roof was impermeable.

But not impermeable from underneath; attacking it from underneath was a different matter.

Just a hole – that's all I need, she told herself. Working as fast as she could, her knife slit through twine, severed hazel twigs. She thrust her fist through. The sharp ends of the sticks drew blood, but she felt nothing, just widened the gap as much as possible, and then sliced again and again. Now the hole was big enough to get her son's head through; enough to enable him to take some pure air into his lungs.

The fire from below roared, the smell of turf smoke now

overlaid with the aromatic scent of old oak timbers. The floorboards must be on fire. There would be only minutes before the second floor would go up in flames as well. There was a crash from underneath – the wooden opening had collapsed and the boards had fallen into the space below. Instantly Mara was off the cupboard and had seized Cormac in her arms.

He was a well-grown child of nine, but she picked him up as if he was a baby in the cradle. Still holding him, clasped close to her, she managed to get one knee on to the cupboard. If only he was conscious, if only he could help. He was breathing, though, breathing with long, deep sighs. She squirmed around, sat on the cupboard, holding him on her lap. The cupboard was barely wide enough to hold her; she could not seat Cormac beside her. And she could not rise to her feet while holding him within her arms. She needed to attach him to her. If only he would put his arms around her neck as he used to do when he was little.

In a moment her knife had slashed the back panel of the devil cloak that he wore. She pulled the loose ends under his armpits, then tied them behind the back of her own neck. Now he was attached to her. She doubled one leg under her and then the other. Eventually she was kneeling. She reached up with one hand and found the central mullion on the window. Her nails dug into its chiselled edge and just as sometimes a hand on a twig will enable a person to vault over a gap, this contact with the stone steadied her and lent power to her leg muscles. With a mighty effort she managed to stand up, feeling the weight of her unconscious son bending her neck almost to breaking point and keeping him clamped to her body with her left arm.

He was about shoulder height to her when he stood straight, but now, slumped as he was, his head hung down well below that. She wobbled for a moment and then managed to stand straight. With an almost incredible effort she got her two arms around the top of his legs and hoisted him up, pushing his head through the hole that she had made.

A tremendous shout from below told her that the rescuers had seen the boy's head appear. Pushing against the broken thatch with the top of her head, she managed to get her own face clear of the straw and to see down to the crowd below. Nechtan was there, and so was Father MacMahon, and Sorley, too. Why didn't they do something, she thought, with a moment's irritation, why just stand around below like spectators at a horse race? If only Ardal O'Lochlainn had been there; he would have organized them into a proper rescue team.

A crackle from below warned her that she had little time to waste. She could not see down and did not dare lower her head or relax her grip on Cormac in any way. She guessed, though, that the wooden boards of the second floor were now ablaze. If the thatch caught fire – as it inevitably would – well, then, her son would burn to death.

'Bring water from the well,' shouted Nechtan. 'And a ladder.'

Mara tightened her lips. Water from the well had worked when a small fire had smouldered on a velvet cushion, and when a powerful man had managed to break the mullion and reach in with his bucket. Now it would be of little use. And a ladder would not work with the almost lifeless boy in her arms.

'Cormac is unconscious,' she screamed down at them.

'Bring mattresses, feather beds, anything like that!' The voice was high and sweet, but the words were in English and there was a sudden baffled silence among Nechtan's men, who had been shouting orders about buckets. It was Grace, the scarred woman pilgrim, Mara realized, and she knew that the idea was a good one. Perhaps Grace herself had escaped from a fire like that.

'Bring mattresses, feather beds, bundles of straw, rushes, reeds, anything soft,' yelled Mara in Gaelic. There was a risk of fire spreading to such things, but the circular walls of the building were four feet thick and built from stone; it would take a long time for the fire to spread. There was no door on that side; she guessed that the door on the other side was now on fire as clouds of smoke were blowing around the half-lit churchyard. She held her son close to her, listening desperately to his heavy breathing. If only he would wake up. Surely by now he had breathed enough pure air into his chest?

But the crowds below were busy. She saw Blad running across from the inn, lantern in hand. He vaulted the fence around the churchyard and she breathed a small sigh of relief. He was a practical, sensible man and would take charge. Nechtan seemed bewildered, but she heard Blad shout orders to the stable boys who were with him, sending them back to the inn for feather beds and mattresses. Even old Father MacMahon was dragging a feather bed and Sorley was behind him carrying a heavy-looking mattress. Nechtan's men were bringing thatching sheaves from the barn and piling them up.

And where was Father Miguel? Had whoever was thundering on the first-floor door managed to get him out? She could see no sign of him and cast an apprehensive glance down. But she could not see through the hole in the thatch and put him from her mind, promising herself grimly that she would kill him if he tried to pull her child back down into the fire that crackled below. She turned to look out again. By now the pile was about six feet high. If only Cormac were awake and conscious, he could easily and safely vault down on to that.

But he was too heavy for her to lift up and drop.

'Cormac,' she pleaded. 'Cormac, wake up. Cormac, you're safe now. Cormac, please wake up.' She tried to hoist him up in her arms, but he was a dead weight.

'He's unconscious, Blad,' she called down, 'I can't . . .' What does one do to rouse an unconscious person? Shake him? Slap his face? Pour water? Desperately she hung on to him, but felt that there was nothing she could do except keep his head outside the thatch and allow him to breathe clear air.

'Don't worry, Brehon,' shouted Blad. 'I'll be with you in two shakes of a lamb's tail. Just you stay there and keep the little lad's head up. He'll be fine. Good man, yourself, Seán, that's just what I need – that's the longest ladder in the place. Two of you stand at the bottom of the ladder and keep it firm. Don't let it sway when I lower him down.'

And with that Blad began to climb. Mara could see that he had a looped rope slung around his shoulders. Now she knew what he was going to do and her heart failed her for a moment. What if Cormac slipped? What if he broke his neck?

But the pile beneath had grown higher. Grace had seemed to take charge, widening the base as more mattresses and sheaves arrived. Once the hay was saved and the turf drawn home, September was the time for renewing the thatch before winter set in, and most households had accumulated bundles of dried reeds from the river or from Inchiquin Lake, and now these were strewn around the pile of mattresses close to the wall.

But the ladder was too short. Too short by about six feet.

It was probably the same ladder that Ardal had used on the day when Hans Kaufmann set fire to the relic. It reached to the small window slit but no further. The top of the ladder and Blad's knees were a good six feet below.

'Just keep on holding him, Brehon,' he said reassuringly. 'Can you catch this noose?' He threw a length of rope. She missed but unperturbed he threw it again. This time she managed to catch it. 'Just slip this noose under his arms, no hurry, now, Brehon, we'll have him safe. Over his head, over his shoulders. That's the way.'

Mara held Cormac tightly to her with one arm and tried to do Blad's bidding with the other. The rope was stiff and unyielding, but she managed to get it over her son's head, over his shoulders. It was now over her child's elbows, and then one by one she lifted the heavy arms, praying that she would not let him slip.

'Done it,' she said, and recognized that her voice was shaking almost uncontrollably.

'That's the way,' said Blad calmly. By now he was on the top rung of the ladder, balancing with one foot wedged into the mullion in the centre of the window slit and the other on the ladder.

He reached up a large hand and seized the rope. Mara could feel how it tightened around Cormac's chest.

'Come on now, little fellow, let's be having you,' he said. 'How about one of Mór's cakes now, how would you like that for a late supper?'

The light wasn't good enough to see Cormac's face, but Mara could have sworn that there had been a flicker from his eyelashes against her cheek at those words. She held him very firmly, with her two arms around his waist while Blad, quite at ease on top of the ladder, held the rope from further down.

'That's nice and tight and firm now,' said Blad after a minute.

'We just need to lower him down; they're ready for him down there. Don't you worry, Brehon.'

'Let me take his weight, Blad,' said Mara firmly, throwing every ounce of authority into her voice. It was too risky, she thought, for Blad, swaying precariously towards the top of the ladder, to dangle a well-built nine-year-old boy from the end of the noose. 'I won't drop him,' she added.

'Just hoist him up as far as you can, Brehon. Hold the part of the rope near his chest and play it out – let it run through your hand.' Blad's voice was soothing. For a moment he wobbled then straightened himself again. He was balanced very precariously and despite the weight of the men at the bottom, Mara saw the ladder sway. Blad continued to hold the rope himself, quite near to the noose, but by stretching up as far as he could he now steadied himself by putting the fingers of one hand inside the conical wooden framework of the small roof. 'Ready now, lads,' he sang out to the watchers below, 'we're going to lower him down. One of you stand out there on the mattresses and catch him as he comes.'

'I'll catch him; I'm very strong.' Again it was the English voice. Grace was standing below them, balancing on top of the mattresses and feather beds. One of Blad's men stood beside her, but she had her arms stretched upwards and Mara, with Blad's help, played out the rope, gradually lowering Cormac until he ended up in Grace's arms. There was an excited cheer.

'Now you, Brehon,' said Blad, going ahead to give her space, and Mara wrapped her skirts around her legs and went down the ladder as quickly as she could. Cormac was still in Grace's arms when she got to the ground, and the look on the woman's face made her fight the impulse to snatch her son back into her own arms.

'He's coming to himself,' said Grace softly. She bent her face down and placed her lips next to the boy's mouth. 'He's breathing strongly and well,' she said.

'So he is,' said Nechtan, holding a lantern up. 'The colour is coming back into his face.'

Cormac's eyelids fluttered and Mara held her breath. Was he coming back to full consciousness, or was he still drifting in and out of a stupor caused by the amount of smoke that he had inhaled?

'Where's Father Miguel?' came Finbar's voice, unmistakable with its lilting Cloyne accent.

Then Cormac's eyes opened fully.

'You *amadán*, Finbar,' he said in clear, strong tones which held a trace of annoyance, 'you've made a mess of things; you shouldn't have let him into the tower.'

Eighteen

Cáin Lánamna
(the Law of Marriage)

There are two kinds of rape: 'forcor', forcible rape, and 'sleth', where a woman was subjected to intercourse without her full consent.

'Sleth' of a woman who normally frequents alehouses, without a male member of her family in attendance, will carry no penalty.

In the case of 'forcor', the rapist must pay the honour-price of his victim's husband, father or son. He must also be responsible, if necessary, for any children that result from the rape.

In addition to the honour-price, the 'éraic' or full body fine must also be paid in the case of a rape of a nun or of a 'girl in plaits'.

The burned remains of Father Miguel's body had been recovered and hastily buried by the time Mara returned to Kilnaboy the following day. Blad and Mór had given Cormac the promised midnight supper, which had turned into an impromptu feast. No beds were sought and they all remained there in the big hall of the inn, some sleeping, some talking, some eating, some sipping wine until dawn had begun to show at about five o'clock. Then Mara had taken the boys back to the law school at Cahermacnaghten, leaving them to sleep for a few hours and then to be supervised by Fachtnan and Brigid, with instructions to Brigid that Cormac was not to play at hurling, if Brigid could prevent it, but was, if possible, to spend the day sleeping or reading quietly in his bed. He seemed well, but Mara was worried about the amount of smoke that he had breathed in. He was to be excused lessons for the day, she told Fachtnan when he arrived, and if he seemed to be unwell, Cumhal was to take him down to be checked over by Nuala.

It took a strong effort for Mara to tear herself away from her son, but the pilgrims were due to set off on their postponed visit to Aran at noon and she wanted to see them before they left, to tie up the loose ends of the case of the false pilgrim.

It was about an hour before noon when she reached Kilnaboy. She had a quick word with Father MacMahon who was shaking his venerable old head at the idea that the Spanish priest could have lit a fire in the tower, almost burning to death the son of the King and his Brehon.

'Poor man,' he said charitably. 'His mind must have been turned by the terrible events of the last few days. Do you think, Brehon, that he had anything to do with the death of the sacrilegious man who burned the relic of the true cross? It does seem as though he had, doesn't it?'

Mara shook her head sadly. 'I think,' she said, 'that Father Miguel believed that death to be the work of God himself.'

And, she thought, that was what the Spanish priest had truly believed. God alone knew what he had had in his mad, perverted brain as he set fire to the tower when a boy had summoned him to see the devil mask and silhouette of a nine-year-old capering around by the light of the lantern, but as to the death of the German, of the false pilgrim – of that crime she truly believed that Father Miguel had been innocent. His belief that it had been the work of God had completely convinced her. And if he really believed that God had struck down the guilty man, well, then it followed that he himself was blameless.

Brother Cosimo had not committed the murder either, she thought. A man who would steal a jewelled cross would not let a pouch full of coins remain untouched.

And Father MacMahon himself – too old, too helpless – how could he have stripped a man, killed him and then taken out the body and placed him on a tomb? Neither he nor Sorley would have had the intensity of hate to do a deed like that.

And Blad – no, of course not. He would not have had the time to set up the elaborate display; he was busy with his guests – and why do it? His business could only be brought back if another relic was purchased in the place of the one that was destroyed. If Blad had resorted to violence, he would have threatened the pilgrim, then taken the valuable bag of coins in recompense and allowed the man to go free. Or, more likely, he would have trusted the king's Brehon to impose a suitable fine and hoped that the money would be used to buy another relic.

Mara took leave of Father MacMahon and walked across to the inn to see Mór. The kitchen was empty of all when she looked in there, but Mór herself was sitting on a bench outside the window looking across at the river running calmly down through the meadows. She had an unusually meditative expression on her face and it did not change as Mara sat beside her.

'You're back, Brehon,' she said, and the words were a statement, not a question.

'I'm back,' agreed Mara. She noted an apologetic note in her voice and sought to explain it.

'It would,' she said ruefully, 'probably seem good sense to you that I should abstain from more enquiries and that the matter should be allowed to die, that the story of the night of the Feast of the Holy Cross should be buried in the grave where Hans Kaufmann now lies, but I cannot leave it like that. I must know the truth and only you can tell me what happened in the early part of that night.'

She stopped and waited, but Mór said nothing. After a minute, Mara resumed. 'I suppose it was your words about the breakfast that first took my attention,' she said apologetically. 'There were only two reasons why there should be no arrangement about breakfast for the man who had claimed sanctuary – the first was that this man was going to escape during the night and therefore would need no breakfast . . .' Mara glanced sideways at Mór, but the innkeeper's daughter showed no change of expression.

'The other,' she continued, 'and I do believe this to be the true explanation of the facts, was that there was no question of breakfast because you were going to see him again long before that.' She paused for a while, thinking about Mór's amused expression when she had last asked about the breakfast. And then when the woman still said nothing, she added quietly, 'You and he had a good supper together – you had carried across from the inn two covered baskets; witnesses related this.

One, of course, would have held food, but the other, I guess, would have held a couple of flasks of your father's best wine – and a couple of goblets. And then, somehow or other, the wine got spilled.'

A smile curved Mór's lips. Mara could picture the scene – the supper, the hand holding, the kisses, and then the spillage of wine on top of the precious crimson carpet. Then the frantic cleaning, the water brought from the holy water font, the scrubbing with cloths, and then . . .

'He told you you owed him another flask of wine,' she ventured, and saw the smile broaden on the lips of the innkeeper's daughter. Of course, Mara thought, looking back; the carpet had smelled of wine as well as incense, but at the time she had assumed it was the communion wine – *a holy smell*, had said Finbar, who had been an altar boy for the monks at the abbey in Cloyne where his father's school was located.

'Let me guess,' she went on, purposely keeping her voice to a non-committal, non-judgemental tone, 'he wanted to make love. You are a pretty girl, he was a virile man who had drunken quite a bit of wine, you were already . . . friends, lovers. He proposed to do it there and then, but you . . .'

'I knew that they were all around, Brehon.' Mór suddenly threw caution away. 'It was not that I minded, you understand; we . . . we had been together before, but who knows, one of those busybodies, Father MacMahon, or that old woman, Sorley, or even the O'Lochlainn, any one of them could have come along to check on him. And if they found the church locked and knew that I was inside . . .'

'I know,' Mara nodded. Of course she knew that Mór and Hans Kaufmann had been together before. She thought back to the missing key and the convenient little windowless chamber on the first floor of the round tower. Hans Kaufmann, she reflected indignantly, had used Mór; she was to him not just a recreation, but a tool in his fanaticism, a means to an end.

'The missing key,' she said aloud.

Mór's eyes fell before hers. There was a short silence, but then she raised them. 'That's right, Brehon,' she said.

'And you wished to be together again; I can understand

that.' Mara's voice was soothing. There would be, she knew,
no trace of censure in her tone. She felt none. Why should Mór
not enjoy the company of a handsome young man?

Mór stared at her for a moment, but then she nodded
emphatically. 'Yes, I wished for it as much as he,' she said defiantly.
'It might have happened there and then if the wine had not
been spilt, but that broke the mood. I knew that Father
MacMahon would throw a fit; I just had to get that carpet
clean. And by the time I had got most of it mopped up then
I thought of other things. And I told him that I would come
back later.'

'So you took back the basket and the cloths that you had
used to swab the crimson carpet,' stated Mara. That carpet, of
course, had been of vital importance. Unfortunately it had
taken the comment of the serving boy to make her realize that
– his comment and that of her daughter Sorcha, Domhnall's
mother came to her mind.

'*Blood is brown when it dries,*' he had said.

And sometime, away back among unremembered trivia, was
Sorcha's voice saying: '*Mother, you must treat a red wine stain instantly
or else you get a blue-black mark even on a red cloth.*'

The stain that was left on the carpet had been blue-black.
So no blood had been spilled within the church . . .

'Go on,' said Mara, looking across at Mór, 'you cleaned up
the wine stain, it spoiled the mood, but you promised to come
back later with another flask full of the best Burgundy.'

'That's right.' Mór nodded.

'And you kept your word?'

'I told him,' said Mór, 'that I would delay for a while before
I came back. It was already starting to rain and I thought that
the O'Lochlainn and his steward would seek shelter. *Wait for
a couple of hours*, that was what I said to him, Brehon.'

'And you came back about midnight, did you?' Mara asked
gently. She was certain now in her own mind about the truth,
but all of the incidental details had to be cleared out of the
way.

Mór nodded. 'He had told me to come straight back, but
I knew it was not safe, not with all that patrolling. I had an
excuse the first time – it had been agreed that he should be

fed – but to come again, well, I would have to be careful and to choose my time. I did think that it would be best just around the time the O'Lochlainn handed over to Nechtan O'Quinn.'

'And when you arrived at the church at the hour of midnight?'

'I waited until Sorley sounded the bell. I saw him go back to his own house. I heard Nechtan and the O'Lochlainn talking together over by *Crooked Moher* and then I went across the churchyard with my new flask of wine.'

'And you went through into the unlocked church?'

Mór nodded. 'That's right. I opened the door and I went in. All of the lights were still on, every candle blazing. For a moment I thought that he was hiding behind the altar and that he would spring out on me; it was the sort of thing that he would do. But . . . it's a funny thing, Brehon, but there was an empty sort of feel about the place.'

'And he had gone?' Mara knew the answer to that question, but followed it up with another. 'What did you think?'

Mór shrugged her plump shoulders. 'I thought that he had made a fool of me; that he had stolen out and somehow got hold of his horse and managed to get away – perhaps at the time when I told him that the O'Lochlainn would be handing over to Nechtan O'Quinn.'

'You didn't think to search the church?'

Mór shrugged again. 'Why should I? It wouldn't be the first time that I was let down. He wasn't there and that was that.'

'And when you saw him dead the next morning, what did you think then?'

For the first time Mór did not meet Mara's eyes.

'I didn't know what to think, Brehon,' she said firmly.

Mara smiled. 'I didn't know what to think either,' she admitted. 'It was one of the most puzzling cases that I have known. Thank you for telling me everything so honestly, Mór, and don't worry. Nothing that you have said to me will ever be made public.' She got to her feet, noting the relief in the woman's eyes.

Grace was not with her two sisters and Brother Cosimo who were having a farewell snack with Blad in his spectacular hall. Mara did not go in, but went swiftly across the churchyard

and down the small passageway until she reached the tomb
– the *gabhal*. Grace was there, just standing, not looking at the
capstone but below it. Mara saw that she had removed the
limestone plug. She turned her head and then seemed to feel
that an explanation was needed.

'An old lady showed me this place on the first day that we
came here,' she said softly. 'She saw me limping and beckoned
to me. I couldn't understand her and she couldn't understand
me, but we both had lame legs and that made the bond. She
brought me here and showed me how she put her leg into
the hole and then said a prayer. I did the same and she patted
me on the shoulder and said something and mimed how she
had been so terribly crippled and now was improved.'

Mara smiled. A dry, hot summer had probably improved lots
of rheumatic arms and legs in the elderly, she thought cynically, but did not say so. Who was she to judge?

'I wondered how you knew about it,' she admitted.

Suddenly the last piece of the picture slipped into place. She
looked down at the hole and knew what had happened.

'You were sorry for him, weren't you, perhaps a little in
love with him?' The girl, she thought compassionately, was
probably very young for her age. While fourteen-, fifteen- and
sixteen-year-olds were out flirting and trying out their wiles
on young men, Grace would have been hiding indoors, afraid
to show her scarred face and her marred body among the
pretty Welsh girls of the neighbourhood.

Mara bent down and touched a scratch mark on the stone
that had been removed from its socket. Badger, she thought,
and wondered whether some other frightened creature had
tried to get inside the hole.

'Will it be easier if I tell what happened?' she asked, looking
into the white face. 'Don't worry. I mean you no harm,' she
added, her heart melting as she heard the stifled sob. This tale
should be told quickly, she thought. She knew its beginnings,
soft words spoken on board ship, jealousy awoken by the flirtation
with Mór, girlish, romantic love turned to horror.

'You went to the church – perhaps you brought the pilgrim
something, or perhaps came to bear him company. You knocked
on the church door, is that right?'

'I knocked a couple of times. I was going to go away, thought he must be asleep. And then he suddenly opened the door.' The words were barely audible.

'And he had taken his clothes off.'

Mara hardly waited for the nod. That must have been the way it was. Hans, roused, wanting to make love to Mór, would have taken the knocking as flirtatious by-play – he had already stripped because of the hot night, perhaps, and then at the knock removed his braies.

'And you got a fright and ran.' Once again there was a nod.

'And he chased after you.' Undoubtedly the false pilgrim was drunk – perhaps he did broach the communion wine after Mór left. It was extraordinary that no one had seen him, but of course Ardal and Danann were sheltering with their backs to the oak tree looking towards the road, not towards the church. They would have been too far away to hear anything.

'I ran.' The words were barely audible. 'I could hear him behind me. I ran towards the darkness, out of the churchyard.' Grace, Mara remembered from Bess's explanation, could when frightened run as fast as any other girl of her age. The sight of Hans would have terrified her into forgetting the pain of the scar tissue on her thigh.

'And you suddenly thought of the hiding place, the empty space under the capstone.'

'I thought that I would be safe there. I still thought I was, even when I heard him come after me.'

Mara put out a hand and touched the girl on her arm. 'You must have been terribly frightened.' Not for nothing, she thought, was the rape of a young girl considered to be such a serious crime under Brehon law; although technically Grace was not 'a girl in plaits', emotionally she was. Her terribly scarred face and lame leg kept her away from the experiences that helped other young girls to mature.

There was more to be said, though, she knew that. She had a picture in her mind of the terrified girl crouching in that small space beneath the capstone. It was obvious what would have happened next.

'You took out your knife from your pouch.' All of the women had serviceable strong-looking knives. Grace would have reached for hers once she felt threatened. The trapped animal is dangerous; Cumhal always warned the boys of that, telling them to back away from a cornered rat.

'He heard me breathing, I think,' whispered Grace. 'I couldn't see him, but I could . . . I could smell him. He reached in and grabbed me. He said something . . . something about it being good that it was so dark that he wouldn't be able to see my face . . .'

Vile rapist, thought Mara, but she said nothing. The rest of the story had to be told by Grace.

There was a long silence. And then, quite abruptly, Grace said, 'I didn't know it would be so easy to kill someone. I just drove my knife – drove it into him – and nothing seemed to happen. He made a kind of sound, but he was still there. Still standing. I thought he'd run away.'

'And then?' asked Mara.

'I suppose,' said Grace dully, 'that I sort of knew the truth really. I could smell the blood. It was pouring rain. I could hear the drops pattering on the grass, but even still I could smell that sort of . . . You know,' she said suddenly and unexpectedly, 'there is a copper mine near to where I live and blood smells like that, it smells like copper. And then there was a flash of lightning and I could see his legs – just his legs, nothing else – and I tried to tell myself that he was all right, just standing there.'

'He had slumped over the capstone, was that it?'

Grace nodded. 'Yes, just there. I knew that no one could stand there in the pouring rain for so long without moving. I thought he might be unconscious, that I might be able to escape, so I slipped out past his legs. And then there was another flash of lightning and I saw his eyes, just staring up at the sky, wide open, and then I knew that he was dead. He was there, with his legs on the ground, slumped over, his head turned upwards towards the sky.'

'And the weight of his body was across the capstone.'

'That's right. Once I realized that he was dead, I was terrified. I thought that I would be hanged or burned to death. So the idea just came to me to pretend that he had been struck down by God.'

Mara nodded. The body would still have been quite pliable and the girl would easily have been able to arrange it on the slab, arms outstretched, feet together.

'And then I went back to the church. There was no one around. I picked up the clothes and I carried them back and pushed them well in under the slab and put the stone back. All the blood seemed to be washed away by the rain.'

And then she added the remaining touches – the crown of thorns, the making of the holes in the hands and feet – it all took a certain cool courage, but perhaps it was just desperation, thought Mara.

'Where did you get the prayer?' she asked.

'I had it in my pouch; that was why I went to the church. I was going to give it to him. I wanted him to pray for forgiveness, to save his immortal soul before it was too late.'

God is not mocked. A fitting final judgement . . .

Nineteen

Maccslechta
(Son Sections)

A boy who is adopted into a kin group may be able to have rights of inheritance if the adopting parents pay a fee (lóg fóesma). A contract must be drawn up, bound by securities and agreed by the head of the kin group. He does not gain automatic entitlement to a full share of kin-land, but only to the land under the direct ownership of the adopting father.

Mara stood and waved a farewell. Six pilgrims had come here on the eve of the Feast of The Holy Cross and now only four left. Side by side in the churchyard lay the other two, each in his own way believing intensely in the religion to which he had given his devotion, and yet each lacking in humanity and a respect for their fellow human beings. Hans Kaufmann believed that he knew better than others and was prepared to destroy what they believed in, and yet he himself was a seducer and a rapist. As for Father Miguel, well, he believed so intensely in his own narrow view of God and the devil that he was prepared to be an arsonist and perhaps a murderer. Mara could hardly bear to think of Father Miguel. She would never know whether he had in fact firmly supposed that the small figure capering around in a horned mask was really the devil, or whether he was prepared to punish the audacity of a nine-year-old child by burning him to death. Whatever it was, he had suffered a terrible end, and she hoped that the smoke had rendered him unconscious before the flames reached him.

There was one more thing that she wanted to do before she left Kilnaboy.

Nechtan was standing by his barn talking to his steward when she went past the church and towards the castle. She exchanged a few pleasant words with him and went on to give her thanks to Narait for her hospitality.

Narait was sitting listlessly by the window when Mara came in, but roused herself to make anxious enquiries about Cormac.

'Disgusted with himself for blacking out like that,' said Mara with a smile. 'He'd have much preferred to play the hero and put the fire out single-handed.' She wondered about apologising for the loss of the devil's costume, but decided to say nothing. Cormac had worried about the nature of a recompense for this on his way home, and she thought that she should leave the matter to him. There was something else that she wanted to discuss with Narait.

'Narait, have you ever thought of adopting a baby,' she said, coming to the point in a straightforward way. Before Narait could speak, she went on, 'There is a motherless little boy near here, he'll be the most beautiful child, with golden hair and blue eyes. His mother died in childbirth, his father has deserted the children, and they are with their grandparents at the moment. The older children will be cared for – they will work on their grandfather's farm and help him and their grandmother; they are happy children who have been well brought up, but that little baby needs a mother's love and a mother's care.'

And then she sat back and watched the effect of her words. There would be no problems if Nechtan and Narait decided to adopt the motherless child of poor Aoife. Nechtan would have an heir to his position as *coarb* of the ancient monastic lands of Kilnaboy and Narait would have a beautiful child to love. Mara had not actually seen the baby herself, but all of Aoife's children had, like the poor girl herself, been blond, beautiful and blue-eyed. The wet nurse that Muiris and Áine had found would probably be happy to go on feeding the baby – the grandparents themselves would have their hands full with the other eight children, and Rory, if he ever reappeared, could make no objection. It was the perfect arrangement – a stroke of genius, thought Mara, with a slightly smug feeling of self-congratulation as she watched the colour flood into Narait's face, her eyes light up and her lips begin to curl into a tremulous smile.

'Go and talk to Nechtan, he's out by his barn,' said Mara

indulgently. 'I'll wait here for a moment – I have something to sort out in my mind and would welcome a quiet few minutes on my own. If you and Nechtan are happy about the idea, I'll drop in to see Muiris and Áine, the grandparents, on my way home and then you can ride over to their farm tomorrow. Nechtan knows Muiris well; his lands march with yours on Roughan Hill. You'll have to see the baby, of course, but I'm sure that you will love him as soon as you have him in your arms.'

Narait almost flew out of the room and Mara, watching through the window, saw her run in the direction of the barn. She smiled with satisfaction and turned her thoughts back to the affair of the false pilgrim. The truth had to be told to the people of the Burren, she decided. She owed them that. No man's death in her territory must go unaccounted for. She would tell them of the attempted rape, also, and would tell them what her verdict had been. Few would care that much, she decided, but she would put the legal arguments before them, ask whether there were any questions and then, if there were none, she would move quickly on to the next case. Within a few months the death would be forgotten – unless, of course, this Martin Luther made such a stir in the world that religions changed and a new type of pilgrim arrived at Kilnaboy anxiously seeking the grave of the man who was marked by God with the stigmata of his own son.

When she returned to Cahermacnaghten the school was in session, but Cormac was in the kitchen teasing and tormenting Brigid's fourteen-year-old assistant, Eileen.

'I'm perfectly all right,' he said defensively when he saw her. 'I'm really bored with lying in bed – though I'm not quite well enough for lessons,' he added quickly, and Eileen snorted derisively.

'That's good that you're feeling better,' said Mara calmly. 'Would you like to come for a ride with me?' She didn't wait for a reply but went out to the stable.

'I'll take the cob, Cumhal,' she said. 'Poor old Brig has had her exercise for the day. Let her rest.' While Cormac was saddling his own pony, she took down a pair of wide panniers, woven from supple willow stems, and handed them to Cumhal. Without comment he attached them to the sturdy cob.

'Where are we going?' asked Cormac as they rode across the limestone-paved fields of the high Burren. There was still a defensive note in his voice and after a moment he added, 'Aren't any of the others coming too?'

'No,' said Mara decisively, 'this is just a family affair, just something for you and me, and your father, of course.'

He gave her a sidelong glance of puzzlement, but said nothing, and she reflected rather sadly that very few events or occasions just involved the three of them. During the long summer holidays – between the Trinity term and the Michaelmas term – when the other boys went back to their homes and their families, Cormac spent most of his time with his foster brother Art either on the farm or out in Setanta's boat. He had a good life, and he was a confident, healthy, well-grown boy, but there must be times when he missed a special relationship with his parents. He didn't have much to say to her, she thought sadly, as they rode in silence across the flat land of the High Burren. It was only when they reached the standing stones at Fannygalvin that Cormac stared up at the hillside ahead of them and said in puzzled tones: 'Where on earth are we going?'

'Cahercommaun,' said Mara calmly.

'Cahercommaun – Murrough's place. Why are we going up there?'

'That's right, Cahercommaun.' Mara did not answer his second question. She was looking up at the steep hill rising high above their heads and feeling thankful that she had not ridden her elderly mare.

Cahercommaun was a spectacular fortified household on the top of a cliff near to Carron. Three rings of semi-circular protective walling enclosed the inner site, each ring breaking off exactly at the perpendicular edge of the steep cliff. No enemy could approach this site without being in peril of death, either from throwing knives or from the immense heap of heavy stones that were piled up at every gateway, and on the edge of the cliff itself. As they climbed up the path, the sound of deep-toned barking came to them. No one ever approached

Cahercommaun without the wolfhounds giving good notice to Murrough.

'Well,' said Mara, choosing her words carefully, 'I've been thinking of getting another dog for some time. The trouble is that I don't have a lot of time to spare for training a puppy. But now you are nine years old I think that you could help with that, or even take it over from me. What do you think?'

'What? A wolfhound? A wolfhound puppy!' Cormac's face was blazing with excitement and pleasure.

Murrough was standing waiting for them when they reached the top. He would have guessed, of course, what they had come for, but first they had to be taken inside, given the customary refreshments and exchange news about the turf and the hay. Then there was a pause.

'I was thinking of getting a puppy, Murrough,' said Mara then. It was coming to the point rather too abruptly, she knew, but she was tired and somehow this place brought back sad memories of her beloved Bran.

'Well, I've got just the dog for you!' Murrough beamed. 'I was hoping you might call. You won't believe it, but I've got the living image of your Bran. Come and see them – there are six of them, God bless them, and they're all lovely.'

Cormac was out of the room before either of them got to their feet. Across the yard he flew to the stone stable. It had a small wooden door closed in front of it, low enough for the bitch to get over, but high enough to stop the puppies from wandering and becoming prey to an opportunist wolf.

'Let them out, Cormac,' called Murrough.

The pups streamed out, grey ones, fawn ones, but Mara had eyes for only one: a beautiful little dog puppy, pure white, calm, reflective, with large intelligent eyes. Murrough was right: he was the image of her deeply mourned Bran.

'What did I tell you?' said Murrough, his voice echoing the excitement that was rising within her. This was a lovely dog, a perfect shape, from sloping shoulder to the narrow flanks and down to the long muscular thighs. White in colour, but with dark eyes, long tail slightly curved, a long, arched, strong neck. He was a beauty. Unlike the other pups he did not race around, but stood, collected and proud, looking across at Mara.

'Brehon,' called out Cormac, 'could we have this one? I love him.'

And on a bed of straw her nine-year-old son was rolling in an ecstatic play-fight with an exuberant smoke-grey puppy, who was licking his ears and wriggling in his arms. One of these wild dogs, thought Mara, her heart sinking, who would undoubtedly be a handful, would need a huge amount of exercise and training, would probably cause trouble with neighbours until he got some sense, but would, she thought as a reluctant smile came to her lips, probably always adore Cormac and would provide him with fun and companionship.

'All right,' she said. 'If you want him, you can have him. What will you call him?'

'Smoke,' he said without hesitation, raising his head from the dog's face. 'He's grey – a real smoke colour – and it will always remind me of how exciting it was last night when that mad, crazy, religious freak set fire to the round tower with all that smoky wet turf.'